Branches

Thank you to my beautiful wife and amazing followers.

2

Chapter 1

Lavender Amos couldn't remember the last time she smelled rain in the air. She was so used to the dust and oppressive heat of the Arizona sun. It had been so long since she'd been surrounded by lush greens and blues. She'd miss the forest. She'd missed Branches.

"Ender?" a confused voice called from behind her.

She stopped staring at the woods and turned to her father. "Huh?" Lavender noticed the dark circles under his eyes. They matched her own. They were both exhausted. She'd called at 4am to let him know she'd be landing in Seattle at 7. Add on a 3 hour car ride there and back and the man looked beat. They were definitely going to take a long nap after she got settled. Perks of being the sheriff of a quiet town was that he could take off when needed.

Dean held her backpack out then gestured to the front door with his head. Her other bag was hooked on his shoulder. He felt terrible but he was ecstatic she was here. His little girl had gotten so big. A bitter part of him was furious he was robbed of watching her grow.

Lavender had packed in a hurry. Only her favorite clothes and a few trinkets. It saved her money on the flight. She also didn't want to have time to second guess herself. Also, Lavender knew she had an entire room waiting for her here. She grabbed the offered backpack. "Sorry, just…got lost in thought."

Dean smiled. "I know. Surprised your mom let you come." He swallowed the bile that rose in his throat at the mention of his ex. A righteous fury filled him but he stamped it down. He wasn't going to disparage the mother of his child, as much as he wanted to. "Let's get inside, flower."

The house was the same. A large porch with its well worn chairs. The flaky white paint of the exterior. The old oak door. The big bay window. Speaking of windows. Lavender looked up and saw her old room window. Her wind chimes were still hanging. Beautiful blue and green pieces of sea glass danced behind the window pane. Memories of scavenging those gems on the beach made her smile. Till she recalled her first run in with reality. The reality that her mother despised Branches. Despised her people. Lavender wondered if she despised her too. Probably with how she'd thrown Lavender to the wolves.

Memories she wanted gone, resurfaced. Being dragged from the sand. She'd accidentally dropped Ethan from the force of the pull. Then there was screaming and yelling. The look on her grandmother's face. The wails of Ethan. Being thrown in a car and driven miles away. Lavender would always remember the way Dean chased after her. The way he begged and cried for her mother to turn around. Her throat closed and she buried those memories. She tried to at least. A bitterness filled her mouth but she swallowed it down.

She'd lived in these walls on and off her entire childhood. Lavender wondered how insane her parents had to be to keep trying over and over. For her dad to always let her mom come back after running away. How could he stand it? Why didn't he grab Lavender and tell her

4

mother to go? Why did he keep trying? Why didn't he come for her? As much as she wanted to scream and demand answers from her father, she wanted peace more.

Dean fumbled with his keys and blinked his blurry eyes. He finally got the front door opened. "Home sweet home!" he announced with a tired smile.

Lavender snapped out of her thoughts and followed her father inside. "Yeah," she agreed and kicked off her shoes.

"I'm happy you're here, Ender." Dean turned on the lights. In his rush to get his daughter, he'd forgotten to. He knew her coming here wasn't serendipitous. Something had happened, but he wasn't going to look a gift horse in the mouth. His baby girl was back after so long. "Everything's still the same," he assured, noting her nervousness.

Lavender put her head down. She didn't want her dad to see the pain behind her smile, "Sure is."

Nothing had changed.

She hadn't been here since she was 13, but it was all still the same. It was like she'd stepped back in time instead of forward. The couch was the same. The table was the same. Even the curtain's were the same. The large bay window, which held more sea glass window chimes, was even the same.

Her mom was right.

"Nothing ever changes in Branches!" The memory of her mother's words made her shudder.

Dean noticed her distress, even if he didn't know the reason. "Your room is just like you left it, didn't touch it." Dean set her bag on the table. "Might be a little dusty." He hoped the joking tone of his voice would bring her out of whatever she was under. The loud rumble of their stomachs made the pair laugh. Dean opened the refrigerator. "Okay, I got old pizza and... beer." He gave her a sheepish smile. He hadn't had time to go grocery shopping with the recent incidents. He wasn't about to mention those though. His daughter was finally here. He couldn't stomach the thought of driving her away.

Lavender snorted, "Got a few more years, dad." In truth Lavender was scared of drinking. Something about losing control of your body made her terrified. She then remembered her mother and father's tolerances for the stuff and wondered if it would even have an effect on her.

"You know, I would have been ecstatic if my dad offered me a beer," Dean teased. In truth he knew that this reintroduction was turning into a shitshow. He closed the fridge. "I think Lin's just opened. Want some chinese?"

"Sure. I'll go put my stuff up." Lavender took her bag off the table and started for the stairs. "Get me some Lo mein!" she told him.

"Got it!" Dean flipped open his phone and looked through his saved contacts. There were only 9 or 10. 'Rosemary' sat at the bottom. Dean grimaced and quickly selected Lin's. He hoped he could place his order without stuttering.

Lavender entered her old room. A wave of dust hit her. She sneezed at the particles. Her bags were quickly dumped onto the bed, which kicked up more dust. It caused her to cough. She hurried to open her windows. Lavender took a deep breath of fresh air before turning back to take stock of her old room. Well, her now room, she supposed.

It was so different from her room in Arizona. Cooler in the palette and densely packed with memories.

The fairy lights were still strung up and surprisingly worked. Her bed smelt stale but not bad. The overhead lights came on, as did the fan. The desk was clear, as she left it. She went to her shelf. There were pretty stones she'd found by the river. There were arrowheads she'd made with her mother. Jewelry from Nana. Lavender wondered if the old woman was still alive.

Pictures lined the walls. Some taped, others clipped on to strung wire, some were probably even glued. Her polaroid camera sat on the shelf. She was a fiend with it. Snapping pictures of anything and everything and everyone. All the messiest photos were on display.

Lavender grabbed her scrapbook off the shelf, careful to not disrupt the gems in front of it. Once acquired, she sat on the bed. Lavender found it still had some spring to it. Probably from disuse.

The scrapbook was made of faux leather. Her dad had given it to her to hold her important things. Lavender opened it. Her first fishing hook was taped to the front page. A picture of her first catch underneath. The whole family was together. It was before the running started.

Lavender stared at her mother's face and saw her own. From her golden eyes, to her hooked nose, to her high cheekbones. There was no doubt she was her mother's daughter. There was also no doubt she was her father's. They had the same dark complexion. Their sepia tones were nearly identical. Dean and her also shared long textured hair. Lavender had noticed his now held strands of gray. His face looked the same. There was barely a wrinkle by his eyes. "Black don't crack," she mumbled to herself with a laugh. Everyone had always claimed she was a perfect mix of her parents. She now recognized why. It filled her with pride. They were the perfect family. Reality set in.

That wave of happiness quickly morphed into despair. She'd never have that back. This family in the photo no longer existed. She thought, *Maybe it never did.* A numbness settled in. "Why?" she wondered. Why couldn't she have had it for longer? She was so little in the photo, only 2. It was her first clear memory. If she'd known the next year she was going to lose it all, she would have cherished it more. Lavender used to ask why her mother kept running away. She never got a straight answer.

"My mother and I had a fight."

"My mom loved the pack more than me."

"Branches has nothing going for it."

"Why do you want to know those people?!"

"Why are you asking me these questions?!"

"Drop it, Ender!"

Lavender shook her mother's voice from her mind. Living here now, she'd find out soon enough. Hell, she could probably ask her dad. If Nana was still alive, she could definitely ask her. Lavender remembered the dark circles under Dean's eyes.

She'd save her questions for later.

Lavender turned the page and kept turning. She saw photos of her and Ethan.

God, Ethan.

Lavender would never forgive her mother for keeping her away from him. 4 years. She'd missed 4 years of his life. Sure, they talked on the phone every once in a while, but that wasn't the same. Lavender knew her mother did it on purpose. She didn't know why but she knew. Ethan lived on the reservation. Whatever beef her mother had with the elders extended to the kids too.

Lavender looked at the scrawny boy, who was her best friend. The little brother she'd always wanted. They had been inseparable. Little bear and mama bear, everyone used to call them. Which made them call each other that too. The first photo was of her and him on the beach behind Nana's house. An hour after the photo, Lavender was taken by her mother for the first time. The next picture was 4 months later. For a long time Lavender's mom followed a pattern.

A year here, 4 months gone.

A year here, 4 months gone.

A year here, 4 months gone.

When she was 13 though, something happened. Lavender didn't know what triggered it, but the pattern broke.

A year here, 4 years gone.

Lavender slammed the book shut. She gripped it so tight the fake leather creaked. Hot tears pricked her eyes. What if Ethan and her were no longer friends? What if dad didn't want her to stay? What if the tribe and Nana rejected her?

Dean's voice cut through her spiral. "Ender, food's here!"

"Coming!" she called back. Lavender wiped her face. She left the book on her bed and raced down the steps. She jumped the second to last one, avoiding the horrid squeak it always let out. "Hey, dad?"

"Yeah, flower?" Dean began taking the food out of the brown paper bag. The look on her face made a pit open in his stomach. What if she wanted to go back already? He couldn't blame her. He didn't have the same resources as her mother. He didn't have the same ability to spend one on one time. It had been the reason he'd never fought for full custody in the first place.

"Is Ethan still here?" Lavender picked at the oak chair nervously.

Dean was relieved. "Of course. Where else would he be?" He smiled, "Your little bear is safe and well and very excited to see you tomorrow." Dean had texted Jerry about Lavender's arrival. His friend was surprised but let him know everyone was happy to hear she'd be coming back. Especially Ethan. Ethan had missed Lavender terribly.

Lavender rolled her eyes, trying not to show the relief on her face. "Leave me alone." She took her food and went to the couch. Her spot had firmed up while she was away. Lavender took it as a challenge to break it in again.

Dean scoffed, "Mama bear."

"I can't hear you!" Lavender began to eat her noodles. That nickname would follow her until the day she died.

"Yeah, yeah," Dean sat next to his daughter. He turned on the TV, making sure to avoid the local news stations. An old rerun of Star Trek was settled on. They ate in silence for a time. Neither of them wanted to break the peace they found themselves in. When the episode ended, Dean finally said, "I'm happy you're here, Lavender." He turned to her and she smiled. God, she looked exactly like her mother when she smiled.

Lavender finally relaxed, "I'm happy I'm here too."

Dean wasn't lying, Ethan was excited.

"MAMA!" he screamed and jumped at the girl. Lavender was glad she had gotten that nap in. The boy was bursting with energy. She caught him, wrapping her arms around him. Lavender was strong and big enough to support his weight easily. It also helped that he was a twig. "Oh, little bear! I missed you!" She gave him a squeeze and a few cheek kisses before letting him go.

Ethan hopped out of her arms and began to run around her. "I can't believe you're back! I thought I'd never see you again! Oh, I'm catching up to you!" He teased and pretended to measure their heights. He was almost as tall as her.

"Get bent!" Lavender snickered and lightly punched his shoulder. She couldn't believe how much he'd grown. "How old are you now?"

"14." Ethan had that air of pride every teen held. The fact they were growing older was an accomplishment. It wouldn't be for a long time till they realized how both right and wrong they were. His birthday had just passed. To him, Lavender coming was like a late present from the universe. He'd missed her birthday too. Maybe next year they could celebrate together, like they did as kids.

"Are you going to the town school?" Lavender asked. She hoped to spend her last year of childhood with him. Being 17 was surreal.

"Nah, rez." Ethan shrugged, "Tried town school, wasn't fun." He didn't want to mention that he wasn't allowed to go to Branches' school.

Lavender grimaced. That didn't bode well for her.

"Not that it'll be bad for you!" Ethan reassured, "Just, little kids are cruel, ya know." He hoped his excuse hadn't ruined something before it even started.

"You're a little kid," Lavender teased, hugging him again.

Ethan rolled his eyes, "Little, little kids." He nuzzled into her shoulder. Her smell was calming and made him feel safe. He'd missed feeling safe. His mama was home. Ethan noticed his father's eyes boring into him. The boy stepped back. "I missed you," he whispered, pouring all his love into the words.

"I missed you too," Lavender ruffled his hair. "Anyway, start talkin'! Catch me up!"

Ethan beamed and began telling her everything he was allowed. Slowly, he guided her away from his father's prying eyes. Ethan didn't want to deal with his frown or disapproval. The boy wanted to be wrapped in the warmth of Lavender's aura. The pack could shove it. He led her to an entrance in the woods. The way they'd always used as kids.

"Be careful!" Ethan's father, Jerry, called. The man's face was grim.

Ethan huffed and rolled his eyes. "We'll be careful!" he answered and tugged Lavender into the trees.

Lavender was confused but followed Ethan into the woods. She looked back at Dean. He had a hand on Jerry, as if to hold him back. Before Lavender could ask any questions, Ethan began to ramble on again. His new friends. His crushes. His life. Not much had changed. He was the same little boy she'd left 4 years ago. He was definitely still clingy. The boy was practically trying to fuse into her side. Lavender didn't question it. She'd missed him too. Plus, she didn't mind. Cuddles were nice.

Eventually the words stopped and the fun began. They tossed stones and had a stick battle. They clambered over fallen trees and danced in mushroom rings. It was like they were little again.

Lavender didn't know why her mother would ever want to leave this place. If she could live forever in these woods, she would in a heartbeat. The dust of Arizona was blown away by the moist air of Washington. The sand was cleared by moss. The beaming hot sun was covered by clouds. This was her home. This was where she belonged. The world around her was alive and she finally felt alive too.

A twig snapping made Ethan and Lavender freeze. They turned toward the sound, expecting a deer or a fox.

Instead it was a boy.

Far off but Lavender could see him clearly. Her eyes were always strong. A trait she shared with her mother. The boy looked spooked. A stag in the headlights. He was Native, with long dark hair and obsidian eyes. The air blew and she caught his scent.

It was odd, faint, like he was miles away instead of a few yards.

In her periphery, she saw Ethan was clutching a moss covered rock. The boy looked like he was ready to fight this stranger. Lavender wondered if this boy had been one of the bullies Ethan had mentioned. She looked at the boy again. He was still stockstill. His black eyes were still wide in terror. No, she couldn't see him as a bully, even if he was big. "It's okay," Lavender whispered to ease Ethan. Her hand reached over and took his. She turned on the charm she'd gotten from her dad. "Hi!" she called to the boy warmly, "What's your name?!"

The boy's eyes somehow went wider. He ran into the trees and disappeared into the greenery. His movements were so fast he looked like a blur.

Lavender jumped. She let out an unsteady breath. That was wild. She wondered if he was on the track team. She'd heard small towns made great long distance runners, but that boy was ridiculous. "Have you ever seen him before?" Lavender asked Ethan. The boy was still uneasy, still clutching the rock.

"No," Ethan lied. "We need to leave." He tugged at her arm and the pair made their way back to the house. It felt like the rock he held was now in his stomach. He'd just gotten Ender back and now some bastard could not only scare her away, but possibly take her. He blinked the tears out of his eyes. He should have listened to his dad.

Lavender frowned. The boy was muttering to himself unconsciously. She only made out a few words. "Ethan, hey?" She tried to get him to stop and talk but he kept up his hurried pace.

"Home," he whimpered, tugging at her.

Lavender felt a swell of protectiveness. She planted her feet into the ground to stop them. "Little, calm down." Ethan finally stopped but kept holding her hand tightly. "What is it?" She could feel his nerves. They were like a live wire under his skin. His heart was racing so loud she could hear it over the forest.

Ethan pressed against her again. He'd never noticed before, but she really did smell like lavenders. It was calming. "There's been murders," he whispered in fear. Ethan nuzzled into her shoulder.

Lavender gasped, "What?!"

"Shhh!" Ethan hissed, even though there was no one else around for yards. "A few bodies in the woods, dad told me about it. They don't know if it's a killer or an animal. The bodies..." He squeezed her hand. Ethan remembered the crime scene photos and his stomach twisted. "Don't go into the woods alone." Ethan warned, "Never alone."

Lavender squeezed his hand back. "I promise, little bear. Never alone."

Ethan rubbed his forehead against her shoulder. "I'm glad you're home, mama."

Lavender wrapped her arms around him. She kissed his temple, "Me too."

10

Chapter 2

Branches' high school was small. It wasn't surprising, but it still made Lavender pause. It was night and day compared to Phoenix. She sighed and got out of the old truck. Her first car. It was rusting and dented. The blue paint was fading, but it was hers. Had meant to be hers since she was a child. She used to play in the bed of it. Pretending to be a pirate, or on the back of a dragon, or-

An overly chipper voice cut through her reminiscing. "Where are you from?"

Lavender jumped and turned to the girl behind her. "Um?" The girl was shorter than her, which wasn't unusual. Lavender was on the taller side and loved her swampers. Those boots gave her an extra 2 inches. The girl's crystal blue eyes were boring into her. They didn't hold any malice or ridicule, just pure curiosity.

"Sorry, that was rude. I didn't mean your," she gestured to Lavender's…everything. "I meant like, you're not from here, new face…so." The girl's deep southern accent was surprising.

Lavender hoped the grimace she felt wasn't showing on her face. "I'm from Arizona." She hoped the answer would sufficiently end the conversation.

It didn't.

"Oh, what tribe's out there?"

Lavender sighed, "I'm not a part of the tribe out there. My mom's from here." She noticed some of the other students were staring at her. Some gave her a sympathetic look. Lavender realized this girl definitely had some kind of reputation.

"Oh, cool!" The girl beamed. "Most go to the reservation school. I don't know why, our school is pretty nice. I mean only 3 of the teachers have been rac-" the girl paused, "Well, actually now that I think about it."

Lavender frowned. *How nice, only 3*, she thought sarcastically. "My mom and dad went here. I also don't live on the reservation." She hoped that would end the conversation and she could leave the girl pondering in the parking lot. She shrugged her backpack on and moved toward the school.

The girl followed. "Did you know you're our second new student this month?" She sounded so giddy about this piece of trivia and Lavender didn't have the heart to tell her to buzz off. The girl was harmless.

"Oh yea?" Lavender walked into the building. The fluorescent lights buzzed and made her wince. She hated frequency noises. She especially hated the fact that most people weren't bothered by them.

Even worse than the noise were the other people. So many smells blanketed the halls. From cherry blossom body mist to pubescent b.o. It was a thick miasma she had to wade through. Other people also meant more staring. Some even glaring. Lavender was a drop of color in a sea of white and they made sure she knew it.

"Yea, another Indian…or is it First Nation? Or Native?" The girl was going a mile a minute. "Did I offend you? I'm super sorry if I did." Her apology was earnest so Lavender didn't hold it against her.

"You're fine," Lavender sighed. "I like Native." She hated term debates. She did give the girl props though, most assumed Lavender was fully black or hispanic. Apparently the girl knew enough to see she was Indigenous. Mixed technically, but still, having a part of her acknowledged that most people ignored made her happy.

"Oh, cool beans!" The girl smiled again. "By the way, I'm Belle." Belle offered her perfectly manicured hand.

Lavender gave her a small smile and shook the offered hand. A new acquaintance would be nice. Her only friend was Ethan. "Nice to meet you. Lavender." She dug in her pocket for the note with her combination on it. Her locker looked a bit roughed up. Scraped and dented. Not unusable, but definitely needed a shine. The inside was worse. It was like something exploded and then fused to the walls. She decided to just keep her backpack on instead.

"Oh my god, your name's so pretty!" Belle giggled. "Hey, can I ask something?"

Lavender was surprised by the want for permission. She decided to humor the blonde. "Go for it?"

"Okay, so, is it true you guys have two names? Like a white name and your Ind-Native name?"

Lavender was befuddled and shrugged, "Maybe some do, I don't." She knew for a fact some people had to have nicknames because people outside their tribe refused to learn their real names. Lavender didn't feel like being an educator while in school though.

Belle beamed at the information. "Wow! You know, you're a lot nicer than the new guy. I tried to talk to him and he just froze me out. Didn't even look at me." Belle exasperatedly waved her hands, "Was like he wanted me to leave him alone!" She said it with such disbelief that it stunned Lavender.

I wonder why, Lavender thought. "Yea some people are loners," she closed her locker and tried to ignore the whispers about her. She hated that her hearing was above average. Lavender pulled out her class schedule and map and tried to make her way to homeroom.

"I know but not even a 'Hi'? I'd even take a 'kick rocks'!" Belle followed closely. "Like, no one has managed to get a word out of him! Even the teachers! He's so creepy. He just sits there. Doesn't even move half the time. I don't even think he's breathing!"

Lavender huffed, "Well, he could be shy." She didn't know why she was defending a dude she'd never met, but it felt right to. If Belle was right then the guy probably couldn't stand up for himself.

"I guess, but geez." Belle then smiled brightly again. Changing the subject she asked, "Anyway, wanna sit with me and my friends at lunch?"

Lavender sometimes hated how bubbly people would adopt her as a friend, but it was better than the alternative. Said alternative hit her like a ton of bricks from across the hall. She glared at a couple girls who were whispering snide remarks. They pointed at her, giggled, and whispered again. What they said made Lavender grit her teeth in rage. "Say it louder!" she challenged them.

The pair jumped. They obviously didn't think Lavender could hear them over the sea of students. The two turned tail and rushed down the hall.

"Whoa, what'd they say?" Belle asked, mostly so she'd never repeat it. Her new friend looked very scary and Belle never wanted that anger directed at her.

Lavender growled, "I'm not repeating it." She turned to the blonde, "That might be why he hasn't been talking."

Belle frowned, "I need to stop listening to my tunes so loud. I couldn't even hear them." She pressed against Lavender's side. "I'm sorry, I know some people here suck, and sometimes I suck too, but if you tell me I suck I'll try to suck less!"

Lavender snorted, unable to contain her laugh. Damn this girl and her true sincerity and her pretty smile.

Belle beamed at her joy. "So, lunch?" she asked, far more hopeful in getting a positive answer.

Lavender nodded. The girl was nice and that's all you could ask of a stranger. "Yeah, lunch."

The bell rang and Lavender fell back into the motions of school life. She wondered if she'd get to meet the strange boy Belle had told her about.

Even though the school was small, the lunch room was still loud. Mindless chatter. Clinking of trays. The buzzing of the cheap lights.

Lavender looked for Belle. She spotted the blonde in the center of the chaos. Of course. Belle perked up at the sight of her. The other students around her stared at Lavender.

"This is Lavender!" Belle introduced to her other friends. "She's super cool and from Arizona, and likes the term Native." The blonde looked so proud of herself.

Lavender smiled. Belle was a mess but she was the first real friend she'd made.

"This is Jeremy!" Belle pointed to the boy who was currently playing with a mini skateboard. He gave her a crooked grin and went back to his toy.

"This is Blake!" Belle pointed to the boy who was ramming his skateboard into Jeremy's. He looked up at Lavender and gave her a kind smile. The black boy was sitting next to Belle. The pair were nearly meshed together at the side. She was giving him the type of look Lavender had only seen in romance movies.

The blonde snapped out of her swooning. "And this is Carrie!" Finally pointing to the girl who seemed to be absorbed into her book. Carrie gave her a brief glance and a short wave.

Lavender set her tray down and took the free space at the table. "Nice to meet you all," she greeted the group. Lavender took a bite of her pizza.

"She is nicer," Carrie remarked while turning a page.

"And she's actually eating," Jeremy giggled. "Already better than sad boy." .

"Sad boy?" Lavender took a bite of her fry.

Blake used his head to gesture behind them. "Sad boy, new guy. Belle tried to drag him over here on his first day. Dude was super creepy."

"Still is, we've never seen him eat." Jeremy kickflipped his little skateboard.

Lavender moved to see the boy. The boy's black hair was bone straight, peaking out of his red hood. Lavender could see a sliver of his deep golden face. He was staring out the window. His eyes were far away. He was sitting alone, without food. Her heart clenched. No one deserved to go hungry. "Did you guys ever stop and think he couldn't afford it?"

The other members of the table paused their activities.

"I mean…his adopted dad's a doctor?" Belle offered. "Also his mom's on the council."

Lavender huffed, "Like adopted kids being abused is something new." She stood up, "I'm not letting a kid starve." Tray in hand, she went over to the boy. He was strangely still, like Belle said. It looked like he was holding his breath. Moving round the table, she got a clear look at his face. "Wait a minute."

The boy finally looked away from the window. His black eyes widened in shock.

"It is you!" Lavender set her tray down and sat across from him. "Hello, woodsy boy." She noticed the shock spreading across his face. "I guess you didn't see me the other day but my friend and I were in the woods and-"

"I remember you."

Lavender stopped. His voice was…odd. Deep and smooth, but wrong. There was another voice beneath it. Like a shadow behind his words. It wasn't right. It wasn't natural. Lavender shook off the shivers down her spine. This wasn't the first time she'd heard something strange in a person's voice. She wasn't going to shame a guy, who probably didn't even know his voice was weird, about it. Lavender mentally swore. Her ears were too sensitive for her own good.

"Cool," she forced a smile, "I'm Lavender." The boy was staring into her eyes. She thought they were a beautiful black until light hit them. Normally with black eyes you'd see the brown in the light. His showed red, a deep and beautiful red. They were a pair of teens with Peculiar eyes.

"Your eyes are gold?" His voice was unsteady. As if he was in disbelief at the fact.

14

Lavender snapped out of her thoughts. "Yea, it's hereditary," she explained. This wasn't her first rodeo with that observation. "My mom, her mom, grandmother," Lavender waved her hand as if to say etcetera. "Anyway, you want some?" She pushed her tray toward the middle of the table. "I got an apple, frozen peaches, fries, I kind of already ate some of the pizza but-"

"I don't eat."

Lavender was taken aback by this. "Oh?" She'd heard a lot of excuses to not take handouts before, but never that one.

He nodded and thought before clarifying, "Special…diet?" He tugged at his hoodie cuffs. "I eat a big meal before and after school." The boy gave her a shy smile.

It was adorable and made Lavender's heart skip a beat. Her eyes stared at the food. "You sure?" She gently nudged the tray closer to him, hoping to entice him, even just a little.

The boy was staring at her, studying her. His eyes turned gentle. "Yea." He pushed the tray back toward her. "Thank you though."

Lavender let it go. She picked up her apple and took a bite of it. The boy hopefully knew the offer was still open when it came to her food. "So, what's your name?" she asked. Her motherly instincts were currently screaming inside her and she needed a distraction.

The boy thought for a moment. His head tilted. His eyes looked to and fro. It was like he was trying to do algebra in his head. Finally, he answered, "Silas."

Lavender smiled, "That's beautiful. I'm Lavender"

Silas leaned forward and inhaled, "You smell like it."

Lavender was surprised by the comment. She'd been told it before, mostly by her mother. That was even how she got her name. It was just something she hadn't heard in years. It was nice to hear again. Lavender decided to match his weirdness. She leaned in and inhaled, "And you smell like the woods."

Silas balked but then giggled. His smile was bright, especially under the afternoon sun.

Lavender laughed along with him. She'd made another friend.

Chapter 3

"What's your next class?" Lavender asked.

"Biology." Silas was clutching the strap of his bag.

"Hey, me too!" Lavender dumped her trash and the two headed out of the lunch room. "You want to lead the way?" She gestured with her hand.

Silas looked at it, then took it. "Sure."

Lavender gasped, "Holy shit, dude!" She used her other hand to cover his. "You're freezing!" She tried to warm up his hand with hers. "No wonder you're wearing layers." Lavender let go of his hand once she was satisfied with its warmth. "Here, give me your other one."

Silas looked like he'd been smacked in the face. Eyes wide and mouth slightly open. He slowly handed his other hand over.

Lavender smiled, "Dad says I'm a living space heater. My mom is too." She teased, "surprised you aren't."

Silas forlornly said, "I used to be."

Lavender raised an eyebrow at the comment. She was about to let his hand go. Silas, however, decided to keep holding hers and guided her out of the cafeteria. The bell rang as they crossed the threshold. "Where'd you come from?" she asked.

"Oregan," Silas finally smiled, "Used to live up there with my grandparents."

Lavender looked at their connected hands. When was the last time someone held her hand? She couldn't recall. "How'd you end up here?" Lavender asked. Some of the other kids were staring at them.

Silas's voice was grave, "They died."

The finality of the statement was chilling.

"I'm sorry," Lavender gave his hand a reassuring squeeze. She tried to think of something else to break the ice. "I bet the woods there are beautiful."

Silas smiled, "They are." He looked at her, then their hands. It was as if something had clicked in his mind. "You weren't offering your hand for me to hold, were you?"

Lavender snorted, "No, I wasn't, but it's okay." She shrugged, "I'm used to this sort of thing." Lavender reminisced, "Mom and I used to always hold hands."

Silas teased, "Does the touchiness run in the tribe?"

Lavender shrugged, "I don't know."

"Oh, I thought you were-"

"No, my mom is from here, and she and I lived here on and off." Lavender continued, "I'd see my Nana and pseudo little brother, but we never did any… activities. None of the community stuff. No celebrations. No traditions. I don't even know the history. Aside from what I've found online. This is my first time back in 4 years." Lavender frowned, "My mom had a…"

"Falling out?" Silas offered.

Lavender nodded. "That obvious?" she asked sarcastically.

"Well, I know many don't just leave their families for shits and giggles." Silas guided her into the classroom. "Has to be for some reason."

Lavender let go of his hand and sat beside him. "Yea, her and my Nana had a fight and-," she groaned, "I don't know why I'm telling you all this."

"It's okay, I don't mind," Silas assured.

"I don't even know what they fought about. All I know is she and dad went to the rez together, but only she came back. Then bam! I'm in a car. Didn't even get to say goodbye to anyone." Lavender took out her notebook, "This is the first time I've been here without her. I don't even know if my Nana wants to see me. I'm also kind of scared to see her. So, I only have Ethan and Jerry."

"Ethan and Jerry?" Silas rested his head on his folded arms.

"Yea, Jerry is dad's best friend, also a deputy. Ethan is his kid and my best friend." She noticed the slight disappointed look on Silas's face. "He's like a little brother or, I guess, a son to me. He calls me Mama," she added.

Silas's dark eyes widened a bit then his face became neutral once more. "I always wanted a little brother," he confessed.

Lavender bumped him with her elbow. "Maybe you can meet him, he's always wanted a big brother."

Silas smiled brightly, "I'd like that."

"Alright class!" the teacher wiped off the chalkboard. "Let's get started."

"I can't believe you got him to talk!" Belle cheered. She was bouncing up and down. "Everyone thought he was mute. I have to guess it's cause of," she waved at Lavender's…everything. "Anyway, do you think he's being abused? I know Dean Amos, he's our sheriff.

Lavender snorted, "I know, he's my dad."

Belle's blue eyes went wide. "Seriously?! So you're mixed?"

"Yep," Lavender smiled, "Also, his name is Silas. I don't think he's being abused, just awkward."

"Understatement," Carrie added.

Lavender jumped, "Where'd you come from?"

"She does that sometimes," Belle assured her.

Blake came up and put an arm around Belle. "Hey, babe." He gave her a kiss on the forehead.

Lavender was surprised by the display.

"They only get touchy after school," Carrie explained. "They got in trouble too many times for doing it during."

"Leave us alone," Blake huffed, "Alexis and Mark get to kiss in the middle of the hallways but we hold hands and we get written up. Mr. Johnson is an ass."

Belle rested her head on his shoulder. "I know, honey."

Lavender couldn't miss the contrast of Blake's dark skin against Belle's. She frowned. Small town, small thinking.

Jeremy was already outside. When he saw the group he pointed to the shiny car in the parking lot. "Rich girl's here to pick up the creep."

"Silas," Belle chastised, "his name is Silas, Jer." She smiled at Lavender, "She managed to get through that thick shell. You should have seen it, in Bio, she got him to smile!" Belle squealed, "Maybe we'll have a new friend."

Jeremy rolled his eyes and Blake chuckled, Carrie was still in her book.

Lavender sighed. What Motley Crew had she ended up in? She looked at the fancy car. It stuck out like a sore thumb among the dirty pickup trucks and 80s resales. A woman stepped out. She was…ethereal. Unnaturally beautiful. Wavy auburn hair and a thin frame. She looked like a starlet from the 1930s. Lavender frowned when she noticed the beautiful woman was parked right next to her truck. "Fuck my life," Lavender groaned. She decided she'd wait for the woman to leave. It would save her from humiliation.

"Lavender?"

Said girl whipped around. Silas emerged from the sea of students. "Hey," Lavender perked up again. The gorgeous woman was forgotten.

Silas nervously pulled a folded piece of paper out of his pocket. "Here."

Lavender took it. "Oh, thank you-"

"Okay, bye!" Silas ran off, down the stairs and to the beautiful woman.

Lavender was shocked. She watched him duck into the fancy black car on the passenger side. The woman looked at Lavender. Her eyes narrowed. Lavender watched as the car drove away.

"So…what's the note say?" Jeremy asked, moving to take it from Lavender.

"Obviously something for me!" she snapped and left down the stairs.

"Don't be so sensitive!" Jeremy called after her and was smacked on the arm by Belle. "Knock it off!" the blonde warned.

Lavender got in her truck and drove home. Dean was still on duty so she took the opportunity to open the note in the living room. She gasped at the beautiful illustration of her. The portrait was surrounded by lavender flowers. Silas was quite the artist. "Hell yea, woodsy boy." Under the art was a note.

Thank you,

I had a lot of fun today

~Silas

Lavender smiled and noticed the phone number underneath the signature. She bit her lip and wondered when would be a good time to call. Lavender bounced her leg anxiously. She pressed the letter to her chest.

For the first time, she had a crush.

Lavender found Silas at the same table during lunch. She looked at Belle and her misfits and debated where to sit. Lavender sat across from Silas. "Hey."

The boy looked up at her in shock. "Hey." His voice was soft, like a cloud on the summer breeze. Even the second voice he had was merely a faint whisper.

Lavender relaxed. "You want to sit over there?" She gestured her head at Belle's table. The blonde noticed them looking and waved.

Silas frowned. "They don't like me."

Lavender explained, "In fairness you didn't try to get them to like you." She noticed the shocked look on his face. "I'm just saying, they'd be willing to do a retry if you are." Lavender smiled, "I want my friend to have friends." She leaned in and whispered, "Also they're a lot and I could use a distraction."

Silas smiled cheekily, "So I'm a human shield?"

Lavender pursed her lips. "No, more like a buffer," she teased.

Silas nodded. "Yeah, alright, I'll try again."

The pair went to Belle's table. The group looked Silas up and down. Lavender sat and Silas sat beside her.

Belle turned on her charm. "Well, hello again stranger!" She beamed, "I see you've met Lavender, isn't she awesome?"

Silas nodded, "Yeah, she is."

Lavender snorted, "Shut up!" She began to eat. Her mind prayed to whatever was listening that Silas didn't notice her blush. If he did, the boy thankfully didn't tease her about it.

Silas looked at Carrie. "Is that book good? I read the first one a couple months ago, but I'm scared the sequel might ruin it."

Carrie looked up in surprise. She placed her bookmark to keep her place. "It's pretty good."

"Do Jake and Mary get together?" Silas asked. He didn't want to read the sequel if his favorite pairing didn't get their deserved romance.

Carrie smiled sheepishly. "Well, I don't want to spoil it."

Silas assured, "No, no, spoil it! I need to know."

Carrie sighed, "They go through a lot but they do end up together."

Silas whispered in wonder. "I knew it."

Jeremy leaned forward so he could look past Lavender and see the weirdo. "Are you a fucking nerd too?" Lavender turned so sharply that the boy flinched. "I was just teasing, I promise!" Jeremy thought Lavender's eyes were beautiful, but they were also terrifying. He thought she would and could rip his throat out with her teeth.

Lavender growled, "Better have been."

Belle shuddered, "Oh, I felt that in my bones!" She giggled and gripped Blake's arm. "Wasn't that cool?"

Blake thought it was more horrifying than enchanting. He forced a chuckle, "Yea cool."

Lavender went back to eating. From the corner of her eyes, she could see Silas's shocked face. "What?" she asked, halfway through an apple.

Silas blushed and looked at the table. "Nothing."

Lavender was walking to her truck when Silas ran up to her. She smelt him and heard him before she saw him. Silas moved weird. Almost like everyone else but also…not. Lavender turned around before he could call for her attention. She saw that look of shock for the second time today. "What's up?"

Silas bit his lip. He gently kicked a stray rock. He was fidgety and obviously weighing his words. "Would you…maybe, um."

Lavender stepped closer. "Hey." Those black eyes stared into hers. "Just ask."

Silas sighed. She was giving him a kind smile. The kind of smile that makes you feel safe. Silas realized that's what he was feeling. Safe. Lavender made him feel safe. Silas took his shot, "I found a waterfall the other day. Do you want to see it?"

Lavender frowned a bit. "Is that a euphemism?"

Silas was confused. "Um no…what could that be a euphemism for?"

Lavender shrugged, "I don't know."

Silas tugged at his sleeve. "Well, it's not. It's like an actual waterfall." He remembered his sketch and took off his back pack. "Look," he found his sketchbook and showed Lavender his picture. "It's beautiful right?"

Lavender nodded. She was amazed by Silas's talent. "You're incredible," she whispered.

Silas blushed again. He cleared his throat and took the book back. "So, want to go? My sister isn't picking me up today so-"

"Why isn't she getting you?"

Silas tried to think of an excuse. "She had an appointment."

"You don't live in town though!" Lavender huffed, "They just abandoned you?"

Silas saw that protectiveness again. It was sweet. "Well, the waterfall is near my house, so two birds one stone," he lied.

Lavender bought it. She agreed. "Okay, let's go."

Silas was shocked by how easy that was. "Really?"

Lavender opened the door of her truck and got in. She looked back at the disbelieving Silas. "Yeah?"

The boy's face lit up and he went to the passenger side and hopped in.

Lavender giggled at his enthusiasm. She turned on the radio and the two drove out of the parking lot. Silas gave her directions. They went outside of town and pulled off on the side of the road. It was a rare gravel patch for her to park on. "How did you find this?" Lavender asked as they got out.

"I was running around the woods," Silas explained, "I've been coming every chance I get." He offered his hand to her. "Come on," he urged.

Lavender looked at his hand. There was something off about it. It looked smooth, like a porcelain doll's. Instincts screamed to turn away, to drive off and go home. That voice was drowned out by another. One that screamed to see a beautiful waterfall with her new friend. This strange and beautiful boy. Lavender placed her hand in his. They walked through the trees and into the dense woods.

"Watch your step," Silas warned and pointed to the debris-covered ground.

Lavender stepped over the tripping branches and thick brush. She could hear water. They came upon a stream. Silas let go of her hand to hop across the stones poking out of the water. Once he got to the other side, he turned and smiled. His joy was infectious. Lavender hopped the stones and the pair began walking again.

Silas's hand found its way back to hers again. Lavender took in the greenery. The sound of the birds and the babbling brook. "I missed the woods," she whispered mindlessly.

"Where were you?" Silas asked. He kept an ear out for the rush of water that would lead them to the waterfall.

"Arizona, fucking sucked." Lavender kicked a stone. It hit the tree harder than she'd meant to. She sighed, "It's just sun and dust."

Silas responded without thought, "I don't like the sun."

Lavender chuckled, "Me neither. Too hot." She could hear the waterfall now. Lavender decided to let Silas take the lead though.

Silas looked at her from the corner of his eye. She didn't call out his odd comment. He appreciated it. "It's this way," he pointed toward some trees.

Lavender could make out the falls. She got excited and ran ahead. "Oh, it's gorgeous!"

Silas chuckled and jogged to catch up to her.

The waterfall sat high above them. The sheer rock it was coming off from was covered with moss and brush. Lavender inhaled and felt her entire body relax. There was a rocky bank on the edge of the lake. Aside from the section under the falls, the water was pretty calm. Lavender sat on the rocks. Silas came and sat beside her. "How did you find this place?"

Silas wrapped his arms around his knees and hugged them to his chest. "I was having a mental breakdown and was running around."

Lavender was shocked by the admission. She knew that feeling though. Feeling so overwhelmed and needing to just run. "Hey, at least you found something cool!"

Silas smiled, "Yea, true." He laid back on the rocks. The sky was cloudy and the gray was comforting. Silas looked at Lavender. The girl was odd, like him. Her eyes were gold. Her mind was open. Her skin seemed to shimmer. Every strange thing about her was beautiful. As if hearing his thoughts, she turned.

Lavender chuckled at the boy. "Doesn't that hurt?"

Silas looked at the rocks next to him. "No." The girl gave him a skeptical look.

Lavender tugged off her boots and rolled up her jeans. "I'm going in!" She stood and splashed into the water.

Silas sat up on his elbows and watched her go. "What are you doing?"

Lavender looked back at him. "I want some cool rocks!"

Silas laughed, falling back on the rocks.

Lavender giggled and looked into the water. She snatched up some stones. When she straightened up, Silas was beside her. Lavender jumped, "Holy shit, dude!" She saw he'd left his shoes on the bank. "You scared me."

The boy sheepishly smiled, "Sorry." He reached into the water, kicking up some silt to the surface. "Why do you like rocks?" he asked.

Lavender tossed the stones she didn't want back. "I like making art stuff. I prefer sea glass but…" she trailed off, remembering Nana's house. Silas didn't pry and she appreciated it.

"Why sea glass?"

"Family tradition." Lavender put the stones she wanted in her pants pocket.

Silas noticed she preferred smooth to textured. She liked them rounded and not neutral tones. Silas dug through the spring. He felt like a penguin. Here he was trying to find a pretty rock to impress a girl. Lavender cooed. The sound made Silas stand up straight. The girl had a black stone in her hand. She was holding it up to the gray sky.

"Come look!" she insisted.

Silas stood close to her.

"See." Lavender tilted the rock this way and that. In certain light the black revealed a red. "It's just like your eyes," she mused.

Silas watched as she tucked the stone into the breast pocket of her flannel. He felt a blush creeping onto his cheeks. He had a crush.

Chapter 4

Lavender sat on her bed. The alarm on her nightstand read 7:00 pm. The cordless house phone rested in her palm. A debate began to rage in her mind. The letter Silas gave her the other day was laying in front of her. The stone that reminded Lavender of his eyes sat on top of it. She looked at the beautiful illustration of her then the number.

They had fun at the falls. Silas had found a bunch of beautiful rocks for her. They were currently on her desk. Around 4 o'clock Lavender offered to drive him back. Silas said his house was an easy walk from there though. Lavender didn't believe him but she also didn't push. He saw Lavender off by the side of the road and now here she was. Lavender wanted to make sure he'd actually gotten home safe. It was late enough that he would have most likely eaten dinner and would be free to talk.

Lavender looked at the letter and dialed the number. She put the phone up to her ear and tried to collect herself while it rang.

"Hello?"

Lavender froze. The voice on the other end was female. She didn't know why she'd believe Silas would pick up.

"Hello?" the voice seemed confused.

"Yes, sorry!" Lavender paused for a moment before asking, "Is Silas there?"

"Silas?"

"Yes, um, this is Lavender," she introduced, "Do…do I have the right number, I'm sorry if-"

"One moment, dear." There was some movement on the other end. "Silas! There's a Lavender on the phone for you."

More movement, this time frantic. The sound of the phone being passed then Silas's voice came through, "Hi!" His voice was so excited it made Lavender's heart skip a beat. There were then gasps on Silas's end of the line. Things fell to the floor and a pause followed. "One second," he said. There was more movement. Whispers and hisses but it seemed Silas was racing past them. Then there was a closing of a door. "Sorry, hi."

Lavender was smiling like an idiot. "Hi." She looked at the letter. "Also I forgot to tell you. Thank you for the portrait, it's beautiful." She could practically see Silas's sheepish grin.

"Well, it helps that I had a beautiful subject."

Lavender giggled and relaxed against her headboard. They sat in silence until Lavender thought of something to ask, "So, was that your foster mom?"

"Adoptive, yea," Silas was moving, "she's great. I never had a mom so…"

Lavender frowned, "Well, better late than never?" She prayed her joke would land. It did.

Silas snorted out a laugh. "Yea, I guess!" There was a squeak of bedsprings.

So he's in his room too, Lavender thought. She laid down. "Was she that woman at school?"

"Nah, that was Eden. She's my sister."

"Oh, cool, you have any more siblings?"

"Yea. Matthias, my dad, and Ariyah, my mom, took in a crap load of misfits. I'm the youngest, everyone else is an adult. But yea, there's Everett and Jonathan, they're the oldest. Then Eden, then Hana, and then me."

"So you're the baby," Lavender teased.

Silas snorted, "Yea, they make sure I know it too. They baby me a lot."

"How long have you been with them?"

"Fuck," Silas sighed, "I don't know, 9…11 years? Maybe?"

Lavender frowned, "You don't know how long you've been with them?"

"I…was asleep for a while."

Lavender sat up. "Asleep?"

"I…a coma. I was in a coma." There was shifting. "At our last home, I got…" His voice trailed off.

Lavender frowned. "I'm sorry, Silas." She sat cross legged. "You don't have to talk about it, if you don't want to."

The other end went quiet.

Lavender was scared he had hung up, but remembered she would have heard the dial tone.

"Thank you," he finally said, his voice wavering. "I'm sorry…you're my first friend…in a long time."

Lavender smiled, "I'm happy to be." She relaxed again. "You're a cool dude," she added. Silas gave her a short laugh.

"Thanks, Lavender."

Lavender smiled, "Anyway, I should probably do my homework."

"You didn't do it yet?"

Lavender rolled her eyes. "Listen, I'm a hunter, not a homeworker."

Silas teased, "No, you're a dork."

Lavender scoffed, "A dork that could out fish you."

"That a challenge?"

"Absolutely."

"You're on!" Silas was full of excitement, "This weekend?"

"I'd love that," Lavender felt giddy. "Oh, you could meet Ethan!" She added, "He can help you win."

Silas huffed, "You sure he wouldn't be there to help you?"

"Oh, I'm going to bury you in trout!"

"Can't wait," Silas said, joy in his voice.

Lavender stood, going to her bookshelf to touch her polaroid camera. "We can make some fun memories."

"I'd like that."

Lavender frowned, "I need to go, but I don't want to."

"You could do your homework while I stay on the line. We can keep talking and I can help you."

"I don't want to take up too much of your time."

"I have loads of time," Silas went quiet for a moment before adding, "and I'd love to spend it with you."

Lavender felt her heart skip a beat. "Okay," she sat at her desk and put the phone on speaker. "What subject should I do first?"

"Biology."

Saturday was here and Lavender felt like she would vibrate out of her body with excitement. "He's super smart, nervous, but really sweet and-"

"You've been gushing about him for days!" Ethan groaned and face planted into Lavender's bed. "I've never seen you go gaga over a guy before." He huffed, "Thought you'd be like aunt Lee."

Lavender rolled her eyes, "Listen, he's just-"

"Amazing, I know!" Ethan sat up, "If he sucks I'm going to be so disappointed in you."

"He's awkward at first, but I promise, he's really nice."

Ethan rolled his eyes. "The picture he drew of you is good, I'll give him that." He hopped off her bed. "Can I carry the camera?"

"As long as you don't break it."

"I was 8!"

"And I'll never let you forget it," Lavender teased, ruffling his hair. She finished putting her braids into buns on the top of her head. "How do I look?" She turned to the boy, who gave her a tired expression.

"You're wearing overalls, not going to the Met." Ethan fixed his hair.

"The what?"

"It's a fashion thing. Listen, you look fine. Like a weird forest loner's dream girl." Ethan put the polaroid strap around his neck. "So is he picking us up or…?"

"Yea, he's-"

The doorbell rang and Lavender raced out of her room and down the stairs.

"Wait up!" Ethan called after her. He followed downstairs.

She ran past Jerry and Dean on the couch. "Whoa, where's the fire, Ender?"

"Cute boy. Door," Ethan answered, also running past.

Jerry snorted and rolled into a full belly laugh. "Better you than me," he lifted his beer in a mock cheers.

"Oh you only got a few more years, buddy," Dean growled, pointing an accusatory finger.

"Well, I'll laugh at you in the meantime," he gently punched his friend's shoulder.

Lavender opened the front door. Silas had his long hair pulled back, showing his full face. At the sight of her, his eyes lit up.

"Your buns are cute," he said, a blush on his face.

"Thanks, I like your overalls," Lavender said stupidly and immediately regretted it.

"Oh, thanks, Hana picked them out for me!"

Lavender smiled. *Go, my stupid mouth!*

"Let's go!" Ethan demanded. "You two can flirt after we fish!" He pushed past the pair of blushing doofuses.

Lavender snickered, "Sorry, he's a booger."

Silas shrugged, "Every group needs a sassy little brother."

"Damn straight!" Ethan picked up a bucket, "Come on!"

Chapter 5

Despite Ethan's brazen attitude, he immediately took to Silas. The pair were having fun cheating at fishing.

"Dammit, Ethan!" Lavender roared when the boy tossed a rock near her lure.

"What?" he asked innocently, picking up another stone.

Silas gave her a smug smile. "You regretting your bet?" he called over.

"I'm gonna shove my pole up your ass!" Lavender shook her fist at the boys.

Silas and Ethan laughed at her rage. "All I hear is a sore loser," Ethan teased.

"That's it!" Lavender dropped her pole and ran toward their side of the bank.

"Run for your life!" Ethan screamed, dropping his rock and running toward the forest. Silas dropped his pole and ran after him and away from a sprinting Lavender. The boys laughed as Lavender chucked moss at them.

Ethan grabbed a clump of mud and threw it back. It hit the pocket on the front of Lavender's overalls.

She stopped in her tracks, moss in her hand. "You little!" She threw the clump full force.

Silas jumped in front of it, "I got you, bud!" He got hit square in the chest, dramatically falling to the forest floor.

"Silas, no!" Ethan wailed, falling to his knees. "What have you done?!" he cried. He looked at Lavender, "Have you no heart?!"

She laughed, "Jesus christ, you both can't be dramatic!"

"How am I dramatic?!" Silas flared his arms, "I'm dead!"

Both Lavender and Ethan burst into laughter.

Silas smiled brightly and sat up. He brushed the dirt and moss off him.

"Thanks for taking the hit," Ethan patted Silas's shoulder. "I declare you are good enough for Lavender."

Silas balked. "Good enough?"

"It's okay, she likes you too," Ethan nonchalantly announced. He got a face of moss for his trouble.

"Shut up, Little!"

"What?! I'm helping!" The 14 year old declared, wiping his face clean. "Who knows how long you two doofuses would have taken! Months, years?!"

Silas giggled and stood. "Here," he offered his hand to the boy. Ethan took it, allowing himself to be pulled to his feet.

Lavender took a bandana out of her pocket. She went to the boys. "Stay out of my business," she chastised. Taking Ethan's face in her hand, to wipe it clean.

"God, you're such a mom!" Ethan whined but leaned into the cleaning. He looked at Silas and rolled his eyes.

"And you're such a brat." Lavender finished and turned to clean off Silas's overalls.

"She's always been like this," Ethan said when Silas gave him a confused look.

"Shut up," Lavender twisted the handkerchief into a roll and cracked it at Ethan.

"Ah!" The boy ran off into the woods.

Lavender wound the bandana again and gave Silas a mischievous smile. The other boy dashed after Ethan. She ran after the pair.

"She's crazy!" Ethan declared. "I'm starting to see that," Silas agreed.

"I'm going to get you two!" Lavender declared. The air changed direction and Lavender felt her stomach tighten. A strange smell was on the wind. A foul smell. The realization hit her like a freight train. "Stop!" she called out.

"Got to be faster than that!" Silas teased over his shoulder. When he turned back the smell hit him. He grabbed Ethan by the back of his shirt.

Ethan let out a yelp. "Hey dude, what g-" He saw where Silas was staring and followed his eyes. Ethan gagged. He shook out of Silas's hold and backed away to retch by a tree. "What the fuck?!"

Lavender came to stand beside Silas. Her stomach twisted. The smell of death was so distinct. It was like nothing she'd ever smelled before. There was something in her though, something primal and old, that knew this smell well. Lavender went to Ethan and picked the boy up. "We need to get my dad," she said with finality. Ethan had his face buried in her shoulder.

Silas nodded in agreement. He followed behind her, hoping to shield the still shaking boy from the sight.

The body's eyes had been taken,

and its throat had been ripped out.

The 3 sat on Dean's worn couch. He was in full detective mode. "And you didn't touch it?" he asked again.

"No, dad. Jesus." Lavender huffed.

"What were you doing out there?" Jerry snapped, he looked at Ethan, "I told you-"

"It was my idea, uncle Jerry," Lavender defended, "We were having a fishing contest."

"We won," Ethan declared. Everyone gave him a look. He sunk into the couch. "Just trying to lighten the mood."

Dean rubbed his face. "Okay, so…you?" He looked at Silas.

"Silas."

"Silas, you need to go home. Tell your dad we're going to need him at the morgue."

Silas nodded, "Okay." He stood and looked at Lavender. "I had fun, till…" he shook his head, "I'll see you Monday."

"Bye," Lavender said softly. A part of her wondering if this was how their story would end. With a corpse.

Silas passed Jerry, who was giving him a heavy glare. The front door closed and Jerry immediately piped up. "I don't want that doctor involved anymore."

"His credentials are better than the city boys they send us." Dean rubbed his tired eyes.

"I don't trust th-"

"Enough, Jer, they're good people."

Jerry huffed, "We obviously have two different ideas on 'people'." He then turned to his son, "Come on, Ethan." The boy hopped up and went to his father's side. "I'll see you at the station."

Dean nodded and waited for them to leave before turning to Lavender. "Flower-"

"What did Jerry mean by that?"

Dean massaged his temples. He mulled over his words before deciding to ignore the question entirely. With a sigh he sat next to Lavender. "I don't want you in the woods anymore."

"But dad-"

"It's not just the murders. We also have sightings of rabid animals." Dean took her hands. "Promise me, no woods till we get this under control."

Lavender huffed, "Okay, fine."

"Thank you," Dean kissed his daughter's knuckles. "I love you, Ender, I'd never be able to forgive myself if something were to happen to you."

Lavender smiled, "I love you too, dad."

Dean stood again, "Alright, I'm going to get dressed and head into town. You stay here, I'll give you some money to order something."

"Okay," Lavender stood. "I'm going to shower."

"Alright, I'll leave the money on the table."

Lavender went up stairs and into the bathroom. She stared at herself in the mirror. The smell of death was still in her nose.

She quickly got into the shower.

Lavender was on her bed again, phone in hand. She debated calling. Wondering if Silas would even want to talk to her. She weighed her options, then the phone rang. Lavender immediately answered, "Hello?"

"Hey."

Silas's voice soothed Lavender's racing mind. "Hey," she replied lamely. Lavender wanted to bash her head into the wall. "Are you feeling okay?" she asked.

"What? Oh, yea, that wasn't my first time seeing a dead body." The 'unfortunately' was left unsaid, but was heard in his voice. "Anyway, you alright?"

Lavender nodded. "Yea, I'm okay. Was just…It's weird how you can never smell a dead body before but you know the scent immediately." She laid on her back and looked at the stars taped to her ceiling. Her dad and her had put them up one summer and never took them down. The glow in the dark effect no longer worked, but they were comforting. Lavender needed that right now.

"Do you want me to come over?"

Lavender was shocked, "You reading my mind?"

The other end of the line was quiet for a moment. "I know your dad's out. My dad is out. Plus, my siblings are being…weird." There was shifting and moving. "So it'd be for you and me."

Lavender laughed, "I guess we both need an escape."

"So yes?"

"Yes."

Chapter 6

Silas was unfairly good at candyland.

"This is bullshit, you're cheating!" Lavender snapped. She glared at Silas's colorful game piece. It was squares ahead of hers. The little bastard.

Silas snickered, "I can't cheat at this." He drew a card and moved his piece. "You're so competitive."

"Blame my parents," Lavender said, pulling another card. She noticed Silas's amused smile. He traced lines on the table. "And you could totally cheat!"

Silas snorted, "How?" He moved his piece.

Lavender thought for a moment. "Moving my piece when I'm not looking. Eating the cards."

Silas laughed out loud. "Why would I do that?!"

Lavender sneered, "I don't know! You're the criminal mastermind, not me." She cheered when she got a character card and finally got ahead of Silas.

Silas put his head down and laughed into his folded arms. "I can't deal with you," he said through giggles. He drew another card and moved his piece. He eventually asked, "Is Ethan okay?"

Lavender paused at the question. That was another reason Ethan called her 'mama'. Her face turned melancholy. Ethan and her found Aunt Millie. "Ethan's seen dead bodies before." Thankfully, she wasn't mangled like the corpse in the woods. Granted, the corpse in the woods was less traumatic.

Silas tried to cut through the tension. "Sucks that, that is something we have in common." He gently nudged Lavender's foot, "Aside from having fun messing with you."

Lavender gasped in amusement. "Asshole," she lightly kicked him under the table. The pair began playfully kicking each other under the table. They both laughed and after a time relaxed. The game was forgotten.

"Dad says I can't go in the woods for a while," Lavender bemoaned. She rested her head on her arms. "So our fishing rematch will have to wait for a while."

"Understandable. It'll give you time to practice," Silas teased.

Lavender reached across the table, touching Silas's hand. He opened it and she took it in hers. Holding hands across the table, the pair went silent. The clock ticked by. A drip from the faucet followed the rhythm. Silas's black eyes stared into Lavender's. Black and gold. No, that wasn't right. The light caught Silas's eyes perfectly. Black, blood, and gold.

The silence continued.

It wasn't uncomfortable.

It wasn't tense.

It was peaceful.

Silas broke the quiet. "I like you," he whispered.

The weight of his words settled over Lavender like a blanket. A smile spread across her face. "I like you too," Lavender replied. She squeezed his hand.

Silas wiped his face. He couldn't cry here. "So…what now?" he asked.

Lavender shrugged. "I guess…we can try."

Silas smiled. He nodded slowly. "I'd like that."

Silas went home around ten. She had gotten pizza but he hadn't touched his slice. Lavender wondered what type of diet he had to be on. Dean had called to tell her he wouldn't be home till much later. Lavender decided to clean the house.

Her father wasn't filthy, but he definitely let dust build up. She just needed to keep busy. Her first month here and she already had a boyfriend! There's also a serial killer in the area, which dampened the mood. Lavender was too hopped up on excitement and terror. She needed to get the energy out somehow, so she cleaned.

A knock on the door made her heart rate spike. It was close to midnight. No one should be here.

"Hello?" There was glass beside the door, allowing her to see the porch. The man on the other side looked odd. He was eerily still. His hair was long and wavy, trimmed facial hair, and a blank expression. His eyes were strange. They were a striking blue, but his pupils… His pupils were wide. They were boring into her. They looked her up and down and then a smile slowly spread across his face.

"How lucky am I to find a lone pup? No mama to guard you?" His voice was wrong. Under the southern drawl was a shadow. Like Silas's voice, there was a second underneath. Unrecognizable to most, but Lavender could hear it. "**Let me in, little gold.**"

Lavender furrowed her brow. This son of a bitch wasn't getting inside, come hell or high water. "Get the fuck off my property," she growled.

His eyes widened in wonder. "Oh, those eyes. How I've missed them." He moved his face close to the glass. His pupils now swallowed up the blue. The second voice was louder. It went from a whisper to a roar. "Let me in!" His forehead was against the glass now. "Have you ever been to Paris, little savage?" The man tapped on the glass. "Just come outside, we can go together. I have friends that would love to meet you."

Lavender felt her stomach drop. This creep was probably some trafficker. "Get the fuck off my property!" she demanded again.

The man snorted and laughed. A full belly laugh that made Lavender dizzy with rage and worry. "Oh, you've got bite! My little gold one was a meek thing. Skittish. Quiet." He leaned back in. "How about we play a game? They aren't expecting me back for a while. Those old bastards don't know about modern travel." He tapped on the door. "I bet I can get you out."

You want to play a game?

Lavender jolted. The man's mouth had been closed. She heard the voice inside her head. Lavender was done with this guy's bullshit. She punched the glass, making the man jump back. "GET THE FUCK OFF MY PROPERTY!" She blinked and the man was off the porch. He had retreated to the yard. Still staring at her, he began to laugh.

"Oh, you're gonna make me work for it, aren't you?" His voice was so gleeful. As if she'd given him a Christmas present. "Let's play, little gold!" He began to hop from foot to foot.

Lavender blinked.

He was gone.

Oh shit.

Lavender immediately went to the phone to call her dad. There were sounds from outside, breaking branches and movement. They weren't natural. She grabbed the notepad next to the phone and began to scribble down the man's features. Lavender could hear him racing around. Was he casing the place? Was he just trying to freak her out?

Come out, come out! he taunted. *Come on little savage!*

Lavender whipped around in terror. Where was the voice coming from? It was the man's, but he wasn't inside or behind her. It'd come from her mind. Was she imagining it? She grit her teeth and ignored it. "Focus," she told herself. She began to write down his features. Dean taught her how important it was to write things down while they were fresh.

6 ft.

Blue eyes.

Pale skin.

High cheekbones.

Long hair.

Brown or black?

She wrote as the phone rang, trying to connect.

"Sheriff's department?"

"Miriam, this is Lavender, tell my dad a guy's here. He's trying to get into the house!" she frantically explained. She tucked the phone by her ear. With her back to the wall, she shuffled into the living room. The lights flickered above her. Lavender gasped. This son of a bitch!

Come on, pretty girl, let me see ya! His voice was piercing into her mind. The man was standing in front of the bay window. *I'll be gentle, I promise,* he spoke without moving his mouth.

"Fuck off!" Lavender screeched. She took the shotgun off the wall and began to load it. The man moved out of sight. Lavender kept her back to the wall. "He's running around the house!" she told Miriam. "He's trying to get me outside! He said he wants to take me somewhere." Her heart was practically beating out of her chest.

Miriam tried to reassure her, "Wait there, honey, I'm getting your dad now!" There was movement on the other end. "DEAN!" she called out. "Stay on the phone with me, Ender," Miriam instructed.

The noises on the other end of the line blurred. The lights finally went out. The dial tone began to beep in her ear. Lavender cursed and dropped the phone. It crashed to the ground. The man was still going. Lavender could hear him going round and round. He obviously couldn't come in without her inviting him. She was safe as long as she stayed inside.

Stayed inside.

"Dad," she whispered in horror. He'd show up and this asshole would still be here. The guy moved fast. He obviously wasn't human. What would he do to Dean? Terror gripped her. Lavender shook her head. She wasn't going to risk it. She'd blow the man's head off before he could even think about touching her father.

A rock flew through the window. The speed of it was mind boggling. It turned the glass into shrapnel. Lavender turned her head away from the debris. She caught a glimpse of him as he ran by. He was taunting her.

What a pretty girl you'll be, when you're bouncing on my knee, he sang into her mind. The sound of his footsteps echoed outside. He kept singing and made Lavender's stomach twist in disgust.

"I'M ARMED!" Lavender warned, readying the shotgun. The window over the sink exploded. It made Lavender jump in fright. The glass by the front door was knocked out after.

Come on, pretty girl. The man stood in front of the destroyed bay window. *Just come out. I know a little thing like you can't use that big ol' gun.* His smile was twisted. Still, his lips didn't move when he spoke. *Why don't you invite me in so I can show you?*

Lavender raised her weapon, "Fuck off"! He laughed and ran off again. She kept her back to the wall. This was insane. Was he a ventriloquist? No, no, that didn't make sense either. How was his voice in her head? Hot tears filled her eyes. She took a deep breath. Supernatural or not, she could do this. She would get this bastard down before he could hurt Dean.

The man ran by the bay window again. She aimed her barrel to the far end. Lavender took a deep breath. As soon as he was in sight, she'd pull the trigger. She waited for him to come back. This guy was doing laps and her buckshot was going to be his finish line. She counted as he approached, "3, 2, 1." He emerged at the near end of the window.

She fired.

His head popped like a balloon. The contents splattered on the window frame. A howl rang out as he went down. He began screaming inside her mind. Lavender winced and tried to block him out. To her surprise, it worked. Outside he was still yelling though. Lavender was puzzled. How the hell was he making noise? Lavender went to the window. The man looked up at her. Half his face was gone.

His second voice was hissing in rage as the one most would register gurgled out, "I'll rip off those pretty little arms and drag you back to the cave." The man began twitching and shaking his head back and forth. The contents of what remained hung loose and swayed in the air.

"Good luck, without your head." Lavender raised the shotgun again. "Dad taught me to always double tap," her finger went to the trigger. The man looked up at her in terror.

Good.

There was a wail of sirens and screeching tires. Red and blue lights flooded in. Lavender lowered the gun. The man was forgotten in favor of her father. Lavender needed to warn Dean.

"ENDER!" her father called out.

"Watch out, dad!" Lavender looked at the mangled man one last time. He looked too broken to move. He'd keep. She ran to the front door. She opened it and her father's arms wrapped around her. "I shot him, dad, I shot him!" she cheered.

"Are you hurt?" Dean asked, pulling away to look her over.

Lavender shook her head, "No, promise." She heard the man moving. That wasn't good. She ran past her father, toward the outer side of the destroyed bay window. Her gun was raised as she came around the corner.

Nothing.

Brains and a lot of blood, but no body. Lavender looked around in confusion. A trail of red led into the woods. "Son of a bitch!" Rage filled her. She had him! She had him down! How could she let him get away?!

Dean noticed the gore. His blood ran cold. This wasn't good. "Get some clothes, Ender." Dean took the gun from her. "Pack your toothbrush too," he added. Dean guided his daughter back to the front of the house. "5 minutes."

"Why?" Lavender asked as she was pushed forward and up the steps.

"You're going to Ethan's," Dean answered bluntly. He'd freak out later, right now, he needed his daughter safe. In all of this, the pack had been unaffected. The reservation had suffered no casualties. He was going to use that to his advantage.

Lavender was shocked. She hadn't been on the rez in years. A part of her was excited to finally go back, but the situation at hand was dire. Lavender protested, "I can't just leave you-"

"Lavender, clothes, now!"

Her dad didn't raise his voice unless something was wrong, very very wrong.

"Dean?" A man had exited a patrol car. He was in a suit, unnaturally kempt for the time of night. His voice had a shadow too, incredibly faint, but there. "Is she hurt?" he asked.

Lavender shook her head.

Dean answered verbally for her, "She's fine, Doc." He ushered her inside. "Go, Ender."

Lavender raced through the house and to her room. She piled some clothes and other essentials into a backpack. Lavender looked at the note Silas had given. She grabbed it, refolded it, and tucked it into her pocket.

As she descended the stairs, she heard her dad talking to the suit man.

"I think taking her to the hospital is the best idea."

"She isn't hurt and I'm not dragging her 40 minutes away and traumatizing her further."

"Dean-"

"Listen, Matt, I appreciate you, I do, but my daughter could have been killed tonight." Dean put the shotgun back on the mantle. "If there's a mad man in the woods. She's safest at the rez."

"She could stay with us," Matt offered.

Dean laughed, "I appreciate the sentiment, but your boy has eyes for her. I don't think that's a good idea." Dean 100% trusted Lavender. Silas was new though, and he hadn't gotten a read on the boy yet.

Matt smiled, "I can assure you, my girls would watch them."

"Like I said, I appreciate all you and your family have done, but she's safer with her people."

At the mention of the tribe, Lavender allowed her presence to be known. "You're Silas's dad?" she asked the suit man. He gave her a kind smile and a once over.

"Yes, I am." He offered his hand to her, "Matthias Annora."

Lavender shook his hand, "Your family has a lot of cool names."

The man smiled brightly, "Well, thank you." He patted her hand. "Thank you for befriending, Silas. He's…been feeling a lot better, after meeting you."

Lavender blushed. She bit the inside of her cheek to keep a goofy smile at bay. "I'm glad."

Dean cut in, "Alright, Ender, let's head out, I'll drop you off." He turned to Matt, "The boys have the hounds in the woods. If they find that asshole, they'll probably need your help, since she definitely hit him."

"I hope we find him before he-" He looked at Lavender then changed the subject, "You two should be off."

A man rushed inside. "Dad, fuck, I mean, Doc! The guys just radioed in. Hounds caught his scent. He's still runnin'!"

Lavender took in the man at the door. He was tall, built like a quarterback. His black hair was styled into jaw length braids. A few strands had gold cuffs on them. His skin was far darker than Lavender's. His eyes though. His eyes were light blue, nearly gray. Lavender had never seen a black man with gray eyes before. Now she knew how people felt when they saw her eyes. The man looked at her and smiled. One of those knowing smiles that spelled trouble for someone else who wasn't in the room.

"Oh, is this Lavender?" He batted his eyelashes when he said her name.

"Silas is not even here to tease," Matt moved to the door, "show me the way."

The man nodded, he moved so Matt could exit the house. He looked back at the girl, who had dragged his little brother out of despair. "Nice to finally put a face to ya!" He gave her a mock salute with two fingers before leaving.

The man had a southern accent. Not as deep as the man she'd shot but definitely there. It felt so out of place. Granted, Matthias's accent was very out of place too. Maybe it ran in the family? Lavender turned to her dad with a confused look.

Dean explained, "That's Jonathan, he's a deputy. Good kid, just a goof."

"How much of the family joined the force?" Lavender asked.

"Only Jon. Matt is a doc, his wife's on the council, his other kids do odd things around the town." Dean made sure his gun was secured at his hip. "Come on, you." He took her hand and guided her to his cop car.

Lavender could hear far off hollering in the trees and the barking of dogs. The guy really was running? It should have been impossible. He should have been dead!

"Get in, Ender," Dean ordered.

She hopped into the passenger seat. Dean drove fast. It was like she'd blinked and they were pulling up to the entrance of the reservation. Granted, she probably was dissociating most of the drive.

"Aunt Lee and Aunt Sara will watch you both. I'll come get you tomorrow."

Lavender nodded. They passed the welcome sign. It'd been 4 years. After being barred and screamed at for wanting to come back, it felt surreal to pass the sign again. This should have been monumental. It should have felt good. It wasn't though. A bitter taste filled her mouth.

"Lavender."

She sighed, "Yea, okay, dad." Her hand was shaking. "What about you?"

Dean gripped the steering wheel. "Gotta get that asshole. Then we need to stabilize him so we can interrogate him." He pulled up in front of Jerry's house. "If you nee-" Lavender was looking at him. There were a few cuts on her face and she was visibly shaking. Dean felt his lip quiver, "Your mom's gonna fucking kill me."

Lavender giggled quietly. She reached over and hugged him. "I'll protect you."

Dean hugged his daughter tightly. "I love you." He kissed her temple. "I love you so much, Flower." He couldn't hold back his tears anymore.

"I love you too, dad," Lavender wept.

The radio screeched to life.

"CHIEF, WE'VE GOT A SITUATION!" Then there was screaming and gunfire.

"Fuck!" Dean pushed Lavender away and toward the door. "Out!" he ordered.

She didn't want to leave but knew that look in his eyes. That fire and determination that Lavender saw in herself. She got out of the car and watched him speed away, lights and sirens on. Her lip quivered and fear gripped her.

"Mama!" Ethan swung open his screen door. He ran and hugged her. "You okay? Dad said you-"

Lavender turned and hugged Ethan tightly and began to sob. Her tears ran down her face in waves. Her legs gave out. She kneeled in the dirt driveway. The rocks were bruising her knees through her lounge pants. Lavender coughed and gagged.

Ethan went down with her. He rubbed her back and held her tightly as she sobbed into his shoulder. "I've got you, mama. I've got you."

Lavender clutched at him. She kissed his cheek. "I'm sorry, Little." Lavender pulled herself together. "Come on, let's go inside."

Ethan could feel her practically vibrating. The smell of her distress made him want to cry. "I'm sorry, Mama."

Lavender sniffled. "It's not your fault. I'll be okay." She squeezed his hand. "Is aunt Lee up?"

"Sure am," Lee answered, standing in the doorway. She smiled at the girl. Lavender had gotten so big. "Come on in."

Lavender nodded and led Ethan inside the small house. A part of her expected to find Aunt Millie swinging from the rafter. Lavender shook the image out of her mind. No way was she going to linger on that. Absolutely not. Lavender saw Aunt Sara. The woman gave her a warm hug. She was always so gentle. It was a stark contrast to Lee, who was brash and abrasive.

Ethan clung to Lavender's side. He nuzzled her neck.

Lavender smiled and pulled him with her to the couch. The pair curled up together. Ethan placed his head on her chest. Lavender began to play with his hair and hummed to him.

Lee stared at the pair. She looked at her wife. Sara was making hot chocolate for the kids. Lee sat on the second couch. "I heard you shot him."

Lavender nodded. "I did. In the head. He got back up, it doesn't make sense."

Lee smiled, "I'm proud of you." Lavender preened at the praise. The scanner screeched to life. Dean's panicked voice screamed into the air.

"3 MEN DOWN! SUSPECT STILL AT LAR-"

Aunt Sara clicked the device off and came into the living room with the drinks. "Here we go."

Lavender and Ethan looked at the radio in shock. "Did he say 3 dead?" Ethan asked. Lavender sat up.

"Nevermind that," Sara handed over the hot chocolate. She sat next to Lee, taking her wife's hand. "How have you been, Lavender?" Sara asked the girl.

Lavender looked down at her drink. Before answering, she took a sip.

Chapter 7

"3 dead in a manhunt last night. Branches, Washignton has been-" Aunt Lee turned off the news. She sighed and stood. Ethan and Lavender were curled up together on the couch, still sleeping. Lavender had the cordless phone clutched in her hand.

Lee had given up trying to pry it from her. She pulled out her flip phone.

Sara watched as her wife dialed a number, "Is Jerry-"

"He's alive. I'd feel it otherwise." Lee touched the faint scar on her shoulder. The indents had become blobs over the years. It mirrored Jerry's. Lee put the receiver to her ear. The ring was mind numbing, then there was a click.

"Hello?" the voice on the other end sounded so tired.

"Miriam, it's Lee."

"Oh, hi, sweetheart. Jerry is-"

"I know he's fine. Listen, who was in the search?"

Miriam paused on the other end, as if weighing the information. She did finally answer though, "Johnson, Mallor, and Ryan."

Lee sighed. "Is it bad that my first thought was good riddance?"

"We're all going to hell dear, might as well have fun on the way down."

Lee chuckled. She rubbed her forehead. "Was anyone else hurt?" Lee could hear Miriam shake her head. There was a click of a lighter. Lee wanted to tease her for smoking but Miriam then went on to explain.

"By the time everyone got there, they were dead. Throats torn out. Eyes taken. Guns empty. The guy is officially a serial killer."

Lee collapsed into the dining room chair, her head in her hand. "Jesus Christ." The infamous trio were bastards. They had been on the force since Fontaine. Dean tried to keep them at their desks. Which was easy for Ryan and Mallor. The pair were lazy bastards. Johnson had been trouble since Dean took over. A curmudgeon, like his father. All 3 were racist pricks. Still, Lee didn't think they deserved to be mutilated like that. Sara's warm hand was on her shoulder. It gave her a comforting squeeze. "Okay, fuck, does Jerry want me to come down there?"

"Lee you haven't been on the for-"

"Well there's a few openings now, isn't there?" she snapped. Lee reeled in her anger. She'd hoped to leave the badge behind her. Times changed though. Things changed. Lee apologized, "I'm sorry, I'm sorry it's just-"

"I know, dear," Miriam reassured. "I don't know what he'll have you do, but I know he'd love the support."

"Alright, I'll be there in 30 minutes." Lee hung up, standing to go get dressed. She stopped as if remembering something and looked back at Sara, "I need-"

"I know," Sara gave her wife a kiss. "Go on, I've got them."

Lee let a tear slide down her face. Crying was the worst. The wet feeling. The awful way it clogged your nose. She kissed Sara again, then went into the guest room to change.

Sara looked at the kids and pulled up the blanket Ethan had accidentally kicked off. She tucked them in and managed to gently remove the phone from Lavender's grasp.

She set it back on the hook.

Lavender hugged her father tightly. He kissed her temple and held her tight. "I'm so glad you're safe," she wept. Sweat and fear clung to him like a miasma Lavender tried to rub her scent into him.

"Come on," he guided her to the car. Lavender didn't budge though, she was looking at Ethan. Dean turned to the pair on the porch. "There's a town meeting," he told Sara and Ethan. "You two need a ride?"

Sara nodded, "Lee took the car." She and Ethan had been watching people driving out of the reservation. At least now they knew where everyone was going. "Also, it's good to see you,." she patted Dean's chest. "I'm sorry about last night," she pressed her forehead to his.

"Thanks, Sara." He stepped back and opened the door for her.

They rode into town. A mass of cars were crowded in front of the town hall. The parking lot was overflowing and spilling into the streets.

Dean parked in the fire lane, no one would say anything. There wasn't anyone on patrol. Some cops from the neighboring city had come in. There were talks of the FBI showing up. "Let's go." He hurried out of the patrol car and opened the door for Sara and Ethan.

Lavender looked around at the chaos. There was news, even out of state cars. She clutched at Dean's side. Ethan clung to her's. Like a strange train, they all went to the building. From the door, they could hear the commotion from inside.

"Out of the way! Move aside!" Dean ordered, pushing through everyone. Lavender was tucked under his arm. "Sheriff, move aside!" They got into the main room where the gavel was being banged in an attempt to quiet everyone. It was rabble and chaos. Dean saw Lee next to Jerry. "Lee!" Dean motioned to a table.

Lee nodded and jumped onto it. "QUIET!" she roared, the room went silent. Lee turned to the council members.

"Thank you, Mrs. Vance." The chairman finally sat down. "I know the attack last night has left us all shaken, but we can't fall into hysterics!" He gestured into the crowd, "Port has offered us some of their best and the FBI are on the way."

The crowd began to murmur. Lavender noticed Silas across the way. She guessed the others around him were the rest of his family. They weren't human. He wasn't human. Lavender remembered how the killer was able to speak to her in her mind. She stared at Silas intensely. *If you can hear me, look at me*

Silas turned to her. Lavender's heart skipped a beat. His eyes widened and he quickly turned away. It was like he'd recognized his mistake. The council meeting faded into the background. Voices became muffled and Lavender kept staring at Silas. *You can hear me, can't you?* She noticed how uncomfortable Silas got. *Silas, if you can hear me, please look at me again*

He nervously did. *Are you okay?*

Lavender jumped at the voice. It was Silas's. Clear as day.

"Ender?" Dean rubbed her shoulder.

"I'm okay," she said aloud and in her head. Lavender looked at Silas again. *What happened last night?* she asked.

Silas frowned, *Dad said that guy ripped the cops apart...and the dogs.*

Lavender furrowed her brow. *What the fuck?* She noticed Matthias and Jonanthan near Silas. *Did they see it?*

They got there after the massacre. Silas looked at his mom. She sat next to the rambling councilman. *Dad and Jon followed him for a while, till he went up into the mountains,* Silas explained.

Jesus christ. The mountains were at least an hour away. The new information was making her head spin. Apparently the man could take a shot to the head. He could rip out throats and steal eyes. He could apparently run for over and hour and climb a fucking mountain. Lavender pulled away from her dad. "I need air," she declared.

"Stay on the front step," Dean instructed.

Lavender nodded. She turned to Ethan. "I'll be back in a minute." The boy merely nodded and rubbed the side of his face against hers. *I'm going outside*, she told Silas. The crowd was kinder to someone leaving then coming. She got through the near crush and into the open air. She sucked in a deep breath. Her back pressed against the carved marble of the wall. She sank to the stone.

Can I come see you? Silas asked.

His voice was soft in her mind. The question in itself made her heart melt. He cared enough to ask. *Yes*

Soon footsteps could be heard. Lavender looked up and saw Silas emerge from the building. She gave him a sheepish smile. "Hey."

Hey, he sat beside her.

"Have you been talking to me this whole time?" Lavender asked, resting her head on her knees.

No, Silas admitted, *I didn't think I could do it yet*

Lavender was puzzled, "Can the rest of your family?"

Yes

She teased, "So all of you are odd?" Lavender noticed how Silas began picking at his sleeve. His dark eyes were darting around.

More than you know

Lavender smirked, "I think I could hazard a guess." She joked, "You're superheros."

Silas tried to bite his smile back, but he couldn't. *You're good at that*

"What?" Lavender reached out, taking one of his hands. They were cold. Lavender wondered what made him sometimes room temp versus freezing like he was now.

Breaking tension with humor

Lavender snorted, "I get it from my dad." She scooted closer to him, trying to share her warmth. "My mom said he'd made her almost piss herself laughing the first time they met." Her eyes studied his hand. His fingers were well manicured, though his nails were sharp. Lavender turned his hand over. His hands were smooth. No lines. No fingerprints. Just smooth.

I can't blame her, Silas pressed his face into her hair. He nuzzled into the black tresses. "Your sad smell is strong." It wasn't a scent he particularly enjoyed.

Lavender burst out laughing. His voice had sounded so forlorn. "Oh yea?" She bumped her head into his. "What does my sadness smell like?"

Silas thought for a moment, "Like cold but with salt. Damp moss and fog." He kissed Lavender's temple. "It's heavy. I don't like it."

Lavender kept examining his hand. She ran her textured fingers over his smooth skin. "What does my happiness smell like?" She rested her head on his shoulder.

"Lavenders," Silas admitted. He breathed her in again. "You smell like it now." He laid his cheek on the top of her head. *Can I not talk for a while?*

Lavender nodded, "Course."

They sat there in silence. Lavender continued drawing lines on his palm. Silas continued to bask in the scent of her happiness.

School was hell.

The eyes. The whispers. The accusations. Lavender wished she had headphones to drown them all out. The day was spent with tears constantly in her eyes. Lunch was at least going well. Everyone at the table was happy she was alive. They were impressed she'd managed to shoot the guy.

The mood was lightening. The air felt clearer.

Then Mr. Johnson showed up. He was an older teacher. In every way, shape, and form. "Miss Amos, I need to speak with you."

Everyone glared at him. Belle piped up, "She's eating right now."

Mr. Johnson huffed. "Do you want detention, Miss Clark?"

Belle made the most prissy face. "Do you want another call from my daddy?"

The older man glared at her.

Lavender didn't think she was worth the trouble. "It's fine." She stood up. Silas gave her hand a squeeze. Lavender smiled before turning to the man. "Lead the way."

Mr. Johnson guided her out of the crowded lunchroom and down the hall. He opened an office door and gestured for her to go in.

Lavender felt the hairs on the back of her neck stand up. "I'm not going in there alone with you."

The man sneered, "Don't flatter yourself."

Lavender felt her stomach churn. "Just say what you want. Lunch is almost over. I've had a long day."

Mr. Johnson slammed the door. "You've had a long day! You?!" His wrinkled face twisted in rage. "My son is dead because of you!" He stabbed one of his bony fingers into her chest. "You and that mulatto daddy of yours killed my boy!"

Lavender stepped back. "What the hell are you talking about?!"

"Don't play dumb with me, girl. My boy and his friends were the only members left on the force after Fontaine. Your daddy didn't like them and they sure as hell didn't like working for a colored bastard high on his self righteous horse."

Lavender clenched her fist. "The fuck did you say about my dad?!"

Mr. Johnson didn't even entertain the question. He continued on his tirade. "A so-called killer gets shot in the head and survives? He just gets up and kills some more? The only survivors are you, your daddy, and that fruity little rainbow family? A likely fucking story." He grabbed Lavender by the front of her shirt. "Just admit it! Just fucking admit it! You and that queer daddy of yours wanted my boy out of the way. You knew he was going to try and run and get this town back in order. Admit it!"

"Fuck off!" Lavender roared and kneed the man in the nuts.

Mr. Johnson howled and fell to his knees. "You little bitch! I knew you were trouble, just like your mother! Rez rats don't belong here!"

"Wow, Mr. J, trying to fight kids again." Belle had her Cybershot out. "This'll be interesting to show Mrs. Winslow."

"Are you recording?" The old man stood on shaky legs.

"Not just her," Carrie smiled, her Razor out.

Silas came over and wrapped a protective arm around Lavender. *Are you okay?*

"Fine," Lavender answered aloud. She tucked her head against Silas's neck.

Blake and Jeremy came on the scene with Principal Winslow behind them. "He dragged Lavender out of the lunch room," Jeremy pointed to Mr. Johnson. "Lavender's been through enough!" Blake nodded in agreement.

Mrs. Winslow glared at the man. "Mr. Johnson, what is going on?"

The teacher pointed an accusing finger at Lavender. "That little savage assaulted me!"

Silas caught Lavender before she could lunge at the man. "He's not worth it!" Silas hissed. Lavender gripped the arm he had around her chest.

Mrs. Winslow's face pinched. "Mr. Johnson! We do not use that kind of language." She then turned to Lavender. "You are definitely Rosemary's child." She huffed, "I didn't think your first fight would be with faculty."

"He grabbed her, Mrs. Winslow. I got it on video!" Belle held out her phone. "He was accusing her of killing his son and called Sheriff Amos names."

Mrs. Winslow watched the video. She grimaced. "Trenton," she groaned.

"What?!" Mr. Johnson went over to her. "Martha, you know this girl is nothing but trouble." He pointed to Silas. "Him and his little 'family' are nothing but trouble. They don't belong here."

Mrs. Winslow sighed. She turned to Belle. "Delete this video Mrs. Clark."

Belle gave her a sly smile, "Sure, Mrs. Winslow." She took her phone back then gripped it tight. "Right after Mr. Johnson is fired."

Mrs. Winslow balked. "Excuse me?"

Belle raised her brow. "Oh, would you like me to go to the news? My dad has connections at the Times and I know they'd love a juicy story like this. Especially with a video."

Mr. Johnson took a step toward her. "Listen here, you spoiled brat. I'll-"

Blake stepped in front of the man. He was taller than him and definitely more fit. "You'll what?" the boy asked through gritted teeth. "Touch her, see what happens."

Belle placed a hand on Blake's arm. "Not just from him, but also my daddy."

Mrs. Winslow sighed. "Trenton, you're fired."

Mr. Johnson whipped around in shock. "Martha!"

The principal hissed. "We can't have another scandal!" She pointed to Blake and Belle. "We already had one incident," she pointed to Lavender and Silas, "We can't afford another!"

The bell rang and everyone looked up. "Class, all of you!" Mrs. Winslow commanded. She then pointed to Mr. Johnson, "You, follow me!"

The group all took a sigh of relief as the halls flooded with other kids. Belle came over and hugged Lavender. "Oh, honey, are you okay?!"

Lavender nodded. "Yea, thanks, Belle."

Belle smiled, "You don't have to thank me." She wiggled her phone. "Might as well put this privilege to good use." Blake kissed her on the cheek. Belle giggled.

Carrie was typing on her phone. "I don't know about you, but I'm saving this. Just in case." She tucked her phone back into her bag.

Jeremy nodded, "You're so smart."

Carrie shrugged. She turned to Lavender and Silas. "Are you guys going to class?"

Lavender shook her head. "Hell no. Thanks guys." She pushed through the sea of students to get out. No one stopped her. Lavender walked faster and faster. She could feel the tears in her eyes. There was no way she was crying here. No way was she going to let them see they got to her. Lavender raced to her truck and locked the door before screaming.

She screamed and screamed until her throat was raw. Lavender slammed her fist into the dash. "God dammit!" she roared. Rage. Sorrow. Hopelessness. Everything. A deep dark pit that swallowed her mind. The worst part was she couldn't run. She didn't want to but she also didn't have an option. Her poor dad. This town was more fucked then she'd ever realized. How bad was it when her parents were kids? Lavender tried to shake the heartache out of her.

Lavender?

The girl jumped and looked out her window. Silas was there. His eyes were a strange red. Like they were heavily irritated or had a popped blood vessel. Lavender rolled down her window. "What?"

Silas tugged at his shirt sleeve. "I just…I'm sorry." He looked at the ground. "I should have…"

Lavender frowned. "No, no," she opened her door, "No, Si, it's not your fault." Lavender hugged him. "I'm not mad at you." She cradled his face in her hands. "Look at me. You came. You kept me from ripping that bastard apart. That means a lot."

"I should have let you go," Silas growled. "I should have let you kick his ass. I should have kicked his ass! I'm sorry."

Lavender had never seen Silas angry. His eyes were even more red. Lavender knew. From his body language to the way he spoke. She knew. Lavender kissed his cheek. "You're a good boyfriend, Silas." Lavender rested her head on his shoulder. She rubbed up and down his biceps. His arms wrapped around her.

"I'm making this about me. I'm sorry. Are you alright? What do you need?" Silas kissed the top of her head. "What do you want to do?"

Lavender sniffled. "I really want to go to the waterfall." She nuzzled into his neck. He smelled like the forest and copper. His heartbeat was slow. Far slower than Lavender's. She sighed. "That guy wasn't human."

Silas nodded.

Lavender hugged him. "Are you human?"

Silas didn't answer. He didn't need to. "Do you want me to drive?"

Lavender nodded, "Yea." She handed him the keys and got into the passenger side. As they drove, Lavender reached over and took his hand. Silas squeezed it and didn't let go.

Uncle Jerry was outside her house.

Lavender hopped out of her truck. Jerry stood from his seat on the porch. He walked over to her and Lavender hoped the tear stains on her face had lightened up.

"Hi, Ender."

Lavender smiled and hugged him. His warm arms wrapped around her. God, she needed that hug. "Hi, Uncle." Lavender looked up at him. His smile was always small but very warm. "What's up?"

Jerry sighed and rubbed the girl's shoulders. "Ethan and I are going away for a bit."

45

Lavender felt her heart crack. "What? Why?"

Jerry cradled her face. "It's nothing you did, Ender. I promise." He explained, "This has been a long time coming. We weren't supposed to do it till he was a little older but…things changed."

"What things?" Lavender asked.

Jerry gave her a bewildered look. "Your mom never…" He sighed and looked away, "Of course she fucking didn't." Jerry looked at Lavender. "This is something for the pack. She should be the one explaining this to you." Rage. Sadness. Hurt. Jerry swallowed those emotions and pushed through to explain further. "Ethan and I won't be back till the winter."

"Well, can I see him?" Lavender begged, "I at least want to say goodbye." She'd just gotten Ethan back and he was being taken? Is this what Ethan felt like when her mother would take her? Lavender felt new tears fill her eyes. "Please, can I say goodbye?"

Jerry shook his head. "No, Ender. It already took hours to convince him to go. If he sees you, he won't go, and he needs to."

"But why? You said it wasn't supposed to happen till he was older! Can't you wait? Just for a little while longer? Please!" Lavender begged. She grabbed the front of Jerry's shirt. "Please don't take him!"

Jerry shook his head and pried her fingers off of him. "We're coming back, Ender. I promise." He got free and went to his car.

"Please!" Lavender cried. "Please, I just got him back, Uncle. Please don't take him away." She grabbed his window frame. "Please, Jerry!"

Jerry felt like he was kidnapping his own son. "Lavender, I know you love Ethan. I know you do." He took her hand. "He's been fine for 4 years without you, he'll be fine for a few months. You're not his mother."

The words punched Lavender in the face. Hot tears rolled down her cheeks. "Jerry, please." He couldn't take Ethan. He couldn't! Is this what Dean felt like when her mother would take her?

Jerry started the car and drove out of there as fast as he could. He needed to leave before Lavender got her bearings. He looked into the rearview mirror and saw the girl running behind his car. She was screaming, but Jerry couldn't listen. When she faded into a blur, he finally let himself cry. "I'm sorry," he wept, "I'm so sorry." Jerry wiped his eyes and headed to his house. Ethan and him would need to leave immediately.

Chapter 8

Lavender screamed.

She screamed and screamed and screamed until she felt like her vocal cords would snap. Lavender tried to call Ethan but only got Aunt Sara.

"They're gone, Ender."

Lavender wailed, holding the teddy bear Ethan had given her. He had a matching bear that was smaller. They used to walk around together hand in hand with their bears. Lavender wondered if Ethan took his on the trip.

Dean could hear Lavender's screams from the start of the driveway. He threw his car in park and raced inside. "Ender?!" Lavender was in a nest of blankets on the kitchen floor. "Lavender, flower, what happened?" He kneeled down and tugged her to him. His daughter wailed into his chest. "Ender, Ender." Dean tried to soothe her. He noticed the bear she was clutching. Dean sighed, dammit Jerry. "Flower, he'll be back. I promise. Please try to calm down." Dean kissed her forehead.

Lavender coughed and gripped at her dad. "Today-" she choked and tried to speak again, "I-" Lavender turned her head and continued to cry.

Dean scooted back to rest against the sink cabinet, Lavender still in his lap. "I got a call from Mr. Clark. He said there was an incident at school." Mr. Clark was a strange man. Dean was so used to the rich fucks in town being bastards. Clark was different though. His wife's death softened him. His daughter made him a better man. Dean could relate to that.

Lavender nodded. "Mr. Johnson said we conspired to kill his son."

Dean rolled his eyes. "Jesus Christ." That man and his son were menaces on a good day. "Look at me, Ender," he held his daughter's face. "I know today was a lot. I know it feels like everything is falling apart around you. I promise you, it's going to be okay."

Lavender hiccuped. "I feel like my life's imploding."

Dean nodded. "I know. I know that feeling. I do." He pressed his forehead against hers. "But listen to me. It'll be okay. You're going to be okay. We're going to be okay."

Lavender repeated, "I'll be okay. We'll be okay."

Halloween was weird. It normally was, but especially with new friends. Belle was throwing a party. Lavender knew Belle's dad was rich, but jesus. The stately manor on the top of the hill looked more like a museum than a house.

The whole school was there, which would have been an epic disaster waiting to happen if not for the signs saying in bold letters:

SMILE! YOU'RE ON CAMERA!

Lavender snorted at the posters. They were bolted into the walls and at the entrance. Mr. Clark was a smart man. Lavender wore a witch costume. It was simple but hey, she didn't feel like going all out for that Halloween. Ethan had sent her a couple letters. Lavender had no idea where he was and no one would tell her.

Probably for the best though, she'd run there in a heartbeat. Her dad had been the one to push her to come to the party. She'd been cooped up in the house for weeks. Silas had been talking to her on the wind. Apparently their voices could carry. It was nice, especially for the phone bill.

"Hey, you!"

Lavender turned and saw a girl in a cheap Indian costume. She even had a plastic headdress on and her face painted red. Lavender felt her cheeks grow hot in anger.

"I'm dressed as you!" the girl giggled. She began a mocking dance she probably saw in some old western. The other girl's around were equal parts amused and weary. Some faded into the crowd when they noticed Lavender's glare.

Lavender wanted to knock the girl's teeth in. Fuck it, she was going to. She clenched her fist and stalked over.

The girl stopped laughing when she noticed how pissed Lavender was. She put her hands up in panic. "Whoa, whoa, was just a joke. Lighten up."

Lavender spat, "Oh, really?"

The girl jumped back. Her friends moved away from her. Obviously not wanting to be caught in the crossfire and not really caring about the girl's safety. "I said I was kidding!" she cried.

"No you aren't!" Lavender roared.

"What is going on?!" Belle asked. She was in a Cinderella like ball gown. She looked from Lavender to their classmate. "Katie, what are you wearing?" Belle asked in horror.

"It's just a joke!" The girl, Katie, defended. "Teach your little Indian friend to take out!"

Belle gripped the sides of her dress. Her chest puffed out. "Get out!" she ordered. Belle ran up to the girl. "Right now!" She took the cup from Katie's hand and splashed the contents on her face. "Out!"

Katie gasped and wiped her eyes. The paint was dripping off and into her eyes. She screamed, "What the fuck, Belle!"

Belle dragged the other girl to the door and pushed her into the night. "And stay out!" She huffed and smoothed out her dress. All eyes were on her. The only ones she cared about were Lavender's. "Come on," she took the girl's hand and led her down a quiet hall. The party went back into full swing behind them. "You okay?"

Lavender nodded. Still a little shocked at being defended like that. "Thanks, Belle."

The blonde giggled. "Don't mention it. I had to kick out Aaron Thompson earlier for black face. Those two assholes can party together." Belle grabbed a tissue and wiped her friend's face.

Lavender hadn't even noticed she'd been crying. Belle was kind. Not the fake kind Lavender had encountered so many times in her life. Actually kind. She hugged the other girl.

"Oh! Lavender?" Belle chuckled. She'd never been hugged by the other girl before. Belle returned the embrace.

"Belle, you alright?" Blake asked, peeking around a corner.

Belle stood up straight. "I'm okay, baby!" She gave Lavender one more quick hug. "Wanna dance?"

Lavender chuckled, "Not right now." She urged Belle back to the party and her boyfriend, "Go on." They walked back to the light and revelry.

Where are you?

Lavender jumped at Silas's voice. "In the hall on the left, then turn right." She sat on the ground, against the carved walls. Footsteps came closer and closer. Lavender looked to see someone in a Guy Fox mask. She giggled. "V for Vendetta, really?"

Silas shrugged, lifting his mask. "I like the movie." He sat next to Lavender. "I saw a girl crying outside." Silas bumped her shoulder with his. "What was that about?"

Lavender chuckled. "She played a stupid game and got a stupid prize."

Silas nodded. "Should have known from the costume." Speaking of costumes. "A witch, huh?"

Lavender shrugged. "Can't hate the classics." She leaned back against the wall, even though the patterns made it uncomfortable. "I shouldn't have come."

Silas frowned. He knew how badly Ethan's absence was hurting her. "Well, I'm glad you're here." The hallway muffled most of the cheering and chatter, but not the beat of the music. Silas mindlessly swayed to the tunes.

Lavender noticed his wiggling. It reminded her of a snake raising itself up. "You're adorable," she whispered.

"Huh?"

Lavender got to her feet. Later. She'd sulk and pout later. Not right now though. "Come on, groovy man, let's go dance."

Silas snorted, "Groovy man?!"

"Shut up, come on." Lavender pulled him to his feet. His hand was room temperature this time. There was a rough patch of skin though. Lavender looked down and examined his hand. "What happened?" she asked, tracing the marks. They weren't there yesterday but they seemed days into healing.

Silas frowned. "I was out…hunting."

Lavender raised an eyebrow. "You hunt?" She looked at the marks again. "These are from claws."

Silas looked down the hall. He decided to just confess. "Animals are coming from the mountain. They aren't…right. I've been helping with the hunt."

Lavender looked up in shock. "You mean the rabid animals?"

Silas bit his lip. "If that's what they're calling them, yes." He wanted to snatch his hand away but Lavender's soft eyes made him pause. God, he loved her. He loved her wild curls and golden eyes and her-

"I should help." Lavender unknowingly cut into his enamoration.

"No," Silas said firmly. "You shouldn't have to be involved in this. My family and I got it."

Lavender frowned. "I can help."

Silas gripped her hand. "Lavender, you can't get bit. Do you understand me? Let us handle it."

The command was so firm, Lavender didn't have a defense against it. She wanted to argue. Silas's eyes were pleading though. There wasn't a thirst for control in them, only fear.

Lavender nodded. "Okay."

Silas immediately relaxed. He smiled. "Come on, let's go dance."

Lavender let him lead the way. The pair made their way to the dance floor. The rest of the night was spent dancing and laughing. Lavender went to bed with a smile on her face. It was a rush. A high.

The next morning Katlyn Fields was found mutilated in the woods.

Lavender found herself in the office. Two men in suits sat across from her. Tacky Thanksgiving decorations were lining the walls. Halloween had just happened three days ago. Lavender huffed at the tacky turkey. Mrs. Winslow sat at her desk. She was glaring at the teen. Lavender knew the woman had organized this little sit down.

"Do you know why you're here, Lavender?" one of the men asked.

Lavender knew the basics of an interrogation. "No, Mr. Officer, why?"

The older of the two men smiled. "I'm Agent Kent. This is Agent Wright, we just have a couple questions, off the record."

Lavender glared at the pair. "Oh?"

The younger man, Wright, nodded. He flashed his badge. "We're with the FBI, we want to know more about the murders."

Lavender rolled her eyes. "If you're trying to pin this on me, you're barking up the wrong tree. I got here *after* the murders started. Find another scapegoat." Lavender stood to leave.

"Miss Amos, you will sit down or you will be expelled!" Mrs. Winslow warned.

Lavender glared at the woman. "Oh, really?" She looked at the two men. "Stop playing games, just ask what you want. Plainly."

Agent Kent cracked his neck. "Fine, where were you that night?"

"Belle Clark's party."

"Can anyone verify your whereabouts?"

"Probably half the school?"

Wright chimed in, "Mrs. Winslow says you have a history of violence."

Lavender rolled her eyes. "You mean the *1* incident where a teacher assaulted me, I defended myself and that teacher was fired?"

Both men looked at the principal. Mrs. Winslow didn't crack under scrutiny, she never did.

"Is it true you got in a fight with Miss Fields?" Kent asked.

Lavender rubbed her face. "Yelled at her, nothing physical happened. She was being racist. Belle threw her out. Shut the door on her."

"Miss Clark?" Wright asked.

"Yep, Belle Clark, host of the party!" Lavender groaned. "Can I go now?" She didn't want to deal with this.

"You seem pretty agitated," Kent observed. He gave his partner a look.

Lavender laughed, "Yea, I'm agitated. My racist principal dragged me out of class for an illegal interrogation with the FBI's dumbest." She pointed to the window. "This guy is ripping out throats and scooping out eyes. I shot him in the head! He killed 3 cops while I was 40 minutes away! You two are morons if you're trying to pin this on me. Not even the most corrupt judge in the country would take this case!"

"I suggest you sit down," Wright ordered.

Lavender growled, "I suggest you-"

Dean kicked in the door. "MARTHA!" he roared.

Mrs. Winslow jumped in shock.

Dean glared at the two men. He looked at Lavender, "Outside, go to the cruiser." Dean waited till Lavender was out of ear shot. He marched up to the suited men. The pair stood as he approached. "That little girl is a child. 17. You can't interrogate her without a parent present, and you sure as fuck don't come to her god damn school!" He pointed to the door. "Out of my town, both of you. We have this handled, the FBI can fuck off!"

Wright chuckled. "Listen sheriff-"

Dean cut him off. "I was elected to protect this town. Not you. You two have done nothing except smell your own farts since you got here!" He pointed to the door again, "OUT!"

Kent stood got in the sheriff's face, "Listen, boy-"

"Boy?" Dean sneered.

Matthias came into the room. "Hello everyone!" His chipper mood made everyone pause. "Matt," Dean warned.

The doctor smiled. "Dean, please step outside." He pushed the man out the door.

"What are you doing?" Dean hissed.

Matthias began closing the door. "I'll take care of this, trust me." He winked.

Dean huffed. "Fine, go for it." The door shut and Dean fought the urge to place his ear against the wood. The school bell rang and a bunch of kids spilled into the halls. Dean then watched as the kids cleared out and the halls became empty again. Boredom was just settling in when the door finally opened.

Kent and Wright walked out of the office. They both tipped their hats to Dean. "We see you've got this under control, Sheriff Amos," Kent said. Wright nodded, "We'll head back and let you keep up the good work." They walked out of the school robotically.

Dean was taken aback. He went back into the office. Matt was drawing a mustache on Mrs. Winslow's face with a sharpie. "What are you doing?" Matt looked up at him and smiled.

"Drawing!" The blond capped the marker. He snapped his fingers and Mrs. Winslow came out of her trance. "Have a good day, Mrs. Winslow." Matthias walked out the door, dragging Dean with him. "Come on, before she asks questions," the man whispered.

"The fuck was that?" Dean asked, "Don't tell me you're a hypnotist too!" The blond looked both smug and nauseous. "Are you okay, Matt?"

Matthias shook his head. "I do not like doing that. However, needs must." He sighed, walking a bit faster. "It is very…icky." The new terms nowadays were so odd. Matthias hoped he was using that one right. "That means distasteful, correct?"

Dean wrinkled his nose in amusement. "Sure does, bud." He knew Matt spoke more than 5 languages. Dean was only bilingual and that could be a challenge sometimes. "I once forgot how to say 'eyes' in English. I had to run up to Jerry and scream 'What are these?!'" Dean pointed to his eyes and recreated the distressed face he'd had.

It had the desired effect.

Matthias laughed, having to stop his walking to collect himself.

Dean chuckled, "Jerry's never let me live it down." As they exited the building Dean thanked the man, "I appreciate… whatever it is you did. Those agents have been looking at the rez more than the evidence." Granted, the evidence they had was minimal. Still, Dean thought federal agents would at least look at it!

"The human mind befuddles me," Matthias admitted. Prejudice had always confused him. Even in the 14th century, he found it odd. It was illogical and Matthias couldn't deal with such foolishness. "That is why I specialize in the body."

Once outside, they saw Lavender was sitting on top of the cruiser. Dean went to his little girl. "What did you say?"

The teen shrugged, "Nothing incriminating." Lavender looked at the empty space that had held the agents' car. "How'd you get them to leave?" she asked. The pair hadn't even looked at her. You would have thought she was invisible. It was odd.

Dean tilted his head to Matt. "He got them to go, not me." The sheriff was kicking himself for not listening in on the conversation. "Used his doctor magic."

Matthias waved his hand dismissively. "It wasn't that hard. I do not understand the mind, but I know how to mold it."

"Did you guys hear, the FBI pulled out," Jeremy informed, scrambling to set his tray down. The lunchroom was all abuzz about the news. "Also Sheriff Amos was here." He looked at Lavender. "Tell us the hot gos, killer."

Belle kicked the boy under the table.

"Ow!" Jeremy hissed, "I was kidding!" He rubbed his bruised shin.

Belle snapped, "Well it wasn't funny! Lavender is dealing with enough without you being an ass." She stabbed her salad with her fork. "Those agents were useless anyway. They tried to get me to say Lavender had left early." Belle growled, "I should sue the pants off them."

Lavender frowned, "I'm sorry, Belle." People were dying. The town was in hysterics. Now her friends were being harassed. Lavender felt like everything was her fault. She told them, "They were here yesterday. I guess Mrs. Winslow called them and said I was violent or some bullshit." Lavender grit her teeth.

Silas wrapped his arm around his girlfriend's shoulder.

Lavender let out a shaky breath. "I shot him." She whimpered, "He should be dead. Why couldn't he just fucking die?!" Lavender got up from the table. "I need to go to the bathroom." She rushed to the restroom before anyone could grab her. Lavender burst into the room.

Some girls were by the sink. They jumped at the sight of her and quickly left.

Lavender tried to block out their whispers and accusations. It was all too much. The buzz of the lights hurt. The weight of the world was heavy. Her vision was blurring. There was a sweet smell in the air. A strange and sickening smell. Lavender felt her mouth salivate. That salivation that came when you were about to throw up. Lavender ran to the sink and splashed water on her face.

She gagged and went into a stall. Lavender dry heaved and coughed. Her body felt too hot. She laid on the cold floor and tried to breathe. The dirt and grime below her was promptly ignored in favor of the coolness of the tiles. "Please, please stop," she cried.

Belle came into the bathroom. "Lavender?" She found the girl on the ground. "Oh honey!" Belle kneeled next to her friend. "Lavender, Lavender," she whispered and pulled the girl close. "What's wrong?"

Lavender bit back a scream. "Everything hurts!" she wept. "It's all my fault."

Belle shook her head. "Hey, none of that. You're not out there killing people. You tried to keep us all safe. Yes, it didn't work, but that doesn't matter. You've done more than those government bozos!"

Lavender hugged the girl. "I don't know why you're my friend?"

Belle sighed. "Because I like you, Lavender." She brushed the other girl's curls back. "You're funny and spunky and you've taught me a lot." Belle smiled, "You make me feel all safe and warm." The blonde relaxed against the wall of the stall. "Would you have let them pin Katie's death on me?"

Lavender furrowed her brow. "Of course not! You didn't do anything!"

Belle smiled, "See! I'm just doing what you would. Just cause you haven't needed to defend me yet, doesn't mean you're not a good or worthy friend." She reached out and squeezed Lavender's hand. "You're a good person. Abrasive sometimes, but definitely good."

Lavender sniffled and wiped her face. "You're a good person too, Belle. I've never had a friend like you." Her friendship with Ethan was definitely more familial. More paternal if she was honest. Lavender frowned. Now she was thinking of Aunt Millie. "My aunt killed herself when I was 6. Ever since then my oldest…and for a long time only friend has seen me as his mom." Lavender felt like a weight was lifted off her chest. It was so strange to say it outloud to someone. "So, having friends who see me as a friend is…weird. I don't know how to be normal."

Belle sat back in shock. "Well, that explains a lot." She sadly smiled. "My mom died when I was 3." She added, "Not suicide, just…cancer."

Lavender felt her heart ache. "I'm sorry, Belle." She scooted closer and opened her arms to the other girl. Now she felt ridiculous for her weeping.

Belle smiled and accepted the hug. She sighed. "It's okay. It's one of those things that happened. Daddy got me a lot of therapy and he's always there for me. He had ignored mom when the pain started. He was one of those old school guys that thought she just had 'woman problems'." Belle sat back. "My mom just grinned and bared all the pain. Till her hair started falling out." Belle wiped her eyes. She looked at Lavender. The love in her golden eyes made her feel warm. "Your friend is lucky," she whispered, "I would have killed to have someone like you."

Lavender nuzzled her face against the girl's.

Belle jumped at the action. She didn't understand why Lavender was doing it. "Is this a Native thing?"

Lavender snorted. Now that she was thinking about it. Objectively it was weird. "It's something my family does…I guess. Ethan says my smell is calming."

Belle tilted her head in confusion. "No offense Lavender but you smell like Old Spice."

That made Lavender laugh. It caused Belle to laugh too. The pair left the bathroom after reining in their giggles. Both Blake and Silas were waiting for them. Lavender took Silas's hand. *I'm okay,* she told him. That seemed to soothe the boy's worries. She hadn't been lying either. Lavender was okay.

Chapter 9

The snowflakes looked beautiful. Silas was having a time catching them on his tongue. Lavender giggled at him. She was loading another log onto the stump. The axe was buried in the ground next to it. Winter had set in and with it a quiet melancholy. She was glad school was out though.

Lavender looked at her boyfriend. She knew if it weren't for Silas she'd be buried in her sheets. In the dark. In despair. He'd pulled her out of her depression. Not a yank, but a gentle guide. The world may be dead, but she felt mended.

Silas had finished his pile of chopped firewood. He'd wanted to do it all but Lavender insisted. Something about fairness that he didn't fully understand. It wasn't a hassle. Was pretty easy actually.

Lavender took up the axe and chopped the log. "You sure you aren't cold?" she asked, grabbing another log. He was only wearing a hoodie and jeans.

"I'm fine." Silas came over and grabbed the split wood and stacked it for Lavender. They had made an impressive stack against the house. He was glad Lavender was feeling better. It had been a longtime coming.

"Thanks, Si." She raised the axe and cut the next log. Honestly the chopping was helping with her pent up rage. Because of the murders, everything was on lock down, especially her. She loaded a new log.

"You sure you don't want me to do it?" he offered again. Silas stood a few feet away as Lavender brought the axe down on another log. He went and took the split wood again.

"I got it," Lavender put on a new log, "Besides, I need a workout, since the woods are still off limits." She gave him a knowing smile.

Silas gave her a tight lipped smile. "Hopefully everything will be fixed by spring."

Lavender brought down the axe again. "Hopefully." The man's face flashed into her mind. She stuck the axe in the ground. "Have you seen him?"

Silas frowned. "Briefly. He hides in the caves." He stacked the pieces. "If it weren't for the murders, they would have thought he died in there."

Lavender's lip quivered. "Why is he coming here to kill though?"

Silas shrugged. "Maybe he has a bone to pick with this place. I don't know. We tried asking the tribe but…" he trailed off. Memories of screaming and curses flooded his mind. "Didn't end well."

Lavender was perplexed, "What, why?" Before Silas could answer, a familiar voice cut through the winter.

"Mama!" Ethan rounded the corner. He was drenched in sweat. His breath was coming out in giant clouds.

"Little?" Lavender raced to him. She cried out in joy. Ethan was scalding hot. A walking inferno. He looked so different. Hair longer, grown taller, and insanely fit. "What happened to you?" she asked.

"Training!" Ethan cheered. "As soon as we got back, I ran over."

"You ran here?!" It explained why he was so sweaty, but the tribe was at least a twenty minute drive from her house. Despite the salt on his skin, Lavender smelled something sweet. "Jesus, Ethan. Let's go inside."

The boy didn't argue. Happily following Lavender indoors. He noticed Silas. "Heard you tried to talk to Nana yesterday." The other boy looked uncomfortable.

"Yea."

Ethan glared at him. "That was fucking stupid."

"Sure was!" Silas agreed. He closed the door behind him.

Lavender pulled out a chair. She was too high on endorphins to pay attention to the boys' banter. "Sit, sit," she insisted.

Ethan smiled, taking a seat. Lavender went to the living room and came back with a quilt. She wrapped it around him. Ethan smiled at the pampering. How long had it been? Dad hadn't brought anything for him to keep track of time. A warm kiss was placed on his temple.

"Want some hot chocolate?" Lavender asked.

Ethan nodded enthusiastically. He saw Silas was sitting across from him. He'd expected the boy to be jealous or angry. He wasn't though. Silas seemed happy to see him too. It was nice. Ethan snuggled into the blanket. "What month is it?"

Silas was shocked by the question. "It's December, Ethan."

The boy's eyes widened. He knew he was gone for a while, but… "Holy shit." Ethan looked at the table. He'd missed so much. Ethan looked at Lavender. She was standing in front of the stove, humming to herself. It was worth it. It'd all be worth it if he could protect her. She had her hair in a long braid. The cardigan she wore was a hand me down. The smell of cooking milk and the fireplace made Ethan want to cry. "Mama," he said without meaning to. Lavender turned around in an instant. Ethan felt his heart clench when the face he was expecting wasn't there. "Sorry," he looked back at the table. His emotions were all over the place recently. Ethan blamed his upcoming shift.

"You okay?" Silas asked. He reached out to take the kid's hand but it was quickly pulled away.

"I'm fine," Ethan growled. "I'm just…I'm really tired."

Silas nodded and didn't push it. He looked at Lavender, who'd gone back to cooking. "We've missed you."

Ethan smiled. "Missed you guys too." He pulled the blanket tighter around him. The months had been a lot of work. Him and some of the other pack kids had been training from sun up to sun down. Ethan expected his body to be more sore. Thankfully, Anna's spirit was with him. Some of the other kids were currently face down in their bed, exhausted. Ethan needed to see Lavender though. He needed to. Ethan hissed and unwrapped a bit to itch his arm.

Lavender came over with some mugs of hot chocolate. She caught sight of Ethan's arm. "Little!" she gasped. There were teeth marks near Ethan's wrist. "What bit you?!" She looked at Silas. "Are those animals still roaming around?"

Silas nodded. He knew that bite wasn't from an animal though. "You're a little young," he commented, staring into the boy's eyes.

Ethan frowned. "Considering the circumstances." He pulled his arm away from Lavender. "I'm okay, Mama. Don't worry, it wasn't rabid."

"What the hell was it then? Does Uncle Jerry know?" Lavender sat next to the boy. "You haven't been feeling sick have you?"

Ethan stared at Lavender. "You…you don't-" he looked at Silas. "She doesn't know?"

Silas shook his head.

Ethan looked back at Lavender. "Mama, dad bit me."

Lavender grabbed his hand and looked at the marks again. How the hell could her uncle make these? "Ethan, that's ridiculous. What are you-"

The screeching of tires made the trio jump.

Dean nearly kicked in the door. He looked at the 3 before sighing in relief and landed on his knees. "Oh my god. Thank god. Thank god," he wept. Dean stood up on shaky legs and went to Lavender, hugging her tight. "My baby, my baby."

Lavender didn't know what was happening. She hugged him back though. "Dad? What's wrong?"

Jerry came into the house. He sighed in relief too. "Jesus fucking Christ." He took off his hat and collapsed onto the ground.

"What happened?" Lavender asked again.

"Another body." Matthias explained. He looked at Silas and tilted his head back to the door. The man was out of the caves, but he didn't know for how long.

Silas sighed and looked at Lavender. Dean wasn't going to be letting her go anytime soon. *I'll be gone for a little while*, he added, *hunting*

Lavender nodded, finally understanding. *Rip a chunk out of him, for me.* Silas smiled and left with his father. There was no sound of a car starting. No sound of tires on gravel. Just the wind. Lavender turned her attention back to the man who was smothering her. "Dad," she whined and tried to wiggle out of his grasp. "What's going on?"

The man finally let go. Dean took a deep breath. "Sorry, I'm sorry." He wiped his eyes with his dirty sleeve and cursed. "We found a body and…" Dean trailed off. He went to the sink to wash the dirt from his hands.

"She looked like you," Jerry finished. "She didn't have a face, but the hair was nearly the same."

Lavender frowned, "No face is a new M.O."

Jerry shook his head. "Wasn't the man, was one of the beasts. A cat, probably." He finally got off the floor. "Ethan." His boy looked up. "Come on, we're going with them."

Ethan frowned, "But Nana said-"

"Nana can stuff it!" Jerry growled. He looked at Lavender. "Do you think we should work with Matthias?"

Lavender didn't know why her opinion mattered over her grandmother's. She didn't know why it felt like Ethan and Jerry were waiting with baited breath. "Yes," she answered. "If they can help, if they know more than you, you should be working with them."

Jerry gestured to her. "The mother has spoken. Come on, boy."

Ethan looked at Lavender. There was a pang in his chest. "She doesn't know, dad."

Jerry grumbled, "We'll explain when we get back. Now come on! The trail's growing cold."

Ethan stole a quick hug from Lavender before heading off. Leaving the girl even more confused. There were some puzzle pieces fitting together. Not a whole picture yet, but almost.

Lavender decided to ponder later and instead focus on her dad. He was over the sink. His shoulders were shaking. "Dad," she placed a hand on his back. Dean straightened up and looked at her. His nose was runny and the tears had made lines through the dirt on his face. "Go shower, I'll cook us something."

Dean swayed a bit. "No, I...I should." He tried to head to the door but Lavender stopped him.

"They've got it, dad." She ushered him to his room. "You've been running yourself ragged. You can't protect anyone if you're not on your A game." That got him to stop resisting.

Dean nodded. "Okay, okay." He went the rest of the way on his own.

Lavender smiled, satisfied. She went to the front door and made sure it was locked and bolted. Everything replayed in her mind.

She'd need to talk to Nana soon.

---

7 days. A whole week with barely any contact and being locked up inside. Prior to this, the isolation Lavender had was minimum. She'd also done it herself, instead of it being forced upon her. Dean had found out that the poor girl who was mauled was from out of town. That caused a whole lot of chaos. Another girl that looked like Lavender was found. However the cat that killed her was caught outside the reservation.

It wasn't rabies.

Lavender knew it wasn't, but a part of her was hoping for a normal explanation. There was no studying to be had though. The cat was quickly cremated. Lavender had asked Silas and his only reply was 'So they don't get back up again'. That answer made Lavender shiver.

Speaking of the reservation, what she'd said was not only taken to heart by Jerry. Silas told her they had a proper militia now. Apparently Silas and his family were solely on 'Catch that bastard' duty while everyone else handled the animals.

On the topic of animals, Lavender felt like a caged one. Her dad had ordered her to stay inside until he got back. Which would be hours from now and would then be dark. She definitely wasn't allowed out at night. The town now had a curfew. It wasn't set to a specific time, just when the sun went down.

Lavender groaned and tossed the book she'd been trying to read. The clock read 2:00 PM. This was ridiculous! She wasn't meant to be stuck in one location like this.

I'm going for a walk, she told Silas. She needed fresh air. She needed to actually stretch her legs. The information got the fastest response she'd had in a week.

Don't.

Lavender rolled her eyes. *Not far, just behind my house.*

I'll be back in a few, just wait.

Lavender already had her layers on. *You can catch up with me.*

Lavender.

It's fine, she asserted. *Most of the animals have been put down, right? I'll be okay.* The crisp winter air was refreshing. Like a glass of water in the desert. Lavender rounded the house and saw the axe. It was exactly where she left it. Stuck in the ground, handle up. *I'm taking an axe with me, if I'm going down, I'll at least get a few licks in.*

Not funny.

Lavender huffed and headed into the woods. She swung her axe by her side. A few of the trees were bending under the weight of the snow. The crunching of her footsteps seemed deafening in the stillness around her.

Lavender had been taking stock of all her gathered knowledge for the past few days. *You're the same thing as the killer, aren't you?*

Silas replied, *I'd rather talk about this in person*

Lavender frowned and kicked some snow. *I'll take that as a yes.* She looked back. The house was still visible. *Are Jerry and Ethan the same as you?*

No. The answer seemed nearly offended.

Lavender mused. *Am I human?*

Silas didn't respond. Which made Lavender frown. *I'll take that as a no.* She decided to give it a rest. Lavender looked up at the sky. She fell back into the snow. Mindlessly, she made a snow angel. It felt wonderful to be outside. Lavender hummed. An old song she'd sung since she was young. It was a rumble that came from her heart and rattled her ribcage.

A twig snapped.

Lavender sat up to see a cougar. It was yards away but Lavender could smell the rot. Between its teeth was a twitching rabbit. It looked like it was trying to suck on it. The bloody maw moving and undulating. The rabbit was staring at her with its frantic eyes, like it was screaming for Lavender to run.

The cougar dropped the rabbit in the snow. The body made a sickening thump into the snow. This cougar was sick. Unquestionably sick. Its fur had chunks ripped out of it. Lavender could count every one of its ribs. She slowly stood up. The wood of the axe dug into her skin. The Mountain Lion stepped forward. Its eyes were blazing. An insanely bright red. The growl it let out was distorted. Clippy and unnatural.

Lavender sucked in a deep breath. Fight, flight, or freeze. Freezing wasn't an option, so fight or flight. She couldn't outrun it. She had a chance with her axe. The thing looked weak but looks could be deceiving. While weighing her options, the cat began to move closer.

Lavender planted her feet and set up for a swing. She wasn't going down without a fight.

The cat was in front of her in a flash. She gasped and swung on instinct. Luckily, she got it hard in the jaw. Unluckily though, it only pissed the cat off.

It turned back to her. Jaw broken, but rage still intact. It squared its shoulders to pounce. The snap of bones sounded like thunder in the silent forest. Its jaw clicked back into place.

Lavender shuddered in horror. She gripped her weapon tighter. Caution to the wind. Time of the essence. Lavender screamed into the void and hoped the wind carried her words. *I'm going to die, and I want you to know I love you*

She hoped Silas heard her. She hoped her dad didn't find her. She hoped Ethan would be unaffected. She hoped her mom wouldn't find out. Jesus christ, she shouldn't have come outside.

The cat screamed and charged. It was lightning fast.

Lavender swung again. She got another hit but it didn't slow the thing down. It rammed into her. Her back collided with a tree. The cougar snapped its maw at her. She placed the axe handle into its mouth and tried to push it away. Its canines were huge. Soaked in blood and sinew. Lavender kicked at its stomach and groin. Her steel toe boots should have had some effect, but it didn't. Its paw went up. Lavender braced herself for impact, but it didn't come.

The cougar was thrown off her. Lavender fell to her knees. There was a scream. She whipped around and saw the cat in a headlock. Silas behind it. She watched as he opened his mouth wide.

Fangs.

Silas had fangs, and he buried them into the cougar's neck. The cat screamed and thrashed but Silas held it tight. Slowly its voice died. Its limbs stopped moving. It went limp. Silas pulled back, his mouth bloody. He dropped the cat. He went to one of the oak trees, ripping off a thick branch. The cougar's body was still twitching. They didn't have a fire, so he'd have to do it the messy way. Silas plunged the limb into its heart.

Lavender gasped when the cat exploded. Like a vile flesh and blood balloon, it popped.

Silas shuddered and stepped away from the carnage. He had hoped draining it would make it less gross. What a bust. Silas gasped, face splattered with blood. He tried to wipe it clean but couldn't. His shaky hands were only making it worse. "Fuck!"

Lavender stood, shocked to her feet by the curse. Silas rarely cursed. Her legs still felt shaky, but Silas was here. He was here and he saved her. Right now, he needed help. She'd help.

Bending down, Lavender grabbed some snow. It began to melt in her feverish hands. She pulled Silas's hands away from the mess on him. "Let me." She gently rubbed the snow onto his skin. He didn't even flinch. The mess was now easier to manage. Lavender pulled off her scarf and used it to wipe off the watery gore.

"Why the fuck are you out here?!" Silas roared. Lavender flinched away from him. He quickly apologized, "I'm sorry. I'm sorry. I-" Tears filled his eyes. "Fuck, if I hadn't-" Silas tried to wipe at his face, but it was useless. The somewhat clean mess was messy again. "I love you too," he confessed, pulling her into a hug, "I love you so much."

Lavender's gasp was shaky. She tried not to break down, "I'm sorry I didn't listen." She gripped him tight. "Thank you," she wept. "Thank you, thank you."

Silas's hug became tighter. "I love you. I love you." He couldn't stand the smell of fear on her. The scent was stinging his nose. Acidic and unforgiving. Silas wanted it gone. "Are you okay?" he asked, pulling back.

Lavender nodded. She noticed the bloody tears. "What are you?" She asked.

Silas chuckled. "You already know."

"I know you're not human, I don't know the name for you though."

Silas nodded. "We have many. Most common one is vampire." He expected the scent of fear to come back, or for her to scream. She didn't though. Lavender just smiled.

"Oh, dearheart," she whispered, cupping his face and pressing her forehead against his. "I thought it would be something crazier."

Silas laughed. He couldn't help it. It was so ridiculous. "Vampire isn't crazy enough for you?"

Lavender giggled. "Nah, it is. I just wanted to make you smile." She kissed his nose, which was thankfully clean.

Silas felt his heart melt. He nuzzled into her neck. The itch to bite came on full force. Her veins sung with a rush of blood. The blood of the girl he loved. Silas turned his head and sucked in some winter air. Her scent was still calm. She didn't even realize the danger she was in. "You really aren't scared?"

Lavender chuckled, "Why would I be scared?" She rested her head on his.

"I'm a monster," Silas whispered.

Lavender scoffed. "You're literally a gentle giant. A teddy bear like 90% of the time." She hugged him. "You're adorable and I won't listen to any lies someone told you." Lavender asked, "Do you even eat people?"

Silas shook his head. "No, animals only."

"See!" Lavender teased, "Teddy bear." Even covered in blood, his little smile and blush was adorable. "How long have you been a vampire?" she asked, mindlessly playing with his hair.

Silas shrugged, "I don't know."

Lavender pulled back, "What. How do you not know?"

Silas explained, "I was asleep. Dad and mom said it couldn't have been more than a couple years. They aren't too sure though." he looked at the bloody snow under them.

Lavender thought for a moment. She then remembered, "The coma?"

Silas nodded.

"I want a full recap, but first." Lavender jumped up and offered her hand. "Let's go home. We need showers and I need hot chocolate."

Silas smiled softly. He took her hand and let her help him up. "Do you have any clothes I can use?"

"Dad's given me some hand me downs over the years. Something's bound to fit." She began to lead them home.

"Why'd he do that?"

Lavender shrugged, "Waste not want not." She then gave Silas a sly smile, "Also to wear during skinning."

Silas nodded, "Yea, that makes sense." Lavender being a hunter was the least surprising aspect about her.

"There's gonna be stains."

"I figured."

Silas's eyes grew heavy as Lavender dried his hair. No one had done this for him in years. He'd forgotten how soothing it was.

"Alright you," Lavender finally said, "start talking." She threw the towel into her hamper. Lavender sat against her headboard.

Silas sighed and laid down between her legs. His back to her chest. Lavender's hands went back to his hair. "I lived with my grandparents in Oregon," he began, "We were happy, just the 3 of us, barely saw anyone else." His grandfather had built the cabin he was raised in. It was in the center of the forest. Isolated, but never lonely.

"No tribe?" Lavender wound her fingers in his still damp locks.

"Nah, pops said he was retired," Silas smiled, "and that meant from everything."

Lavender giggled.

Silas clarified, "There was some drama, because of my parents apparently. So he packed up and moved him and Ma out to the woods. I came along a few years later. Parents died. It was either them or some white family in Montana. My Ma apparently told the social worker 'No white lady is taking my baby' So to their house I went."

Lavender buried her nose into his hair, "I'm glad they got you."

Silas smiled, "Me too." He went on, "I wanted for nothing. I needed nothing. I was happy. I was loved."

Lavender could feel the 'but' coming.

Silas sighed, "But murders started happening. Bodies piled up. An unending maw, always consuming, never full." He shook off his grandfather's haunting words. Tales of a monster that lurked in the wood, gorging itself on helpless victims. "One night, a man came, asking to be let in."

Lavender tensed. That sounded too familiar.

"Ma and Pops and I all went to the door. I remember his voice. His unnatural and terrible voice." Silas looked out the window. "Ma opened the door. He pounced on her. Pops got his gun. He shot the man. It got him off Ma but he started to move and shake. Pops told me to run. I was fast, I knew the land well. He knew I was the only chance of getting help. He reloaded his gun as I ran from the house." Silas audibly swallowed. "I was 8."

Lavender continued to play with his hair. She knew it was calming to him and he needed all the comfort he could get.

"As I was running, I heard Pops scream." He wiped at his face. "I still hear him scream."

Lavender moved her hands and instead held him tight. "I'm sorry," she mumbled into his damp hair.

Silas turned his head and nuzzled into her neck. The smell of her made him sigh. Silas took a deep breath and kept going. "I used the land. The pitfalls, trees, and even traps to keep the bastard from catching me, at least for a while. He eventually got me though. I remember the smell of him. The copper and bile and rot around him. It burned my nose." Silas smiled. "Then Eden came. The family came. They saved me, ripped him apart, burned him."

Lavender rubbed his biceps.

"Then they took me in. A human among vampires. Matthias and Ariyah told me, when I became an adult, I could choose if I wanted to be turned or not. I didn't get a choice though." The fire flashed before his eyes. "When I was 17, we moved to this nice town. I met people. I had friends. I had a big family." Silas clenched his fist. If Lavender didn't leave him for being a vampire. He hoped she wouldn't leave him for being… "There was a boy. He…we…" Silas weighed his words and tensed.

Lavender knew that hesitancy by heart. She knew that pause like the back of her hand. The fear of rejection. The fear of disgust. "Silas, my mom and dad are bi. My auntie's gay with a wife," Lavender smiled, "I'm bi too." She kissed the top of his head and felt him melt against her.

Silas chuckled, "Really?"

Lavender snorted, "Yea, dude." She gestured to herself, "Isn't it obvious?"

Silas giggled and tucked his face into her neck. "Well, now that you mention it…"

Lavender pinched him, "Watch it, woodsy boy."

Silas scoffed, though he was still smiling. "You said it!"

Lavender rolled her eyes. "You got me there."

The pair shared a laugh before silence took over. The glow of the moment faded and Silas asked, " Where was I?"

"Ex boyfriend," Lavender recalled.

"Right, right," Silas got back to his tale. "So, he and I were together for a couple months. I thought he really, really liked me." He took Lavender's hand. "It was my first relationship. First time being in love, so I did something stupid." Silas intertwined his hand with Lavender's. "I told him about my family. About them being vampires. How they took care of me and loved me and he…" Silas looked at a sea glass wind chime. It glittered even in the gray light of winter. "He got scared. Genuinely scared. All of a sudden, that nice town turned horrid. People started glaring at us. Graffiting the house. I went from the entire school loving me to hating me over night."

Lavender squeezed his hand. She kissed the top of his head.

Silas began to cry. He didn't even bother wiping his face. "We were going to leave. One night, he…" Silas couldn't say his name. It clogged his throat and choked him. "Him and his friends came. Some of them used to be my friends!" Silas laughed, tears streaming down his face. "They threw some toilet paper, then eggs. We just ignored them and kept packing. Then they threw a molotov."

Lavender inhaled sharply. "You're kidding me!"

Silas shook his head, "They were already drinking. I guess they just…" Lavender hugged him tightly. "I remember burning. The feeling of the fire." Silas shuddered. "The smoke choked me. Stung my eyes. I remember Eden's face, then it was just black. I passed out, then I woke up like," he stared down at his cold hands, "This." Silas used the shirt he wore to wipe his face. "I can't even be mad at them, because I would have done the same thing. If you had the ability to save someone wouldn't you? They tried just their blood, but it didn't work so… Eden just-" Silas gently snapped his teeth.

"Their blood?" Lavender was confused, "Does your blood do something?"

Silas nodded. "It can heal most things, but fire is a big weakness. Burning a vampire is one of the few ways to kill us."

"Huh, something you guys share with nearly everything," Lavender teased.

Silas giggled, "Yea, you're right." He rubbed his face against her shirt. Making her shoulder bloody. "Shit, sorry," he moved to sit up.

Lavender gently guided him back down. "I'm a girl, I'm not afraid of bloody clothes."

Silas smiled widely, "You're ridiculous." She shrugged and returned a hand to his hair. "They want to meet you. Have wanted to, for a while." He looked up at her. Her golden eyes looked beautiful in the winter light. He reached up and traced her high cheekbone with his knuckle.

Lavender turned and bit it. Her grin was wide as her teeth didn't even make an indent on Silas's skin.

The boy laughed, pulling his finger back. "Rude!"

Chapter 10

Dean was mad.

Lavender couldn't blame him. She knew she could have lied, but didn't see the point.

"I told you to stay inside!" Dean scolded. "Was shooting a serial killer not enough for you?! I swear you and your mother have no self preservation skills!" He grabbed a beer out of the fridge.

"I'm fine, dad, and one of those animals is out of our woods." She added, "I see it as a win-win." Lavender reached for the remote. She was laying across the couch. Silas left through the window when they heard her dad pull up. A part of her was curious why her dad just believed she could kill a cougar by herself. She decided to just take it as a compliment.

"I see it as you being an idiot," Dean took a swig from the aluminum can. He gently moved her legs and sat down. "Ender, I know being stuck inside is making you," he waved his hand near his head, "but I'm trying to keep you safe."

"I killed it!"

"And it could have killed you!" Dean sighed, "Listen, you have to be lucky everytime you go in there. They only have to be lucky once." He rubbed his tired eyes. Dean knew the Annora boy had been over. Was probably who helped Lavender with the cat. He felt like he should have been more angry about a boy in his house. He wasn't though. Silas was a good kid. A strong boy with a heart of gold. Silas was definitely better to have around Lavender than away. Dean let his head fall back against the couch.

Lavender frowned, "You know it's not rabies, right?"

"Obviously," Dean growled. He chugged his beer. "Fuck it!" he declared, "It's pizza time!"

Lavender laughed. She reached to the side table and grabbed the phone, handing it to Dean. The man took it gratefully.

"You're already 'grounded', so I can't do that. So your punishment is no stuffed crust."

"What?! This is outrageous!" Lavender slammed her fist into the arm of the couch.

Dean snorted and doubled over. Laughing for so long, the phone timed out. He'd needed that. That levity. That joy. He was so happy his daughter was home. "Dammit, Flower." He gently punched her arm. "How am I supposed to be stern when you're like this?"

Lavender shrugged, "Guess you gotta keep being the fun parent." She flopped back into the couch.

Dean sighed. If she was going to be a brat, he'd be one too. "So, your boyfriend was over today?"

Lavender blushed, "Um, well, he-"

"Do I need to buy you condoms?"

"Ew, dad!" Lavender kicked him.

"I don't want to be a grandpa yet!" Dean cried, "It's too much pressure!"

Lavender sighed, "Jesus christ!" She stood and went to get a drink. "We haven't even kissed!" Lavender grabbed a soda. "I don't think we'll be doing that for a while." She placed a hand on her hip. "We aren't really…interested in it." Dean gave her a face that said 'yea right'. "I'm serious!" Lavender went back to the couch. "We just… like each other. Just being around each other is nice."

Dean pursed his lips, "So…condoms or?"

"No dad, not right now!"

"Gottcha!" Dean dialed the number for the pizza place.

Lavender sighed and chugged her Fanta.

Lavender was drifting off. That sweet spot before entering deep sleep. Where the world and her mind blended. Outside and inside sounds weaved around her. Spinning a web until finally tying her down into REM sleep.

"Lavender!"

Said girl jumped up, swinging her fist into Silas's face. "Ow!" Lavender hissed, shaking her hand. "Holy shit, what are you made of!"

"Sorry, sorry," Silas took her hand. It was definitely broken. "Ah, shit." He let his fangs pop out.

Lavender watched as he cut his arm.

"Here."

Lavender looked at the trail of blood. It was a striking crimson. "Um?"

"Drink it." Silas quickly added, "It'll heal your hand."

Lavender gave him a questioning look, but did lick the line of blood. It was…well blood, but it had a hint of something under it. Fruity, but still blood. She gasped. Shock ran through her. It was like chugging an energy drink or getting an adrenaline shot.

Lavender shook her head, like when she ate sour candy. Gold eyes wearily looked at her hand. She could feel it repairing. The bone fragments mending and snapping back into place. It wasn't painful but it was a sensation unlike any other. She uncurled her fingers. They moved smoothly. "Whoa." Lavender smiled and looked at Silas. "No wonder your dad is an awesome doctor."

The boy was sitting on the edge of her bed with a small smile.

Wait a second.

He was in her room.

He'd woken her up!

Lavender smacked him in the face with a pillow. "What are you doing here?!" she hissed, hitting him again. "You think breaking into my house is a good idea?! There's a killer on the loose, you doofus!"

"Ah!" Silas used his arms to shield his face from the assault. "Sorry, sorry! I was worried." He whimpered, "Dad told me about the venom-"

"Venom?" Lavender set the pillow down. "What venom?"

Silas frowned. "Did the cougar bite you?"

Lavender frowned, "Silas, if I'd been bitten, I'd be bleeding, right?"

Silas nodded, still wearing his empty headed expression.

"And you're a vampire, right?"

Silas nodded again.

Lavender sighed, "Dearheart, if I was bleeding, you'd know, right?"

"Yes."

Lavender stared at him. She watched in real time as he connected the dots. His black eyes went comedically wide. A blush spread across his face.

"I'm sorry," he mumbled. Silas moved to stand and leave, but warm hands grabbed his wrist.

"Come here, stupid boy," Lavender giggled. She pulled him back to sit. "Now, tell me about this venom."

"We have- dad, told me we have this poison. It's a defense thing."

"Are you guys snakes or cats?"

Silas frowned, "We're vampires."

Lavender snorted. She stuffed her face into a pillow and scream-laughed.

Silas tilted his head. That sound was new. He liked it. How it'd make her breath hitch. The nasally snorts and little hiccups. The silly screech. He reached out his hand and touched one of her finger's clutching the pillow.

She looked up at him. Her gold eyes shining in the moonlight. He felt the pads of her fingers. The grooves felt so strange against the smooth pads of his finger. Every human etch in his body had disappeared. All the little things. Tiny hairs, finger prints, Little random bumps of skin.

Gone.

All gone.

He'd never noticed how inhuman he'd truly become. How human she still was. Silas took her hand. It was warm. Burning hot on his frigid skin. Her palm had lines, while his had none.

"Silas?"

He broke out of his examination. "Sorry." His brain was so different now. Wired even worse than it was before. He was already… Silas sighed, "I'll go home."

Lavender frowned. She squeezed his hand. "You don't have to go just yet." Pillow discarded, she scooted closer. She played with his fingers. "Are you always cold?"

"Unless I gorge myself, yea."

"Gorge?"

"Drink a lot of blood," Silas smiled, "like an insane amount. If I drink normally, I'm at room temperature." He used his other hand to trace her palm. They fell into a pattern. "Jonathan and I can't get heat like the others. Dad theorizes it's because we don't have a lot of fat.."

"Does Matthias try to science vampirism often?"

"I mean, he's been a doctor for over 600 years. He knows everything about humans. Might as well research vampires."

That made Lavender break the pattern. "Holy shit, talk about dedication to the craft." She moved back to sit against the headboard. "Thanks for coming to check on me." She patted the space beside her.

"Sorry I broke in." Silas crawled over to sit beside her. "I got scared. I didn't know we had venom."

"Can it be cured?" Lavender let her head rest on his shoulder.

Silas shook his head, "No, Matthias said you'd need a blood transfusion. Otherwise, I'd have to suck it out, which could kill you."

"How so?"

"Cause, I might not be able to stop," Silas frowned. "I've never had human blood."

"Is that bad?" Lavender nudged him.

Silas shrugged, "Depends. Apparently, some…fledglings?"

"Fledglings?"

"Matthias and Ariyah say fledgling but everyone else says baby vamps."

Lavender snorted, turning her head to giggle into Silas's shoulder.

The boy smiled as well. "There's a chance of going nuts, from the blood. It's called a frenzy, but it mostly happens to the unmentored." Silas bit his lip, "The one that killed-" He kneaded the pillow beside him. "The one that took my grandparents was in a frenzy. Most of the animals we've been killing are too."

Lavender asked, "What do you mean unmentored?"

Silas explained. "Matthias said it's like babies and breastfeeding. Some latch naturally, some don't. Those that don't need to be taught or they can't drink properly. If that happens, they're like a toddler with a capri-sun and no straw." Silas waved his hand, "They make a mess."

Lavender snorted. "What an apt analogy," she teased.

Silas shrugged. "Best one I have."

Lavender asked, "What if I had been poisoned? Like, if by some miracle, I had and was still alive."

Silas mused, "Well, I was going to throw you over my shoulder and run home. Matthias has a blood transfusion thing." He turned toward Lavender. "I was scared when you were laying there, all still."

"I was almost asleep."

Silas hummed. He nuzzled her. "I'm sorry."

"Don't break in again."

"I won't, unless you call me."

"Deal," Lavender nudged him. "Alright, out you go."

Silas smiled. He kissed her forehead, "Night."

"Night." Lavender watched as he climbed out the window he'd gotten in from. He pulled it closed behind him. She shook her head. "I love you," she whispered into the night.

I love you too, Silas whispered back

Chapter 11

Dean sighed and sat at his desk. He looked at the photo they'd managed to get of the killer. Was a slimy looking bastard. One of those wild west mustache twirling villains. "Should be tying damsels to railroad tracks," Dean huffed. The fluorescent lights above him were buzzing and made his headache worse. The feds were out of his hair, but this killer wasn't. "Fuck my life." Cool fingers appeared and began to rub his temples. Dean hummed and let his head fall back. He looked up at Matthias. "How are you doing, doc?" he asked with a gentle smile.

Matthias huffed, "Not much of a doctor as of late." He took the seat across from Dean.

"The photo came out good," Dean placed it on his desk. "You know him?"

Matthias frowned, "Unfortunately. Colonel G Combstock." Dean motioned his hand for him to continue, so Matthias did. "We first met him in 1863, then 1945, last time I didn't see him but Jonathan did in 1973." The doctor leaned forward.

Dean furrowed his brow. "Why those dates?"

Matthias looked up at the man. "I enlisted as a medic in nearly every conflict. Even in the sun, we are harder to kill. Our strength is diminished but not fully lost."

Dean asked, "How much can you push in the sun?"

Matthias thought for a moment. "I can not say exactly, but in Buchenwald I flipped a car." He remembered the SS officers' faces when he grabbed the front of their escape vehicle. Normally, Matthias didn't indulge in human blood. However, he'd make some exceptions.

Dean sat back in shock. "Holy shit." The mentioned location wasn't familiar. He asked, "What's Buchenwald?"

Now it was Matthias's turn to be shocked. The memories made him feel sick. It was something no one should forget. "It…was a concentration camp. Did they not teach you this in school?"

Dean frowned. "We didn't learn about the Holocaust. At least in my first History class in high school. My teacher was a-" Dean shook his head. "When I got older, I learned there were more camps, but my teachers only named Auschwitz." Dean wondered how much he wasn't taught.

Matthias frowned. "That's very sad." He looked at Combstock's photo. "Combstock was an SS officer. We were unable to kill him at the time."

"We?"

Matthias nodded. "Jonathan normally enlists with me." He smiled. "We found Eden there. She had gouged out one of Combstock's eyes." The memory of Eden's turning made him smile. He was so sure she would die in his arms. Die in that horrid crematory. She lived though. They all lived. "I lost much while over there, but I did gain a daughter."

Dean smiled. Matt was a good man. Unequivocally good. "You get a new kid every time you go?" he teased.

Matthias giggled. "Not every time. Just the 3."

Dean raised an eyebrow, "I thought you had 5 kids."

Matthias nodded. "Jonathan and Everett were in the Civil War. Eden was World War 2. Hana was Vietnam. Silas was found outside of conflict."

Dean whistled, "Damn. How can you stand all that fighting?"

Matthias shrugged. "Vampire minds work differently. It is a blessing and a curse." He tapped on Combstock's photo again. "After everyone has had rest, we will need to go on the hunt again."

Dean nodded. The thought of going back into the National Park made him nauseous. "How's the pack doing? Anything new?"

"The grandmother is mad. She doesn't think she should be usurped so summarily. Especially since Lavender has not come to take her place." Matthias stretched. He needed rest. He needed to feed. Jonathan was probably face down in his bed cuddling Everett. Matthias couldn't wait to do the same with Ariyah. "I do not understand pack traditions."

Dean shrugged, "Join the club." He took Combstock's photo and pinned it to the cork board. Some of the victims, evidence, maps, and other odd ends littered the board. Dean rubbed his face. He'd need to shave soon.

Jerry came into the room. He nodded at Matt in lieu of greeting. Dean was standing in front of their 'evidence'. Jerry wondered if he and Dean would be so close if Millie hadn't- Jerry stopped that thought in its tracks. He was here to get something done. It would be done. "If you two are going to discuss the pack, you should at least include an active member."

Dean smiled. The other man looked like he was going to fall over. "Aw, come on Jer. You know you're always welcome to join us." He looked at the face of the murder victims, then the ones of the animals. The difference was striking. One side was randomized. Poor souls just going out at the wrong time. The other side all looked like Lavender. "If he wants to take her, why have animals kill her?"

Matthias piped up with a theory. "He is not trying to kill her. He is mad that his fledglings can not find her."

Jerry huffed, "Fledglings?" His eyes felt like they were on fire. From the tears or the tiredness, he couldn't tell.

Matthias sighed, using the term his children came up with. "Baby vamps."

Dean chuckled. He stepped back from the board. "So, they find a look alike, but it isn't her, so they kill her?"

Matthias nodded. "Turned animals can not drink properly. They are starving. That is why the attacks are so brutal." He went to stand beside Dean. "Maker's can see through their fledgling's eyes and into their mind, if they choose. His plan was probably to have an animal incapacitate her."

"Why can't he do it?" Jerry asked.

"If she is in a home, he can not get to her. We must be invited in."

Dean looked at the pale man. "You've come in without an invitation."

Matthias smiled, "We only need to be invited once. Unless the person revokes it, of course."

Dean smiled, "Good to know." He tilted his head. "So why not come and grab her himself? He's coming to drop off bodies."

"He knows we know what he wants." Matthias pointed to the map. "He is hoping if he kills enough, we will give him Lavender. It is a tactic that has worked for him before. Until he gets desperate, he'll most likely keep this, how you say, M.O."

Jerry snorted and joined the two on their feet. "Your boys have been roughing him up though."

"Oh yes," Matthias smiled. "Silas ripped off his arm yesterday, so we should get a break in killings."

Dean was shocked. "Ripped it off?"

"He made an unsavory remark against Lavender. My boy does not anger easily or often, but he is protective of your girl." Matthias tapped the photo of Combstock. The last time he saw the man was in 1945. "He is a disturbed man. But he is not a complete moron. He will be licking his wounds under the earth for some time."

Jerry huffed, "Some good news, at least." This was going off the rails. He'd come here for a reason and before they got too bogged down with all of this. "We need her, Dean."

Said man looked at his longest friend. "Jerry-"

"We lost River."

Dean's eyes widened in shock. "What, when?!"

"During the hunt, he started shifting and…" Jerry closed his eyes and collected his thoughts. "Ethan's going to on the full moon. He needs her. The other kids need her too, Dean. You need to tell her. The whole pack will be there. He gestured to Matthias. "His family's invited, please, Dean." Jerry grabbed the shoulders of his oldest friend. "I can't lose him. I already lost Millie, I can't-" Jerry broke down in tears.

Dean hugged him close. "I'll tell her. She'll be there. I promise you, Jerry."

Ethan was on the doorstep.

Lavender nearly jumped through the door to get to him. She ripped it open instead and pulled him into a tight hug. "Oh, Little, Little." She kissed his cheek. The sweet smell on him was overwhelming. It was like he'd doused himself in a sugary perfume. "What are you wearing?"

Ethan was confused by the question. He ignored it and held her close. "I missed you too, Mama." He breathed her in. "I missed you so much." Ethan kissed her cheek. River's mangled face flashed into his mind. He let out a shaky breath and unconsciously dug his nails into her. "Sorry, sorry," he whimpered.

Lavender pulled back. "Hey, hey are you okay? Did you get hurt?" She knew the recent 'hunt' had been a lot. Dean had said they killed over a dozen 'rabid' animals.

Ethan shook his head. While doing it, he caught sight of his healing mark. "Mama. I need you to know something."

"Of course, come inside." The pair went to the kitchen once again. Lavender grabbed a blanket for the boy. He was shaking, which Lavender didn't think he had noticed. Something had happened. "Here, Little."

Deja vu was such a strange thing to experience. Ethan didn't think he'd ever get used to the feeling, but here he was. Once again sat with his drink and Lavender beside him at her kitchen table. Ethan began, "Mama, you need to know that Silas isn't human."

Lavender smiled, "I know."

Ethan balked. "You knew?!" He'd expected more of a reaction then the simple shrug he got.

Lavender nodded. "We've been talking telepathically for months. He also told me the other day too." She took a sip of her drink. "I'm also assuming you're here to tell me I'm not human either."

Ethan nodded. "Yea. That's right." He leaned back in his chair. "I thought your mom didn't tell you."

Lavender snorted, "Oh, she didn't!" A bitter taste filled her mouth. "I just picked up some clues. I don't know what I am, but I know it's not human." She reached over and took Ethan's hand. "Please, tell me."

Ethan swallowed. "You're a Den Mother."

Lavender had no frame of reference for that. "A what?"

Ethan sucked in a deep breath. "Okay, here goes." He began his tirade. "So we're werewolves and the Den Mother is the leader of the pack. She has this special call that can help shifters and the born to turn into wolves. They're bigger and stronger than a normal wolf. Like 10 feet tall, kind of big! They also give birth to werewolves every time. Apparently with born male werewolves it's a crapshoot. Anyway! Nana is too old to call now and you need to come and do it because if not we could get stuck like River did and have to be shot because you can't fix getting stuck and-"

"Ethan, breathe!" Lavender squeezed his hand. The poor boy was hyperventilating. "Calm down, Little."

Ethan sighed and face planted into the table. "I…I need you to come. I need you there, Mama, please."

Lavender frowned. "What would I have to do?"

Ethan rested his cheek against the hardwood. "You just have to use your call, then my wolf will come out." He rubbed the back of her hand with his thumb. "Nana said you'll just…know how to do it."

Lavender didn't have a lot of confidence, but she was willing to try. "Okay, now. Why can't Nana help anymore?"

Ethan mused, "Menopause, I think? Everyone just says she's too old. I'm pretty sure that's what it means." The consequences of the snag Rosemary caused in the chain were in full swing. He shouldn't be having to explain this. "Your mom was supposed to…" Ethan took his hand back and rubbed his face.

Lavender realized it then. "What, was my mom supposed to be the Den Mother?"

Ethan nodded.

Lavender looked down at her drink. She clenched her cup. "She ran away though."

Ethan nodded again.

Lavender swallowed. Her throat made a clicking sound. "River's dead?"

Ethan's lip quivered. "You wouldn't have been able to save him, Mama. We were miles away."

"If I'd gotten there though."

Ethan shook his head. "Mama, we were an hour away. He would have died in agony before you got there." Tears streamed down his face. Rivers' twisted form was still fresh in his mind. The half elongated jaw. The tufts of fur. The blood and muscle. His spine was exposed and arched. Ripped skin and cracked bones. The disgusted churn in his stomach made him dizzy. "Dad had to…" Ethan wept. He'd looked away when Jerry fired. River's head was gone when he looked back. His mouth salivated. That salivation that came from when you were about to vomit. Ethan rubbed his eyes. "We need you, Mama. I'm the next to shift. I'm scared. I'm scared for all of us. We need you."

Lavender growled. "Why didn't anyone tell me?"

Ethan shrugged. "I guess they thought you knew? I did. Or your mom told everyone to keep quiet. I don't know."

Lavender's face twisted in disgust. She knew Dean didn't know her mother had thrown her here. Maybe he thought she'd be going back. What else was kept from her? Who else died because she didn't know? So much of her life had been hidden from her. So much of *her* was hidden from her. Why? Why would her mother do this? Lavender gripped her cup. "GOD DAMMIT!" she screamed and threw her cup across the room.

Ethan jumped, pulling his limbs inward.

Lavender screamed and flipped the table. "GOD FUCKING DAMMIT!" She covered her face with her hands and then ran them through her hair. Lavender looked at Ethan. The boy jumped. He looked terrified. No, no. Lavender took a deep breath. "I'm sorry," she went to him, "I'm sorry, Little."

Ethan nodded and shakily relaxed. "It's okay, Mama."

Lavender shook her head. "No, no, you didn't-" She wiped her nose on her sleeve. "I shouldn't have done that." Lavender kneeled on the floor in front of him. "I'll be there. I promise. I won't let you get stuck."

Ethan nodded. He leaned forward and wrapped her in a hug. "Thank you, thank you," he whispered into her curls.

Lavender hated that he felt the need to thank her.

Silas rubbed his eyes. He was tired. So damn tired.

"Sleep, Si," Eden urged. She rubbed the boy's shoulder. "You deserve it."

Silas frowned. "I'm so tired but I'm so restless."

Eden hummed. "Maybe making something might help?" She sat beside the boy. The manor was eerily quiet. Most of the family was asleep. "I know, when I can't rest, I paint. After a bit, I feel more relaxed and ready to sleep."

Silas nodded. "Well…there is something I do want to do."

Eden smiled knowingly. "Don't propose too early, you maye scare her off."

Silas snorted. "It's not an engagement thing. It's like a-" he huffed and tried to think of the term.

Eden offered. "A promise ring?"

Silas nodded, "Yea, that! It's like that but more of a family version." He tapped his foot. The craft itself didn't feel like enough. "Could you…maybe come with me?" Eden raised a brow at him. "I want to get some flowers too."

The woman snorted. "I wish the world had more boys like you." She tucked a stray hair behind his ear. "Alright, come on." Eden stood. "I can think of a lovely arrangement for your little wolf."

Silas blushed. "Thanks Eden." He followed his sister out of the house.

Eden mused. "Maybe I should open another floral shop." She smiled at the boy. "Would you be my helper, again?"

Silas snorted, "Hell no. Ask Everett, he was better at it then me."

"Yes but you were so fun to have in the shop. You used to dance with the tissue paper." Those adorable memories warmed her slow beating heart. Eden put on her sunglasses and unlocked the car. "You also ate a tulip."

Silas groaned, "I was nine!" He got in the passenger seat. Eden was laughing at him. The memory was funny, objectively. Silas looked out the window while they drove into town. He hoped Lavender would like the gift.

Chapter 12

"Did you know mom is a werewolf?" Lavender asked as soon as Dean opened the door. The house was back together. Table upright and shattered cup thrown away.

Dean looked at his daughter. She had that look on her face. The 'We're going to talk, right now' face. "Can I get a beer first?" he begged.

Lavender nodded. She waited hours, she could wait a few more minutes.

Dean upholstered his gun and took off his belt. He grabbed a can from the fridge and walked back to the living room. He sat on the couch. "Alright." He took a few big swigs of his beer. "Ready."

"Did you know?" Lavender asked.

"Yes."

"Why didn't you tell me?"

"I thought your mom would, or did."

"Do you know about the tribe?"

"I dated your mom and Jerry, I know all about it."

"Why'd mom keep coming back and leaving?"

That made Dean pause. He sighed and chugged his beer down. The can was then crushed in his hand. "It's complicated."

"My best friend might fucking die, dad. Uncomplicate it," Lavender hissed.

Dean put his hands up in submission. "Okay, okay," he sighed. He rubbed his face. "Alright, your mom and I. Well-" he stopped short. "Your mom was a rebel. Was the first thing that attracted me to her." Dean went on, "If I'd known some of the ways she rebelled you might not have been born."

Lavender winced at that.

Dean quickly added, "Was definitely worth it to have you though. Honest, flower." He reached out and squeezed his daughter's shoulder. The man took his curls down. It thankfully helped his growing headache. "Anyway, your mom is a female born werewolf. Which is apparently important. The pack needs them to exist. Your mom hated that she had to lead and take care of everyone."

Rosemary used to scream about how much she hated her mom. Dean used to let her vent and rage. They were dumb teenagers. He was a dumb teenager. Only a year older than Lavender at the time. He wanted to support the girl who'd been his friend for years. "Your mom didn't want to lead the pack, nor listen to her mother. At first everyone kind of just thought she was a punk but…" Dean frowned, he didn't know how much to divulge. "Your grandmother tried to get her involved with helping those going werewolf for the first time." Dean swallowed the lump in his throat. "Your mom got mad that she was dragged there. She was mad she had to do it. So she chose not to…and to let the other kid die."

Lavender's eyes widened in horror. "She…killed someone?"

Dean shook his head. "No, no, her mom didn't allow it. I wasn't there but I heard and saw the aftermath." Dean tapped the side of his can. "Your grandmother beat the shit out of her."

Lavender winced. "Jesus," she whispered in disbelief.

Dean nodded. "That was the first time she ran off. The tribe let her go, because everyone was pissed." He finished his beer and placed it on the table. "She came back a few months later. Begged me to get married. We did. Had a wedding on the rez. Her mom was overjoyed."

Dean remembered the heartache he felt at Jerry's wedding. How being the best man was a rekindling but also very loud rejection. He hadn't fully cut off Rose. He hadn't fully condemned her. Granted, he hadn't known the whole story at the time. Dean was just glad Jerry and him were friends again. Even though the wound was nearly two decades old, it still stung.

"A few months later," Dean continued, "she got pregnant with you." He laid his head on the back of the couch. "We were okay for 3 years. Then Jerry said-" Dean covered his face with his hands. "It was completely innocent but your mom flipped out and that's what started the cycle of you coming and going. On and off." Dean looked at his daughter. "This past time was the longest she ever went away." He reached out and took her hand. "I wanted to find you. I did. I tried." Hours of crying at the kitchen table. Days on the phone searching. Begging for help. "I'm sorry, Lavender."

Lavender rested her head on the back of the couch. A pit was growing in her stomach. "What happened last time?"

Dean sniffled, "Something your grandmother said. They got into a fight. A real fight." The screaming. The claws. The biting. "They turned into wolves and started ripping at each other." He pulled up his shirt. Claw marks ran across his side. "I tried to stop them."

Lavender jumped up in horror. "Dad!" Her eyes flooded with tears. She reached out but stopped short before touching the marks. The scars were huge. Each one the size of a hand. "She did this?"

"She didn't mean to, Ender." Dean put his shirt down. "I went into an active war zone. I knew I was going to get hurt." Dean chuckled, "Didn't think it'd be that bad though. I obviously got hospitalized. She left with you then."

Lavender growled. "She never told me that! She said you didn't want to say goodbye!" The girl felt hot tears flood her eyes. "Are werewolves just fucked up?!" A panic ran through her. "Am I going to do that?!" What if she hit Silas, or dad, or Ethan. She wouldn't be able to live with herself if she did that. The thought of losing control like that made her nauseous.

Dean took his daughters heaving shoulders. "Ender, no. No honey." He pulled his daughter into a hug. "Sweetheart, It's nurture, not nature. There's plenty of amazing level headed werewolves who've never laid a hand to anyone. Your mother and grandmother are the exception, not the rule." He kissed her temple. "I know for a fact you'd never do that."

Lavender cried into her father's shoulders. "I'm sorry, daddy. I'm so sorry."

Her voice sounded so small. Dean hugged her tight. "You did nothing wrong, flower," he assured. "I never blamed you. I only wanted you to be safe. I'm so happy you're here. You can't imagine how happy I am that you're here."

Lavender clutched at her dad. She buried her face in his shoulder. "I love you," she cried.
Dean smiled, "I love you too, flower. I love you too."
Lavender decided to come clean. "Mom threw me out."

Lavender sat on her bed that night, phone in hand. She'd called Ethan after dinner. It was 3 hours of talking. Ethan felt more assured though, so it was worth it. Dean agreed to come with her to Ethan's shift. Maybe she'd be able to speak to her Nana. Maybe she could teach Lavender how to help with shifting. She wished she could talk to her mom. Well, in actuality, she wanted to scream at the woman. That wouldn't be useful though. Her mom would just scream back and hang up. Jeez, there were so many unanswered questions. A bitter taste filled her mouth. Lavender wondered if her mom would even pick up. Probably not. She groaned and fell back on her bed. Lavender wanted to scream and cry. She rubbed her tired eyes.

A pebble hit her window.

Lavender furrowed her brow. She got up and went over to it. The moon was big, nearly full. Another pebble hit the glass in front of her face. She looked down. Silas was looking up at her. She smiled and opened her window.

With an unnatural grace, Silas jumped up to the sill. "Hello, motek." He offered her a bouquet of flowers. "Surprise!"

Lavender could feel the blush rush to her cheeks. "Oh my gosh." All the sadness was washed away. All her anxiety vanished. She took the flowers. "Silas," she looked at them in awe. No one had ever given her flowers before. "They're beautiful!" Lavender grabbed the front of her boyfriend's shirt. "Get in here!"

Silas giggled and clambered into her room.

Some of the flowers she knew. The roses and actual Lavender. "What are these?" Lavender asked. She touched the soft purple and pink petals.

"Well those are lavender stock and pink stock. They're kind of filler flowers." Silas felt the gem in his pocket. The amount of giddy energy he had was pouring out of him. "I also made you," he pulled the necklace out, "this!"

Lavender nearly dropped the bouquet. She minded her manners and gently set the flowers on her bed. It was beautiful. She took the carved gem from Silas. It was a purple stone, smoothly shaped to look like a flattened donut. It fit neatly in the palm of her hand. Etched into the stone's face was a ring of lavender flowers. It must have taken hours to create, if done by hand. Lavender looked up at him in wonder, "Where did you get this?"

Silas beamed, "I made it!" He was so proud of the necklace. "It's an amethyst. My Ma gave it to me. The stone, I mean. She said to save it for someone special." Ma had told Silas that if he loved someone enough, he'd be able to take the time to shape and carve out the Earth for them. Silas knew it was probably too soon to declare his unending love, but he hoped Lavender got the message. From the way her golden eyes gentled at him, she did. Silas's chest got tight. He wanted to cite all the poems he wrote for her. He wanted to show her all the paintings he made of her. He wanted to tell her all the daydreams he had about spending his life with her.

Instead he explained, "We've been together for almost half a year now, so I thought-" He gasped when Lavender hugged him tightly. She was so insanely warm. Her heart was beating against his chest. Silas wrapped his arms around her. "Do you like the gifts?"

"I love them," Lavender confessed. She looked up at him. There was so much she wanted to say. So many things she wanted to declare. Words didn't feel like enough. They never felt enough. Instead she acted. Lavender went on her tip toes and kissed him.

It was quick, a peck, but the world seemed to stop. Time let them breathe. The wind let out a sigh. The moon shone brighter. Unfortunately, Lavender's poor toes could no longer bear her weight. She set herself back on her feet. They were on the ground but Lavender felt like she was floating.

Silas fell out of her arms and collapsed into the desk chair. His face was a bright red. He burst into a fit of giggles. His smile was infectious. Lavender was beaming too.

The world began to spin again. "Crap, I didn't get you anything!" Lavender began to wonder what she could give him.

"Well," Silas gave her a sheepish grin, "there is something you could do."

"Oh?" Lavender was hoping it wasn't what she thought.

"My family wants to meet you."

Oh thank god. Lavender felt a rush of joy wash over her. She nodded eagerly, "Yes, yes, yes!"

Silas joined in with her joy. "Okay, okay, I'll- will tomorrow work?"

Lavender nodded, "I'll tell dad "

The boy got to his feet, "Hell yeah!" He went to the window. "I'll pick you up tomorrow!" Silas began climbing out. He stopped before jumping down. "Um…could I have another?"

Lavender stared at him. His black eyes looked beautiful in the moonlight. "Another?"

Silas bit his lip. "A kiss?" He added, "It's okay if n-" Lavender pressed her lips to his again. Silas accidentally let go of the ledge and fell. He landed with a harsh thump onto the frozen ground. He had a besotted smile on his face.

"Are you okay?!" Lavender put half her body out the window. Silas was flat on his back. He was looking up at her. You would have thought she'd hung the moon and the stars. The love in his eyes was so endearing.

Silas gave her a thumbs up.

Lavender sighed in relief. *I love you, crazy boy*

Silas's smile grew bigger. *I love you too* He got up and waved, *Goodnight*

Lavender beamed, *Goodnight*

Dean chuckled as the Annora boy ran into the woods. He flipped open his phone and dialed a number. Every ring made his heartbeat quicken. The voice on the other end made it stop.

"Hello?"

Dean tried to keep his tone even. "Rosemary."

"Dean?"

The man felt his throat tighten. He hadn't heard her voice in years.

"Hello?"

Dean shook off his sorrow. "Sorry, here, fuck. Lavender…Lavender knows." He could feel her fury through the phone line.

"What?" she growled.

"It wasn't me. It was Ethan, apparently. Rosie-"

"Don't."

Dean sucked in a breath. "She needs you, she needs her mom."

"I'm not coming back."

Dean rolled his eyes. "I'm not asking that. I'm asking you to talk to her! She deserves answers, Rose." The other end was quiet for a time. Dean hoped she hadn't hung up. Before he could speak again, she finally did.

"I can't, Dean."

Dean felt his mouth twitch. Tears pricked at his eyes. "Did you really throw her out?"

"She wanted to go, I let her," Rosemary said bitterly.

A hot tear rolled down Dean's face. A righteous fury filled him. "How could you?"

"She chose the pack, she got it," Rosemary hissed.

Dean gripped the phone tight. "You gave her an ultimatum?"

"She'll be an adult soon."

"So it's okay to abandon her then?"

"She abandoned me." Rosemary's voice was wavering.

Dean laughed. His bitterness spilled out. "It hurts, doesn't it?" He heard her gasp of pain. It both burned and soothed him.

"Fuck you, Dean." Rosemary hung up.

Dean threw his phone across the room. It smashed into the wall, but didn't break. Thanks Nokia. He wanted to scream at her. Lavender would've heard that though. She didn't deserve to hear that.

"Dad?"

Dean looked at his door and sighed. Of course she'd hear him throwing shit. Dean wiped his eyes. "You can come in," he told her.

Lavender peeked her head inside. "Do we have a vase?"

Dean chuckled through his tears. Guess she didn't hear the phone. "I'm a small town bachelor, Ender. I don't have a vase."

"Damn." Lavender stepped inside. Her dad's room was so sparse. "Is that my old fishing pole?" she asked, pointing to the makeshift curtain rod.

Dean looked at it. Its pastel colors heavily clashed with the deep gray and blues of his room. "Yea, didn't have the heart to throw it away." He looked at his daughter. The memory of finding the old pole in the garage hit him. Rosemary had taken Lavender across the country. That summer had been hard. If that pole was ever tested, they'd find a concerning amount of tears on it. Lavender sat on his bed. Criss cross applesauce, as she used to declare. God, when did she stop saying that? When had she lost the baby fat in her face? Dean reached out to her. She came easily. His daughter was a cuddle bug. Always wanted to be in someone's arms or have someone in her arms. It was a trait she got from him. Dean decided to give her some good news. "We know who the killer is," he told her. "Apparently Matt has met him before."

Lavender looked up at her dad. "Oh?"

Dean nodded. "Combstock." He rested his back against the headboard.

"He's not human," Lavender whispered.

"I'll protect you," Dean promised. He kissed the top of her head.

This distraction wasn't enough. Lavender had heard her dad's phone call. Her mother's voice weighed heavy on her. "Does she still love me?" she asked.

Her voice sounded so small. Like when she was 13. A little girl. His little girl. He kissed her forehead. Dean wanted to reassure her. Wanted to tell her she was crazy and that of course her mother loved her. The words were stuck in his throat. They refused to pass his lips. "I love you, flower," was all he could manage. Lavender relaxed against him. They laid back. Dean felt Lavender's breath even out. A steady rise and fall. He finally relaxed too and fell asleep.

Chapter 13

The ride to Silas's house was nice. It was quiet and calm. Lavender watched the trees go by. The radio was softly playing and lulled Lavender into relaxation. This was something she needed. After last night, Lavender needed this peace. She felt like she should have been more nervous. Meeting a person's parents was a big deal. Lavender wasn't anxious though, she was excited.

"Do you not want them to hug you?" Silas asked as they got closer. "I can make sure they don't."

Lavender shrugged, "I'm fine with hugs." She double checked her hair in the mirror.

"What's that style called?" Silas had seen Eden wearing it before.

"They're called Milkmaid braids." Lavender pulled a couple of her loose curls to frame her face. She smiled in the mirror, happy with her appearance. "They're pretty easy to do." With a sly smile she asked, "Want me to do it for you?"

Silas grinned, "Maybe."

Lavender giggled and smoothed out her shirt. It was a simple black blouse and she paired it with some slacks.

"Home sweet home," Silas announced as they pulled up to the mansion.

Lavender looked at the manor. "Holy shit, and I thought Belle was rich. How did you get this?"

"When you've been alive for hundreds of years, the money kind of racks up. Especially if you're doctors." Silas shut off the car. He let out a shuddering breath.

"You okay?"

This was going to be a lot. Silas tugged at his shirt sleeve. Nervous and needing to fidget. He hoped Lavender wasn't too weirded out by them.

"Si?" Lavender took his hand.

"Listen, my family-"

"Silas, my mom's a werewolf."

The boy was surprised, "How long have you known?"

"Since yesterday," Lavender groaned. "Ethan told me. Now, believe me, your family can't be as wild as mine." Lavender got out of the car.

"Wait," Silas followed her out. "What do you mean Ethan told you?"

"He came by to talk about me being a Den Mother." Lavender kicked a stray rock. Silas came to her side and she remembered. "Speaking of which, how long have you known?" She poked her finger into his chest.

Silas guiltily looked to the ground. "Months."

Lavender made an offended noise. "I can't believe you!"

Silas whined, "It wasn't my place to tell you."

"You know, if everyone would just communicate, this dumb shit wouldn't happen!" Lavender huffed. She looked at the staggering house. "This place is insane." The manor looked so out of place in the dense forest around it.

Silas was glad she changed the subject on her own. "Mom designed it, dad had it built."

"Well, if you got the money," Lavender shrugged. "Alright, let's go!" She took Silas's hand and eagerly pulled him toward the door.

The boy chuckled and let her lead the way. Her switch would flip like a light. On and off. "Hana is probably going to jump out at you."

"Who?"

The front door flew open. Lavender gasped when she was lifted off the ground in an embrace.

"New sister!" Hana cried out in glee. She swung the girl around. "New sister! New sister!" The girl was insanely warm. A little living furnace.

"Hana, please!" Silas begged and managed to snatch Lavender back. He placed her feet on the ground. "I'm so sorry," he whispered to his girlfriend. Lavender only laughed and straightened out her clothes.

"I'm guessing she's Hana?" Lavender asked, pointing to the excited Asian girl. Her black hair was short and choppy. There were streaks of color in it. Her black eyes had the same gleam of red in them as Silas's. Her outfit was splattered with neon colors. Rips, fishnets, and splatter covered her clothes. Lavender already liked her.

"Did you cut your hair again?" Silas asked his sister, who in turn became even more excited.

"You noticed!" Hana giggled. She hugged her brother, easily lifting him off the ground.

"Well," Silas tilted his head in confusion, "It's kind of apparent." He looked at Lavender. *She's hyper*, Silas warned.

Lavender giggled, *I can tell*

Hana dropped Silas and turned back to the girl. "Oh, sorry!" she stuck out her hand and beamed when Lavender shook it without hesitation. "I'm Hana, so nice to meet you. Silas talks about you all the time and I've been dying to meet you. Especially since you've met Jonathan, and Matthias, and Eden said she's seen you and-"

"Hana," Silas gently put his hand on her shoulder. She'd sometimes go a mile a second. Wasn't her fault. Her mind was wired for speed.

"Sorry, sorry." Hana tried to calm down. She wiggled and danced in place. "I'm just so happy!" Silas was in love. Really in love! How could she not be excited? Hana turned her attention back to Lavender, "I'm sorry, I'm a lot sometimes." The girl's eyes were a beautiful gold. Silas hadn't exaggerated that. They were warm and kind and helped with Hana's insecurity.

"Don't have to apologize. Sometimes you get so happy it turns electric!" Lavender hugged the girl. She hoped her own weirdness would make Hana feel less strange.

It worked wonders.

Hana squealed and squeezed the girl closer. "New sister!" she declared.

Silas looked at them with a fond expression.

"Why are you all outside? Hana, let the poor thing go."

Lavender saw the starlet on the steps. She was still so unnaturally beautiful, even as dressed down as she was. The last time Lavender saw her in the parking lot, her hair had been cropped short. Now it was past her shoulders. Auburn curls framed her pale face.

"Lavender," Silas pointed to the woman, "Eden. Eden, Lavender." He was smiling, but Eden's face was pinched. Silas gave her a pleading look and her face softened.

Eden walked down the steps. "Hello," she greeted, hoping she sounded sincere.

She hates me, Lavender thought with a whimper.

No, she just has a bitch tone, promise, Silas assured her.

"**Be honest**," Eden hissed, though her mouth didn't move. It was the second voice. The shadow. The echo. One she hadn't been expecting. Lavender had nearly forgotten about them. Silas's had nearly disappeared to her ears. She blurted out, "It's nice to meet you. You're beautiful!" Lavender slapped a hand over her mouth.

"Eden!" Silas snapped. His own voice rising "What is wrong with you?!"

Lavender jumped. She'd never get used to him yelling.

The woman raised her hands in surrender. "Sorry, sorry, I just…" Eden stared off, "last time."

Silas frowned. He nodded, "I know but you can't do that."

"It's okay," Lavender took Silas's hand. "I understand." She looked to Eden, "but don't do that again."

"Fair enough." Eden looked to Hana, "What did you do to your hair?"

"I used dye!" Hana giggled. She hugged Eden. "She's gonna be our new sister~," she sang in glee.

Silas rolled his eyes. "Stop!" he begged.

"What are y'all doing?" Jonathan stepped outside. "You're letting all the cold in!" he scolded. "You know we're using the heat for her!" He pointed to Lavender, then waved. "Hi, Lavender!"

"Hi," she replied with a wave of her own.

Jonathan urged them inside, "Come on!"

"His southern really came out," Hana giggled.

The redhead rolled her eyes. Eden looked back at Lavender. She gave her a final once over. "Let's go." Eden walked inside, Hana following.

Silas sighed and guided Lavender up the steps. *Ready?*

Already came this far, Lavender smiled. The house interior was just as grand as the outside. "Wow." Lavender had seen mansions in movies and pictures, but to be in one was completely different. There was a chandelier. A big staircase leading to the east and west wings. It was warm and cozy, which Lavender was thankful for. It was an act of consideration for her well being. *I see where you get your sweetness from*, she teased Silas. The boy pinched her side and made her squeak.

Lavender turned her head upward. The wonder that filled her couldn't be understated. There were gorgeous works of art on the ceiling. "Did you do that?" she asked Silas, never taking her eyes off the intricate pieces. They bled into one another but any section could also be sold on its own. Suck it Michaelangelo, there's a new ceiling guy in town!

Silas laughed next to her. "Yea," he finally answered, "Me, mom, and Eden are the painters. It really helped…after I woke up." He learned how to use some of his powers while making the mural.

That made Lavender finally look at him. "You did an amazing job." She squeezed his hand. "I kind of want to lay on the floor and stare at it." Her gold eyes went back to the ceiling.

Silas smiled, a blush spreading across his face. "If you really mean it, I'll do it with you."

Lavender felt breathless. The lights in his house were so soft. They made his skin seem golden.

"You look really pretty, by the way. I can't remember if I told you." Silas kissed her hand. He heard her heartbeat pick up.

"Kiss the girl~" Hana encouraged. She was peeking around a corner.

Silas screeched, "Stop!"

Hana giggled and ducked behind the corner.

Lavender snickered, "You really are the baby." She didn't understand sibling relationships. Her only frame of reference was from television. For once, the television seemed on the money with how Silas was ragged on.

Silas groaned, "They're insufferable." He pouted and gently kicked the air.

"I'm sorry," Hana came over and hugged him. "My poor baby vampy!"

"Mom!" Silas called.

"Don't tattle!" Hana ruffled his hair.

"Hana."

Lavender looked away from the siblings and up to the staircase.

Damn.

She had thought Eden was something, but this woman was flawless. Her being radiated beauty inside and out. There was a warmth about her. An overwhelming love. The type of motherly aura you think you'll only see in movies. Lavender immediately felt calm. A wave of contentment washed over her. She felt relaxed. Safe.

The woman's hair was a chestnut brown, wavy but not wild. Her skin was a bit darker than Silas's. Her eyes were a deep green. They shimmered like emeralds underneath the chandelier light. Lavender forgot how to breathe. She blinked and the woman was directly in front of her.

"Hello, love."

Lavender turned to Silas, "Why is everyone in your family pretty?"

The boy shrugged, "Vampirism?"

The woman chuckled. She gently took Lavender's face in her hands.

The girl let herself be turned this way and that. It was obvious the woman was looking for something in her. Lavender wasn't going to protest. She noticed how unnaturally smooth the woman was. How all of them were, now that she thought about it. They didn't have pores. Even marble statues had pits and fissures. Not them though, not a mark on them. All those tiny human things seemed to have been wiped clean. It was like they were airbrushed.

"You have a mothering soul."

Lavender blinked out of her daze. "Huh?"

"A mothering soul," the woman repeated. A smile was on her rose petal lips. "Ariyah," she moved back and offered out her hand.

Lavender shook it. "Lavender Amos." She was surprised when Ariyah flipped her hand over and began to examine it.

"Calluses," the woman observed. "A fighter, no, a protector." She traced the lines on the palm. "A long life line." Her green eyes kept scanning. "You're very loyal," she declared, "and loving." Ariyah beamed, "Welcome to the family, Lavender." She kissed the girl's hand.

Lavender raised an eyebrow to Silas, *She's a little presumptuous*. The boy shrugged, a nervous smile on his face.

Ariyah's eyes widened. "You can hear her?" she asked Silas. Her son nodded and Ariyah turned back to Lavender. Her smile was wide enough to see her fangs. "I'm so glad you've found someone of Other Blood to be yours," she said to Silas.

"Other blood?" Lavender watched as the woman began to sway. Her green eyes were swallowed by her pupils. Weird.

"The inhuman," Ariyah began to glide across the floor. "We are a new thread that has been woven into the tapestry of the universe." She spun around, "I wonder what we look like from above. A mere speck in the void or the piece that brings it all together. Are we the detail that solidifies the picture or art we merely the drop of unintended color."

Silas sighed, "Mom, are you high again?"

"Shhhh," Ariyah hushed, a finger to her lips. She went to her son. "I'm almost down, let me enjoy the ride while it lasts."

Silas rolled his eyes and Hana laughed. Lavender watched as Ariyah spun while staring at the ceiling.

"Look at the beauty we created, my sweet boy!" Ariyah kept up her dancing. "We made our own tapestry."

"Dear," Matthias came from around the corner and to his wife. He joined in on her spinning and led her into a waltz. "Did you steal my mushrooms?"

"What ever gave you that idea?" Ariyah giggled. She kissed her husband. "I am no thief. What is yours is also mine." She waved her wedding ring in his face. It'd been on her finger for over 600 years. "Do you remember our wedding?" she asked, placing a kiss on his cheek.

Matthias chuckled. "Oh yes, I remember, my dear."

Ariyah hugged him. "I'm sobering up." She turned to their guest. "I am sorry, Lavender. Are you hungry? We can fetch you food."

"I ate before I came," Lavender assured. She didn't expect a bunch of vampires to have food. "It's nice to see you again, Mr. Annora."

Matthias chuckled, "Nice to see you again too. Especially since these are better circumstances." He picked up his wife, bridal style. "Come," he invited, "We'll go to the sitting room." Ariyah giggled in his arms and buried her head into his shoulder.

Lavender snickered. She bumped her hip into Silas's. "That'll be us," she teased and followed his parents deeper into the house.

The living room was cozy, thanks to the fireplace. Lavender sat on the plush couch next to Silas. His arm was around her. She learned a lot about the family.

Jonathan got onto the force by arm wrestling her dad and winning. Hana was working at a coffee shop in town. Eden was working at the community college library. Apparently Silas had another brother that Hana asked the whereabouts of.

"Is Everett still asleep?" Hana sounded concerned.

Jonathan sighed, "You know this whole thing hasn't been easy on him." A little creak in the wood made him smile. He looked up, "There you are, darlin'."

Lavender looked to the entrance. The boy standing in the threshold was staring at her intensely. His blue eyes seemed dull. He had wavy, short blond hair. He had to be over 6 feet tall, but he looked so small. The sweater he wore was at least two sizes too big. He nervously waved at her. Lavender gave him a warm smile and waved back.

The boy looked away shyly. He made his way across the room. He sat next to Jonathan and tucked himself into his side. Jonathan wrapped his arm around him.

"Is this mine?" The black man asked, tugging on the large sweater Everett was wearing. The blond giggled and buried his face in Jonathan's chest. "Stop stealing my stuff!" he pinched the blond's side.

"Stop having your stuff in my stuff," Everett huffed, pinching the man back.

Hana giggled. Her legs were over Eden's lap, mostly because it annoyed her sister. "You need to get an out there style. He'll steal less." She winked and showed off her striped arm warmers.

Eden rolled her eyes. "I took one t-shirt." She'd never live down the theft.

"It was a vintage Queen tee and you got blood on it!" Hana hissed. "I wore it to Live aid!"

Eden smiled slyly, "So it's had worse on it than blood?"

Hana pouted and flopped back against the couch. "Not the point! You're the worst."

Eden gave her a sly smile. "If I'm so insufferable, then get off my lap."

Hana huffed, "No."

Lavender snickered. "Vampires are just cats." She jumped when all eyes turned to her. She'd meant to keep that comment a thought. Seems her mouth had other plans.

Matthias perked up. "I actually have a theory about that!"

All the other vampires groaned.

"Dad, please," Everett whined. "I just woke up, I can't take another existential crisis right now."

"Oh this will not cause that." Matthias looked at Lavender. "You know how some say humanity is attached to apes?"

Lavender nodded, "Yea, we're all chimps."

"Well, I have a theory that since vampires were originally meant to consume humanity, that we became combined with species that also can bring down man. Like snakes, lions, tigers-"

"And bears, oh my!" Eden teased, "Must you bring your dissections out of your workshop?" She pointed at Ariyah, "Her philosophy lectures are bad enough. Adding your biology to the mix is just cruel."

"There's nothing wrong with wanting to understand our place in the cosmos." Ariyah kissed her husband's cheek, "I enjoy your theories, darling."

"So do I," Lavender sat up straighter. "Do you think beings like you are tied to the balance of nature? Like how everything is both predator and prey? A shark can eat a seal, but a shark can also be beaten by a blackfish." The idea hit her like a lightning strike. "What if you were formed around when humanity began to separate themselves from nature and began asserting their dominance over animals?"

"Yes, exactly!" Matthias jumped up. "The mother and father of our kind came from Mesopotamia!" He turned to Ariyah, "We must keep this one!"

"She has a family," Silas reminded him.

Matthias put his hands on his hips. "Then I guess you'll have to bring her in through marriage."

Eden balked, "They're children."

"Your mother and I married when we were their age."

"In the fucking 13th century!"

"14th," Ariyah corrected.

"Why do they label centuries like that?" Hana asked in disgust. "It's like they want to piss people off."

"Honestly, that probably is why," Jonathan answered.

The clock chimed.

Lavender jumped. She never knew grandfather clocks were so loud. It made sense for a huge place like this. You could probably hear the deep chime from space. Silas stiffened beside her.

"How time flies," Ariyah stood. She asked, "Will you be staying for the hunt dear, or would you like Silas to take you home?"

"The hunt?"

"We get a few bucks. It's more exercise than anything." Jonathan stood and stretched. Everett was still glued to his side. He wrapped his arm around the blond man. "You could take one home with you. Hell, it would probably save you some time since we'd drain it."

It wasn't a bad idea. Plus, Lavender knew her dad was bummed out he missed hunting season. They normally had a nice stock of jerky in case the weather turned on them. It would be a nice surprise to bring home. "Sure," Lavender answered. She offered, "I don't know how much help I'll be without a weapon though."

"What can you use?" Matthias asked.

"Gun or bow." Lavender shrugged, "Faster with a gun of course."

"I got ya!" Jonathan ran from the room.

Silas took Lavender's hand. He hoped she wasn't just agreeing to appease his family, *You sure?*

Lavender smiled. *Absolutely*

Chapter 14

The night air was so crisp it hurt to breathe. Lavender got a buck in her sights. She sucked in a breath and fired the rifle. It went down. She turned to Silas, "Soup's on, baby vamp." Lavender raced over to the twitching animal.

Silas rolled his eyes, "Thanks." He was beside the buck in seconds.

"Cheater!" Lavender huffed. She jogged over. Her lungs burned and her breath puffed out and crystallized into the air.

Silas giggled. He checked to make sure the beast's heart was still beating. "Thank you," he whispered to it before baring his fangs.

Lavender flinched when Silas bit into its neck. She thought she'd be more grossed out. Surprisingly though, she was only curious. The logistics of drinking was new and she needed to know how it worked. "Do your fangs have straws?"

Silas snorted, blood coming out of his nose. He pulled off the deer and hacked out a cough. "What?!"

"I'm sorry, I'm sorry!" Lavender went to his side and patted his back.

Silas cackled and then gagged. Choking while laughing wasn't something he thought he could feel anymore. "Why have you done this to me?" He put his hands in the snow and coughed up fluid. Red tears were streaming down his face.

"I'm sorry." Lavender hugged his side and tried to keep her own giggles at bay. After he stopped hacking, Lavender declared, "So, new rule, no talking while you eat."

Silas laughed harder. He wiped his face with his sleeve. "Good rule." The buck's heartbeat stopped. "Damn," Silas turned to the animal. "Sorry, big guy."

"What's wrong with it?"

"Once the heart stops, you stop." Silas parroted his father. A rule he burned into every member of the family.

Lavender frowned, "What happens if you don't?"

"Depends." Silas went over and grabbed the buck. He threw it over his shoulder. At Least it wouldn't go to waste. "Dead animal blood will make you really sick, like food poisoning. Everett did that once. He was apparently down for 4 days." Silas grimaced. "Dead human blood will kill you."

"Seriously?" Lavender shuddered. "No wonder you guys prefer animals."

"There's some surprising health benefits." Silas adjusted the deer on his shoulder.

"I'll get you another one," Lavender offered. "Oh! Maybe we can find a mountain lion."

Silas frowned, "I've had a lot of that recently."

"Oh yea, I forgot."

Silas smiled. "I'd still take it. I forgot to eat yesterday, so I'm really hungry."

Lavender frowned. "You shouldn't put off eating, Silas. It's important."

The boy shrugged. "We don't have to eat everyday. With how much energy we're using though has definitely changed that." Silas could hear his family in the distance. He thought there was another set of feet going through the snow. Silas shook his head. He was probably just mistaken because of his hunger. "We have stock at home, but heating it up in the microwave can be a mess."

Lavender giggled. She never expected vampires to warm up blood the same way she warmed up day old coffee. "Have you ever tried doing it like a bottle? Hot water."

Silas mused, "Now that you mention it." He loved the little giggle he got in turn. "So, how do you like them? My family."

"They're super sweet," Lavender answered. "I honestly want to talk to Matthias more. His theories are cool." There were twigs snapping around them. She could hear some of Silas's family laughing in the dark. They were incredibly lively despite being technically dead.

Lavender looked up at the trees. They were bare and the moonlight was shining down brightly. The snow on the ground glittered. It crunched beneath her boots. "You guys are welcomed to Ethan's shift." Lavender looked to Silas. "I know I'd like you there," she added. His eyes widened in surprise. They were shining red. She wondered if it was from hunger. Given the cougar's eyes, it seemed to be. Regardless, Silas was beautiful. His long dark hair was flowing in the icy wind. The buck he was lugging over his shoulder was huge. He made it look effortless. Strong and gentle. Fierce and calm. Lavender wished she was a poet. She wished she could express how etherial he was to her. Too bad her mouth was her worst enemy, "I can't believe you're carrying that thing."

Silas snorted, "Well, how else would you get it home?"

Lavender giggled and bumped her hip into his. "I meant you're strong."

"Oh!" Silas adjusted the stag. He heard someone following them. The wind was going against his face so he couldn't make out who it was. Probably Eden.

Lavender noticed he wasn't blushing. Despite him wearing the smile he did when he blushed. "So, is blood like your water? Is that why you cry blood?" More twigs snapped around them. Lavender grimaced. She hoped one of Silas's siblings wasn't planning to jump out and scare them. They may get a bullet to the face.

"I guess." He teased, "I'd be even stronger if I fed fully."

Lavender winced, "Sorry."

Silas bit his lip, "No, no, that…that wasn't a jab I just meant when I'm fully fed I'm crazy strong." He laughed nervously, "Like Superman." He flexed his free arm.

Lavender giggled. "You're a dork enough to be Clark Kent."

The pair entered a clearing. It was a perfect circle. The kind of natural clearing that seemed so otherworldly. It was no wonder people saw them as sacred. Another twig snap. Silas felt his fangs lengthen unconsciously. The wind changed direction and he stopped dead. That wasn't his family. *Lavender*, he warned.

Said girl stopped too. *How far?* she asked. Lavender slipped the gun off her shoulder. She brought it to an optimal position to turn and shoot with.

Few yards

A twig snapped right behind them. Lavender whipped around, rifle raised. The edge of the clearing was covered in shadows. Dark and foreboding. All she could make out clearly was a set of eyes. Reflecting like a beast's does in the low light.

"Well if it ain't the lone wolf." The thick southern accent was carried on the wind.

Lavender shuddered. "Holy crap," she whispered in horror. A sickening scent of death and decay hit her. Bile rose in the back of her throat, but she forced it down. She could make out his form in the patch of dark he was lurking in. "What's wrong?" she taunted, "Your face still recovering?"

The man stepped out of the shadows. The moonlight made his already pale skin seem snowlike. His movements were janky. A visible limp. His face was still blighted. It was like someone had reopened the wound Lavender had given him and added a few licks of their own. Lavender glanced at Silas. He hadn't been lying about hunting the guy.

Combstock sneered. "No more running around, little one. They aren't expecting me back for a year or two, but I want to have some fun with you." He looked at Silas. "And you, filthy little mongrel. You know you can't beat me while you're like that. Just give me the girl."

Silas dropped the buck and got in front of Lavender. He hissed, baring his own fangs. The man jumped at the sight before laughing.

"You," Combstock snickered, "you blood tainting bastard. Our gift wasn't meant for you!" He stalked forward. "You and that filthy family shouldn't be a part of our kind."

"Funny how you still think that after I ripped your fucking arm off!" Silas roared.

Lavender was shocked, nearly faltering in her stance. She righted herself quickly and kept her sights on the killer. Her finger went to the trigger.

"You got lucky, boy. Have you liked my presents?" He took a step closer. "I thought if your kind could have the gift, why not the other beasts?"

Silas grit his teeth. "Fuck you!"

The man laughed, "Oh you may have won the battle, but not the war. Didn't your daddy ever teach you to finish the job?"

"No, but mine did," Lavender said, pulling the trigger.

The man roared as a bullet lodged in his shoulder. "You little-!"

Silas surged forward. His fist connected with the man's chest. The blow was strong enough to throw the other vampire through the air, smashing him into a tree trunk.

Lavender gasped in shock. Silas had moved faster than lightning. Unfortunately, the hit didn't bring the other vampire down.

The killer crashed into Silas. He sent the boy across the clearing. Smashing him into the frozen snow. "Shouldn't fight on an empty stomach," Combstock taunted. The man was over the boy in a flash. "Especially if all you eat is other animals." He smashed his fist into Silas's face.

Lavender screamed, "Silas!" She raised the rifle and fired again. Once more the man screamed. It hit him in the arm. Lavender shuddered when his icy eyes glared at her.

"You little bitch!" he hissed. The man was in front of her in between blinks. He grabbed the barrel of her gun. "Enough!"

Lavender fired again, getting him in the face.

He roared and ripped the rifle from her hands. With the butt of the gun, he struck her across the face.

The hit knocked her down and blood filled her mouth. Lavender gasped. Her vision swam and the edges were going black. She pressed her face into the ice beneath her. No passing out now. With the shock of cold came adrenaline. She tried to use that to crawl away. Lavender grit her teeth when claws scratched her scalp. The man used her hair to flip her around.

"I missed the smell of dog blood," Combstock laughed. "Anna was always so sweet." He pulled her closer. "I'll only drink a bi-"

Lavender spat in his eyes. He let her go and she tried to scramble to her feet. The man's icy fingers grabbed her ankle. "No you don't," he growled. Lavender screamed as she was dragged back down and through the snow. The man's sharp claws were digging into her flesh. Her hot tears felt like a brand. Lavender turned and kicked his face with her free foot. It only got her other ankle caught in his grasp. Lavender kept trying to kick.

Combstock chuckled. "You sure you're Anna's? She was never this feisty. I like it."

Fear shot up her spine as he leered over her.

Silas tackled him. He violently ripped at the man's body with his claws. He managed to tear off a chunk of the bastard's face. The scream he got in turn felt like Chrismukkah morning. Silas's own body was worn but rage could cause quite a spike in strength. Silas snapped his teeth at the man. He hoped to use his venom. Silas had never used it before but now seemed like the perfect time. Combstock managed to kick him off. Silas took a chunk of his flesh with him. The boy scrambled to get in between Combstock and Lavender. They both stopped and waited for the other's move. Silas could hear his family. His maker was close. He screamed, "Help! HELP US!"

"You calling for your daddy, boy?" the man taunted. He could take the pansy doctor. Jonathan, that ungrateful slave, he could manage. Combstock had gorged himself on human blood. He struck now because he knew they were hungry. They'd neglected their thirst while searching for him. Combstock smiled. "Call your daddy and brother boy, you'll need more than them to take me down."

The forest began to fall around them. Trees were cracking and falling. The snow was being plowed through. The catastrophic noises were growing closer. Eden ripped through the forest like a hurricane. She was on all fours, sliding through the snow to guard Silas. Her curls were wild and her eyes were near black in the moonlight. Fangs and claws bared, she glared at the man. This pathetic, broken man. "You dare lay a hand on MY BLOOD?!"

For the first time, the man looked afraid. He then squinted at her. "Wait a minute. You?" He laughed haughtily. "Well don't you fill out nice." His lecherous eyes looked her up and down, "Shame you're wasting such beauty." A smile split his face, cruel and dripping with venom. He pointed to her chest. "Where are your little triangles?"

Eden snarled. "I was able to rip out your eye as a mortal. Imagine what I could do now?" She smiled when the man shrank back.

Ariyah crashed through the forest behind the killer. Jonathan came from the side. Matthias slid into the clearing. He came up behind Lavender. The scent of her blood made the hairs on the back of his neck raise. He wrapped his coat around her. She jumped, golden eyes wide with fear. "I've got you," he promised.

Everett and Hana followed behind Matthias . The Vietnamese girl came to her younger brother's side. She tried to get Silas to move back and let the others take care of the killer. She looked to Everett for help but her older brother seemed to be in shock. He was staring at the killer as if he was a nightmare made real.

"Adam?" The killer's grisled voice had softened. It was hope filled. "Oh, Adam." Combstock stood. "I've been wanting to see you."

Everett shook his head in terror. Fresh, red tears rolled down his face. Memories flooded in. Horrid, awful memories he'd buried under decades of love and care. They were back now. With it came fear. Fear he hadn't felt in over a hundred years. "No, no, no," he whispered.

Everyone was silent. The forest was silent. Everett was silent. Hana stared at her brother. He so rarely spoke of his past before Jonathan. She now knew why. "Everett," she said to try and pull him out of his spiral.

"It's a reunion!" Combstock cackled. He opened his arms toward Everett. "My sweet, Adam," the killer slowly stood. "Come here, my boy. Come to daddy."

A deer in headlights looked less frozen then Everett. Combstock took a step forward. The sound of the snow under his torn boot made something in the blond snap. Everett shook his head and bolted into the woods.

Combstock sped past his last prey and went after his boy. "Adam!" he roared.

Lavender watched as Ariyah, Jonathan, and Eden gave chase. Everyone was screaming. Silas tried to go but Hana held him fast. "No!" she scolded, "Why the fuck were you fighting while hungry?!" The sounds of destruction began again. Cacophony was a nice way of putting it. The chaos was hellish.

"Be gentle, Hana," Matthias looked at Lavender. "Can I carry you, dear?" The girl nodded and he scooped her up into his arms.

Silas hissed, "I can carry her!" He tried to stand but immediately fell to his knees. Hana caught him before he went down fully.

"Silas, chill," Hana picked her brother up. She threw him over her shoulder. Hana ran beside her dad back to the house.

Chapter 15

Lavender drank the concoction Matthias made for her. It was a chamomile tea with a metallic undertone. Obviously there was blood in it. Lavender didn't care though. It fixed the punctures in her legs and the bruises on her face. She sniffled and wiped at her stinging eyes. Hana wrapped a blanket around her. Lavender snuggled into it.

"He'll be okay," the scene girl assured. "Not the first time dad's had to patch him up." Hana stretched. "All he needs is some blood and he'll be right as rain."

Matthias had taken Silas to his office. The boy was definitely worse off. Lavender hadn't realized the extent of the damage till they'd gotten inside. She shuddered. Silas's face had literally been rearranged, swollen and bloody.

"It's just because he's hungry," Hana rubbed the girl's shoulder. "I promise you, Silas could have taken him single handedly if he'd fed."

Lavender broke. Tears overflowing her eyes. "It's my fault," she wept. "I shouldn't have made Silas laugh. I should have killed that bastard the first time. If I had just-"

"Okay, absolutely not!" Hana took the girl's face in her hands. "Did you know that creepazoid was following you?"

Lavender shook her head with a pathetic sniffle.

"Okay, so stop blaming yourself just because it's easier than admitting the universe is random and shit happens!" Hana huffed. "'What ifs', 'maybes', 'could have beens', are meaningless! You didn't know, so it's not your fault." Hana squeezed the girl's shoulder. "You're alive, he's alive. That's all that matters."

Lavender nodded, "You're right-"

"I know I am," Hana let the other girl go. She scratched her head, ruffling her chopped hair. It had already begun to grow back. At least this style lasted a few hours. She checked on her dyed piece of hair. It was blackening. Hana sighed.

Eden's coming, Ariyah warned her daughter.

Hana moved her and Lavender away from harm's way. Her head snapped in the direction of the door. "Brace yourself," she warned.

Lavender opened her mouth to ask for what, but the back doors flew off their hinges as Eden burst in. The starlet looked crazed.

"Where's my baby?!" Eden screamed. There was blood on her mouth and hands. She had cuts and bruises of her own. Gashes across her chest were bleeding.

Hana pointed down the hall. "Dad's-" The other woman was gone in a flash. She sighed, "You'd think he was fucking dead." Hana got up. Door bits had landed nearby, so she started cleaning.

Lavender watched as Hana went to pick up the blown off doors. "Is she always like that?" She got up and grabbed some of the more manageable pieces of wood.

"Protective as hell over Silas? Yes." Hana frowned. The hinges were irreparable. They'd need a new door, again. "In fairness, she made him." Hana tossed some of the broken door outside.

Lavender looked up in shock. "You mean…she's the one who turned Silas?" She assumed it was one of his parents. Lavender followed Hana's lead and tossed some wood outside. They were forming a strange pile next to the flower bed.

"Well, she found him, so." Hana ripped off the piece of door that somehow stayed on the frame. She saw her mother and brothers coming out of the woods. Without hesitation she raced over to them, dropping the wood. "Did you get him?!" she asked, hugging her mother.

Ariyah shook her head. She looked at her sons. Everett was gripping Jonathan like a vice. Her other boy was cradling Everett's shaking frame in his arms. Ariyah looked at the house. She saw Lavender with an armful of debris. "Oh, yay, we need another door." The woman rolled her eyes. As she got closer to the house, she declared, "It seems the universe does not favor our happiness." Ariyah took the broken pieces from Lavender and tossed the ruins of mahogany into the pile by the rose bushes.

Lavender sadly laughed, "Yea, seems not. Did you get him?" The 3 returning vampires all gave her a sorrowful reaction. "Really?" 3 vampires couldn't catch one mangled bastard?

"He went into the reservation." Jonathan kissed the top of Everett's head.

"So?" Lavender watched as all of them exchanged looks.

Ariyah explained. "They're willing to help us with hunting the beasts and him, but we still are heavily…discouraged from going onto their land."

Lavender was utterly confused. "What, why?"

Everyone exchanged looks again. Ariyah sighed, "Your grandmother is not taking the transfer of power well."

Jonathan added, "Also you never explicitly said we were allowed on so…"

Lavender was dumbfounded. "Great. Just fucking great!" She went back to sit on the couch. The rest followed her. The cold of the winter blew in from the open door. "I need to talk to her. I'll go there tomorrow. This whole situation is fucking rediculous."

"What i don't understand is why that bastard's here," Hana plopped down on the floor. "He normally runs when he sees us. What changed?"

"He's not here for us." Everett uncurled himself from Jonathan. "He's after something else." He looked at Lavender. "But you knew that, didn't you?"

Lavender grimaced. "He keeps mentioning my eyes."

"He's obsessed with them." Jonathan tapped beside his own. "Only thing that saved me."

Lavender looked up. "Saved you?"

Jonathan looked at Everett. His man was still tucked close. Everett hadn't reacted well to the news that Combstock was skulking around. The last thing Jonathan wanted to do was trigger him further.

The blond looked up at his mate and smiled. Jonathan was always so thoughtful. His sweet, kind man. Everett kissed his cheek. "It's your story, darlin'. Tell it, if you want."

Jonathan blushed. He shook off his bashfulness and focused on Lavender again. "Combstock has these strange ideas about souls and eyes." He frowned, "Said a coloured with pretty eyes was a rarity. One he couldn't just kill." Jonathan kissed the top of Everett's head. "Also helped that this one vouched for me." The blond giggled and tucked his head back into Jonathan's neck.

Lavender hoped her and Silas would last as long as them. Speaking of which. "When did you two meet?"

Jonathan thought for a moment. "Was 1859, I'm pretty sure." He looked at Everett, "Right?"

The blond shrugged, "I wasn't watching the time." Everett didn't mention he wasn't allowed to leave the isolated cabin. He especially didn't mention the circumstances under which they met. "Was 1848 when he took me."

Lavender was shocked, "You two have been together for a century?!"

Jonathan corrected, "141 years." He laughed when the girl's jaw dropped. "If you think that's wild," Jonathan pointed to Ariyah, "Her and Matthias have been together for 665 years."

Ariyah beamed, "And I've adored every minute with him."

Lavender felt her heart melt. She looked at Hana. "What about you and Eden?"

Hana snorted. "Eden and I aren't a thing. She's my sister, dude."

Lavender winced in embarrassment. "Oh, sorry."

Hana shrugged. "It's cool. I get it, they're a thing," she pointed to Jonathan and Everett. "I was adopted at 3 so all these fucks are my siblings. I haven't found a mate yet." She shook out her hair. It'd now grown past her shoulders. "Maybe never will."

Lavender was surprised by how nonchalant she seemed about it. "Won't that be lonely?"

Hana laughed, "Please! I got a whole family. Couldn't be lonely if I tried."

Lavender went over what the vampire had said again. "Wait, you were adopted at 3, how?"

Hana explained, "Matthias was over in Nam. My mom threw me at him as his chopper left." Hana shrugged, "One of them wanted to throw me back, but dad said no. He tried to get my mom but," Hana made a gun with her fingers.

"Jesus Christ," Lavender didn't really know how to respond to that revelation. "I'm so sorry."

Hana shrugged again. "I mean, mine's the least traumatic. If you can believe that."

"Trauma's still trauma," Lavender mumbled.

"I honestly don't remember it. My first memories are of mom singing to me," Hana smiled at Ariyah. She crawled over to her mother and rested her head against her leg. "Con yêu mẹ."

Ariyah kissed the top of her daughter's head. "Cũng yêu, Hana."

Lavender felt her heart clench. It was a horrid bitterness at the display of mother and daughter affection. They made it look so easy. Lavender didn't need to know Vietnamese to understand them. Lavender bit her lip to keep it from quivering. She asked Jonathan, "So, you guys know this Combstock well?"

Jonathan nodded, "Yea, old Colonel Combstock."

Lavender frowned. "He was a Colonel?"

Everett nodded. "Yeah. Fought in the French and Indian war." He tried to remember the bits and pieces Combstock told him all those years ago. "He went to Europe after 1812. Came back with a girl. She managed to get away from him in 1833. After that he had a deep hatred for Natives. He said they stole his Anna and his Adam."

Lavender furrowed her brow. "Anna?"

Everett nodded. He stared at the girl. "He used to sing about her golden eyes."

Lavender shuddered. "Wait, who was Adam?"

Everett looked to the ground. "Combstock said she was pregnant, but lost it because of the Natives. I don't believe that though. If I was her, I would have done everything in my power to miscarry." Jonathan rubbed his back. Everett smiled up at him. He was a lucky man.

Lavender fell back against the couch. "He said he wanted to take me to Europe."

Ariyah sat up straighter. There was a look of recognition on her face. She stood and went deeper into the house.

Lavender watched her go. Jonathan and Everett were still snuggling. Hana was staring at her from the floor. All the information she learned tonight was making her head spin. "You guys are so human, but not. It's wild."

Hana chuckled. "In fairness, we're the exception, not the rule."

"What do you mean?" Lavender asked.

"We have to work for our humanity," Jonathan explained.

Everett nodded. "Vampire's are apex predators. Solitary hunters. We're meant to kill what we used to be. We have to keep interacting with humans and society."

Hana chuckled, "Gotta use it or we'll lose it."

"Wait, so, vampire families aren't a normal thing?" Lavender looked between the trio.

"Nope," the 3 answered.

"Some vampires have even become beasts." Everett shuddered, remembering Matthias's stories and sketches. "Others have retained their minds but have lost their souls."

Lavender frowned, "Welp, that's fucking ominous." Jonathan and Hana laughed. Everett just shrugged. Lavender thought this was enough for one night. She's had enough existential crises for one life, thank you very much. "Can I see Silas?"

Hana nodded, "Sure, come on." She got up and left her brothers on the other couch.

The halls of the house were dark. Lavender wondered if they had a form of night vision. Given Combstock's eyes, it was more than likely. She noticed the shape of photo frames hanging on the wall. Later she'd ask to see them. How many places have they been? How many homes have they had? Lavender coughed. A strong smell hit her like a buckshot. "What is that?" she asked incredulously.

Hana rolled her eyes, "Dad's probably concocting something." She smiled, "He gets in these moods. If he's doing that though, it means Silas is fully healed."

Lavender took some comfort in that. There was crying. Loud spine chilling wails. There were frantic voices too. She sped past Hana and to the door where the noises were coming from. She threw it open and the site nearly made her fall over in disbelief.

Eden was weeping and placing kiss after kiss on Silas's healed face. "My baby, my baby!" she wailed.

"I'm okay, E," Silas whined as he was being smothered.

Matthias was rubbing Eden's back, trying to console her. Ariyah was bubbling something in the Frankenstein-esque lab equipment that sat on a giant table. The room was strange, a few chairs and a steel bed. There was a big contraption in the corner. It was obviously medical in nature.

Silas was half rolled off the bed. As if he was making another, of what seemed to be many, failed escape attempts.

"Eden, please!" Ariyah sounded exasperated. "Let the boy get up!" She filled a beaker with whatever brew she had been making. "Drink!" she ordered, placing the glass container in Eden's trembling hands. Her daughter didn't sass and instead gulped down the mixture.

Silas was finally able to break free. "Thanks, mom," he whispered to the older woman.

"You're welcome, dear." Ariyah gave him a kiss on the forehead.

Eden finished the drink while Matthias continued to rub her back.

Silas looked to the door and saw Lavender. She looked dumbfounded. "Hey." He was very embarrassed but Lavender seemed amused.

The girl bit her lip, trying to hold in the laugh she felt bubbling up. While Silas wouldn't have minded, a part of her knew Eden would. With a deep breath, she quelled her giggles. "I wanted to check on you."

"I'm," Silas looked back at a still sniffling Eden, "I'm fine."

Lavender gave him a sympathetic smile. "I think I should be heading home," she admitted. With a serious expression she turned to Ariyah. "I'm going to the reservation tomorrow. I'm going to talk to my Nana." Lavender looked at Matthias. "I'm going to make sure you guys can get on the rez, if you need to."

"Your optimism is cute," Eden wiped her eyes.

"I mean, she did get them to work with us," Hana defended, "First time we tried to talk to them they-"

"They didn't talk to us!" Eden ranted, "Just automatically judged and-"

Matthias interrupted, "Considering how their only reference of vampires is Combstock, I'm not surprised." He smiled at Lavender, "We would appreciate your help."

The girl smiled. "Ethan invited you guys to his shift, I know it'd make us all feel safer if there was some more muscle."

Eden snorted, "Trust me, the bastard will be licking his wounds for a while."

Matthias beamed at the invitation. "I would love to go!" He looked to his wife, "Let's go, motek!"

Ariyah nodded in agreement. "We would be honored."

"Cool beans," Lavender turned to Silas. "You feel okay enough to drive me home?" she asked with a forced smile.

Thankfully Silas did feel okay. Right as rain in fact. "Of course," he turned to his maker and father, "I'll be back soon." He took Lavender's hand and left before the others could stop him.

"It was nice meeting you!" Lavender called back as she was guided out of the house. The night air once again hit her. She breathed it in. The world was quiet. Blissfully quiet. When they reached the car, Silas opened the door for her. Lavender got in. Even after everything, he was still Silas. Still a gentle giant. Just a gentle giant that would also rip off a limb if necessary.

Silas got into the driver's seat and they started off. Doubt and fear were strange things. They made you think and do strange things. Silas was drowning in his failure. He looked at Lavender. She seemed so blissfully unaware of the turmoil he was in. Everything felt like his fault. After a while Silas gripped the steering wheel tightly and took his shot. "Do you think we should break up?"

Lavender's eyes widened in shock. "What?" She looked at her boyfriend. Silas looked like he was going to vomit. Lavender could practically feel his anxiety. His hands were shaking. Doing this while driving wouldn't be smart. "Pull over. Now." There was no way she was going to let him do this to himself.

Silas was powerless to the command. Luckily there was some room for him to pull off. He put the car in park and made sure the doors were locked. The dread he felt was all consuming. It felt like a pit was going to open below him and swallow him whole.

Lavender rubbed her face. She took off her seatbelt and turned to him. "Do you want to break up with me?"

Silas felt his lip quiver. "N-no." He let his head fall back against the headrest.

"So why did you ask that?"

"It feels like Combstock is trying to kill you because of me-"

"No, he's here for me, Silas. You didn't drag me into this, I dragged you." Lavender pressed her back against the door. "I understand if you don't want to be with me anymore but-"

"I don't want to break up!" Silas cried. "I just don't know how to protect you or how to fix this or what to do." He was hyperventilating. He didn't need to breathe, but felt like he was suffocating. "I couldn't protect you."

"You hadn't eaten, Silas." Lavender reached over and took his hand. "I couldn't protect you either." She kissed his hand. "I don't blame you. Do you blame me?"

Silas shook his head.

"Okay," Lavender was relieved. She went over their conversation, "So neither of us want to break up. We want to protect each other. We love each other, right?"

Silas nodded, enthusiastically.

Lavender smiled, "Alright, that's settled then." She leaned over the middle console for a kiss. Silas met her half way. It was gentle. It was sweet. It was what they needed. Lavender pulled back and rested her forehead against his. "I love you."

Silas smiled and stole another kiss. "I love you too."

Chapter 16

It was 10pm when Silas pulled into Lavender's driveway. Dean was on the porch, a beer in hand. He glared at the car and Lavender winced. "Shit." She turned to her boyfriend, "Don't mention the colonel encounter."

Silas was frozen by the look of rage on her father's face. Dean could crack a safe with that glare. "I'll try," he squeaked out. Lavender got out of the car. Silas looked at Dean. The man gestured for him to get out and come over. Silas grit his teeth and parked the car. Aw, shit.

Lavender was surprised to see him out. She looked at her dad's furious face. "Be nice," she mouthed at him.

Dean raised his eyebrow. "It's past your bedtime, flower." He tilted his head to the door. "Go inside." The man stood up. "I need to talk to your boyfriend."

Lavender rolled her eyes. *You want me to tell him to fuck off?*

Silas looked at her then Dean. *No*, he braced himself, *I can take it.* "Goodnight," he said aloud. *I love you*

Lavender smiled, "Night." *I love you too*

Dean waited for the door to close. He moved to the step and sat down, patting the space beside him.

Silas tried to keep his nerves calm. He sat beside the man. The silence was awkward. He watched as Dean took a few more sips of his beer. The man offered the can to him.

"Want some?"

Silas shook his head, "No-no thank you…sir?"

Dean chuckled. "Calm down, kid." The phone call he'd gotten thirty minutes ago was fresh in his mind. He sighed, "Jerry told me Combstock came to the rez. All mangled. He attacked someone. Thankfully the victim was able to fend him off, since the guy was missing an arm. The pack got there and chased him toward the mountains." Dean looked at the nervous boy. Brown eyes sparkled with knowing, "Wanna explain that?"

Silas took a deep breath and tried to keep the truth from spilling out of him. "I think we saw him in passing."

Dean pursed his lips in disbelief. "C'mon, dude."

Silas sighed and put his head in his hands. "You know about my family."

"Obviously," Dean huffed. He then remembered the night before, "Also, did falling out the window hurt?"

Silas shook his head, "Nah, pain is…" He didn't know how to articulate it. "I mean, I can feel it but stuff like that doesn't do much, especially at night."

Dean asked, "You guys stronger at night?"

Silas nodded, "Sunlight makes us weak, nearly human. It also makes our brains," Silas waved his hand by his head. "It's like when you have to push through fear to go into the woods alone at night." He chuckled, "Dad said it's against our nature. That's why the old ones don't like

102

us. We fight our nature." In his hunt for answers, Matthias had met some vampires. Over a millenia old kind of old. Ariyah said when he came home from the encounter, he didn't speak for a week. The shock of it all had stolen his voice. He'd only mentioned them 3 times in Silas's memory. When Matthias spoke about them, Silas could practically taste his father's fear. Whatever the old ones looked and acted like scared his father. Silas never wanted to meet what scared his dad.

Dean decided to ignore the 'old ones' comment. That would be a problem for future him. Present him wanted to lighten the mood. "Huh, so Dracula had it all wrong?" Dean teased, bumping his shoulder into the boy's.

"Oh yea," Silas laughed. "We actually use the stairs."

Dean smiled and visibly relaxed. He asked the boy, "When did you fall in love with Lavender?"

Silas paused. That wasn't a question he was expecting. He thought for a moment before answering. "Everyone at school was scared of me. I did it on purpose, kind of. I didn't want to make friends." Thankfully Dean didn't make him explain why. "She came up to me and offered me her food. She thought I didn't have any. That I maybe couldn't have afforded it or that my adoptive parents were abusing me," Silas laughed sadly. "The first time I spoke again was to her. It felt so easy to talk to her. It still is. She's nice, and funny, and…" Silas picked at the rip in his jeans. "She makes me feel safe." He looked at Dean, expecting maybe disapproval or disgust but only saw a smile.

"You really love her, don't you?" Dean asked, though he already knew the answer. Just from the way the boy talked about his flower, he knew. Dean looked up at the stars. The air was crisp and refreshing. The forest around them was so peaceful.

"Yes, I do." Silas was sure Dean had called him over here to scare him. He was pleasantly surprised by the nice conversation they'd been having so far. Silas felt fortunate that Lavender's father wasn't one of those old school tough guys. That Dean hadn't pulled out a shotgun, like dads in the movies did.

"Well bud, you two seem good for each other, but I need to tell you something." Dean took another sip of his beer.

Silas frowned. Guess he was going to get the old dad threat after all. "Yes?"

"If you ever break my daughter's heart," Dean reached out and touched Silas's shoulder, "I'm gonna fuck your mom and dad."

Silas was dumbfounded, "Huh?"

Dean clarified, "Listen, you're a vampire and I'm not the type to make promises I can't keep. So if things go south, and it's your fault, I won't shoot ya. I'll fuck your parents."

"W-why?" Silas stammered out in horror.

Dean smiled, "Because, you'll heal from a bullet wound, but you'll never heal from that." He gave Silas a friendly slap on the shoulder. "Night, champ. Get home safe." With that, the man walked into the house.

Silas sat on the front porch. He was still reeling from the shock. The worst thing though, was that Silas knew Mr. Amos could do it. He had enough charisma to enact such revenge. Silas let out a shaky breath.

It's a good thing he planned on spending the rest of his life with Lavender.

Said girl had sat herself by a window upstairs so she could hear what her father and boyfriend were talking about. With a blush and a smile, she closed the window. Silas drove into the night.

Lavender snuck back to her room, thankful that her father slept on the first floor. She took off her battered clothes and put on her pajamas. Tomorrow she'd see her grandmother. For now though, she'd replay the words Silas said over and over again. It was a calming lullaby that soothed her to sleep.

The reservation was quiet. Lavender parked her truck in front of the little house. It was just like she remembered. The same white house. The same porch. Lavender looked into her rearview mirror and psyched herself up. She hadn't seen her grandmother in years. She'd avoided talking to Nana since she got here. Would the woman speak to her? Would Nana be mad Lavender didn't come sooner? The girl shook off her doubts. She could do this though. It was for everyone's safety.

When she stepped out a shock of anxiety ripped through her. "Stop it," she growled at herself. The worst thing that could happen was her grandmother telling her to fuck off. Lavender noticed the handmade windchimes on the porch. The sunlight made them sparkle beautiful shades of green and blue. Lavender got lost in them.

"You helped me make that one."

Lavender whipped around to see Nana in the doorway.

"You were so excited to help," the woman reminisced. She stepped onto the porch. Her hair was salt and peppery. It laid loose on her shoulders. Her eyes were a matching gold to Lavender's. The cardigan she wore was handmade. It was covered in intricate patterns.

Lavender smiled. She wished she had her mother and grandmother's ability to make clothes. Lavender had fond memories of being doted on by her Nana and mom as they tailored an outfit for her. From dresses, to shirts, to moccasins, they could make it all. "Hi, Nana," Lavender smiled, a tear rolling down her face.

The older woman came closer. The girl had her daughter's face. Nana felt her heart clench. "Lavender," she cupped the girl's face in her hands. "Oh, my little flower." Her lip quivered and her eyes began to fill with tears. "You're so big," she whispered. With a sniffle, she pulled back and wiped at her eyes. "Your mother said she'd never let you-"

"Mom and I aren't talking," Lavender interrupted. She looked down, examining the old wood of the porch. "She kind of…threw me out?" Lavender laughed. The memory of her

104

argument with her mother replayed in her head. She shook her head. "It doesn't matter, I'm not here for that." Lavender stared into Nana's eyes and saw her own. "I missed you, Nana."

Nana sighed in awe. "I missed you too."

Lavender asked, "Can we go in?" She gestured to the door with her head. She felt ecstatic and terrified.

"Of course, flower." Nana walked inside. Her granddaughter followed.

The inside of the house was as beautiful as Lavender remembered. Reflections of sea glass danced in the afternoon light. Skulls and shells hung from the walls. Lavender hoped her future home would have this much personality. She noticed the simple oak table under a bay window. The shore of the calm sea was beyond the glass.

"Do you remember picking sea glass for me?" Nana asked. She placed the old kettle on the stove. "You loved it out there." The older woman giggled, "You'd spend hours shifting through the sand." She gestured to the table, "Sit, flower."

Lavender plopped into the chair. "I feel like everything has changed, but not physically." She looked out at the ocean. "Everything looks the same, but nothing is how it was."

Nana got two cups out of the cabinet. She placed the handmade mugs on the counter. "Time makes fools of us all," she quoted. The kettle sang and she made two cups of tea. "How is your mother?"

Lavender sighed. "She runs a boutique. Just works, mostly."

Nana frowned. "But how is she feeling?" She came to the table and sat down with the hot drinks.

Lavender shrugged. "I can't say. She doesn't like talking about feelings." Her mother didn't like talking at all. The tea Nana made was really good.

Nana chuckled. "Well, that hasn't changed." She took a sip of her tea. A glitter caught her eye. She noticed the necklace around Lavender's neck. "Where did you get that?"

Lavender looked at the stone. "My boyfriend made it for me." She took the necklace off and handed it over for her Nana to examine. "He carved it himself," Lavender explained with pride. "He's an artist. He can paint, draw, and write poetry."

Nana giggled at the smitten look on the girl's face. She ran her thumb over the etchings. "Where is he from?"

Lavender mused. She decided to only reveal as much as she needed to. "I don't know what tribe, but he grew up in Oregon before being adopted."

Nana nodded. "I knew a boy whose family did this. They said if you loved someone enough, you'd be willing to carve out the earth for them."

Lavender felt her heart melt. "I wouldn't be surprised if he was from the same family. That sounds like a sappy thing he'd say."

Nana felt a small clench in her chest. The boy she knew wasn't from her tribe, but one near the Puget. She handed the necklace back to Lavender. "Well, I know this isn't purely a social call." Nana asked, "What can I do for you, Lavender?"

The teen smiled and took the gem back. Guess it was time to get down to business. "Mom didn't tell me anything about the pack, or about being a Den Mother, or any of that." She looked up and saw the shocked expression on Nana's face. "Can you tell me?"

Nana nodded. She stood and went to her bookshelf. "I can't believe she didn't tell you anything!" The book she got off the shelf was old and worn. The leather was heavily cracked. Some of the pages were too big for the book and stuck out. "Well, best to start from the beginning. Nana sat back down and opened the tome.

Lavender saw a large picture. "Wait, that's Combstock." She pointed at the man. There was a girl beside him. She looked young, no older than 20. Even in the sepia photo, the striking color of her eyes stuck out. Her face was forlorn. Like she had been dragged there against her will. Which she most likely was.

"Yes," Nana pointed to the man. "And this is Anna," she pointed to the girl. "Our first Den Mother." Nana turned the page. The pages were old and stained. Contracts and other odd ins. "He kidnapped her as a child. So young that she had no memories of her family. He brought her here in 1833. Came with the fur trade." Nana pulled out another picture. The girl had a baby bump. Combstock had his hands on her stomach. "Combstock went off for a time. Anna took the opportunity to come to the tribe. She hoped to expel the fetus. She explained what Combstock had done to her. They didn't have the heart to turn her away, so they helped her. She was still early in her pregnancy, so they were able to induce a misscarriage." Nana turned the page and it was a photo of Anna with the tribe.

Lavender's eyes softened. The girl, Anna, was smiling. She looked resplendent while dressed in the tribe's clothes. Anna had her arms wrapped around a man. The man was obviously in love with Anna. His eyes were on her, while everyone else's was to the camera. He wore a soft smile. It reminded Lavender of Silas's. "They're adorable."

Nana chuckled, "Yes. Her and one of the chief's sons. They were devoted and adored one another." Nana turned the page.

It was an illustration. Lavender leaned in closer. It showed a wolf. Twice as tall as the men around it. Its teeth were bared and ears pinned back. The men around it had weapons, but they weren't fighting the wolf. All of them stood in opposition to a single man.

"Eventually. Combstock came back." Nana explained, "They were able to drive him off during the day. He came back at night and began to slaughter the tribe. Anna shifted for the first time. They battled until the sun began to rise." Nana turned the page. It was an old newspaper headline: **MAD MAN GOES ON RAMPAGE**. "Before the sun fully rose, he ran. Killed a few people in town on the way out." Nana huffed, "They didn't care about the deaths in the tribe."

Lavender frowned. "'Course not." She watched as Nana turned the page again. This time the photos were of an older Anna and the man. They were surrounded by children. All of them with striking eyes.

"So began the first pack." Nana flipped through the photos. "A symbiotic relationship formed between them and the tribe." She pointed to a photo of a much older Anna next to a young woman. Both were surrounded by children. "From mother to daughter, the title is passed down. Female born werewolves will always have werewolf children. The male born are," Nana waved her hand, "finicky."

"So our gold eyes mean we're born werewolves?"

"Yes," Nana smiled. She loved teaching about their history. The opportunity came so rarely. She turned the page.

Lavender noticed the photos had less and less children. The final photo on the page was of a young Nana. Rosemary was strapped to her chest. "Why did you only have mom?" Lavender asked.

Nana frowned. "I wanted more," she confessed, "your grandfather died in Vietnam." Nana looked at the photo hanging above the couch.

Lavender looked at the picture. "I never knew that."

Nana swallowed, "It's a painful thing to talk about." She turned the page. "That's the history side." She pursed her lips, "Let's see, what else should you know? Ah, yes." Nana began to explain, "We born werewolves can bite as many as we want. Bitten can only bite once. Most keep it for their child. Once we enter menopause, we lose our call and our ability to bite." Nana sat back, she tried to think of other facts. "Oh, this may be important to you! If there are more than one born female wolf, they can lead together, or one can be appointed." Nana pointed to a picture of two women with their mother.

Lavender furrowed her brow. "Important to me?"

"When you have your children," Nana smiled. "I can't wait to see your little ones."

Lavender was dumbfounded by this. "What if I don't want to have kids?" she asked.

Nana rolled her eyes. "Please, don't be irrational. You'll make up for your mother's mistakes." She stood to put the book away. "We are the last of the born. We have a duty. One which your mother neglected. I had a true reason to stop at one. She did not." Nana shoved the book harder than she needed to. "You'll make up for her selfishness."

Lavender felt like a bucket of ice water was poured over her. Her mother always told her about pressure. The weight that crushed Rosemary from childhood. "Why did my mom run away?" Lavender asked.

Nana stopped. The question hit her like a freight train. She rested her forehead against the bookshelf. "She didn't like the responsibility of being a Den Mother. Of caring for the pack and helping to lead the tribe. She was childish. Jealous. Rebellious." She walked back over to Lavender. "She thought I loved the pack more than her."

Lavender frowned, "Did you tell her you loved her?" She already knew the answer, but she needed to hear her say it.

Nana huffed. "It seems unnecessary. I fed her. I kept a roof over her head. I-"

"That's not the same thing, Nana." Lavender felt nauseous. A bitter bile filled her mouth. "The bare minimum isn't the same as love."

Nana raised her chin. Years of guilt and regret tried to force her to the floor, but she refused. "I was a good mother," she asserted.

Lavender glared at the woman. "You don't get to decide that. She doesn't get to decide that." She felt tears prick her eyes. "You don't get to grade your own parenting. Your kids do."

Nana flared her nostrils and her frown deepened. "Well then, I guess I was an awful mother."

Lavender closed her eyes. She hated that phrase. It stung to know where her mother got it from. Lavender decided she wouldn't entertain it. She sat up straight. "I'm the new Den Mother," she declared. "My first order of business is that the Annora's can come on the land."

Nana slammed her cup down in rage. "Those leeches shouldn't be here in the first place!" She cursed her peoples' bleeding hearts. They'd seen the comatose boy and couldn't justify chasing the cold ones out. Nana had been outvoted, defied for the first time in decades. "They brought that maniac here!"

"He's here for me, Nana!" Lavender roared back. "Combstock came for someone with golden eyes. He's after us!" She pointed between herself and Nana. "And for your information, those so-called leeches have not only been protecting me, but the town, and the tribe! Matthias is an incredible doctor. Jonathan has been working with dad and has actively been helping hunt down the animals and Combstock. Silas is an amazing boy. He's kind and he's gentle, and he ripped the bastard's arm off for me. He's been an amazing friend and boyfriend and-"

"You're dating one of them?!" Nana stood. "I can not believe this!"

"Nana, they aren't like Combstock! Yes, apparently most vampires are all fucked morally, but they aren't. They're a family. They love. They laugh. They don't even drink from people, Nana. Only animals, no different from us. They're good people."

"They're walking corpses!"

"And we're giant dogs!" Lavender slammed her fists into the table. Her face was hot. "Some of them have been victims of Combstock. Hurt by him, just like Anna. They want to help and I'm letting them!"

Nana was shocked. She deflated and collapsed into her chair. Her face turned to stone. "Fine."

Lavender was panting. Her heart was pounding in her ears. She'd expected more of a fight. Lavender let her shoulders fall. "Fine?"

Nana spat, "You're the Den Mother." She snatched up their cups and went to the kitchen. "Do what you want."

Lavender's lip quivered. That cold rejection she'd felt so many times. It stung. It burned. Lavender couldn't help but laugh, which got her grandmother's attention. "You really are my mother's mother." She stormed out of the house. Nana was calling after her but she didn't stop to listen. She peeled out of the reservation and tried to wipe her eyes dry.

Chapter 17

Dean sat next to Jerry on the log. The roaring fire was relaxing him. Ethan was in the house. Dean had never been to a shift before. There were whispers of them. Vague things he'd heard over the years. It was secretive for a reason though. Who knows how the outside world would react to werewolves. Lee and Lavender were in the house with the terrified boy. Ethan had burst into tears at the sight of Lavender. "Will he be okay?" Dean asked the other man.

"Ender is a mother. He'll be fine," Jerry said, but was shaking. Dean's warm hand rested on his shoulder. It helped. It really did. Jerry could see the shadow of Lavender in the window. She was soothing Ethan. "Besides, she's a true mother. Took to it better than Rose," Jerry said bitterly.

Dean flinched.

"Sorry." Jerry put his face in his hands. "I'm just-"

"Hey, it's okay." Dean scooted closer and hugged his friend. Jerry leaned against him.

"Thanks," Jerry sat back and relaxed.

Dean smiled. "No problem, Jer." He wondered where Matthias was. Dean scanned the area for the vampires. He finally spotted them in the center of a crowd. Silas, Matt and Ariyah were being swarmed by members of the tribe and pack. They were taking all the questions like a champ. Well, Matt was. Ariyah merely answered when asked directly and Silas was hiding behind his mother. Dean exhaled humorously. Poor boy.

"You trust him with Ender?" Jerry asked, handing the other man a water.

"He's only snuck in the house twice, both times kept it in his pants." Dean opened the bottle. "He's a softie, don't let him fool you." Dean stood and waved the boy over. "Silas, come here!"

The youngest vampire jumped. He exchanged glances with his parents before treading through the snow. "Yes?" he asked, once he reached the fireside.

"Aw, nothing," Dean admitted and beckoned the boy to sit. He retook his seat. "Just looked like you were going to cry." Dean patted the teen's shoulder. "I know they can be a lot."

Silas's perplexion morphed into understanding. "Thank you," he said. The fire in front of him was roaring. The heat of it paled in comparison to Lavender's.

"Can you feel it?" Jerry asked, gesturing to the flames.

Silas nodded. "It doesn't register how it used to but I can feel it."

Jerry let out a hum and sipped his water.

The front door of the house slammed open. "He's ready!" Lee announced. She stepped to the side. Sara came out after, holding some blankets. She turned back to gesture to the final pair. Finally, Lavender stepped out of the house with the boy. Ethan was glued to her side. He was shivering. Whether from the cold or fear, Dean couldn't tell. Lavender had a protective arm around the other teen.

Everyone was watching as the pair descended the stairs.

Jerry stood. He went to his son and hugged him. Ethan placed his forehead over his father's heart. Jerry then turned to Lavender. "Please, take care of him," he begged in a whisper.

Lavender nodded.

Lee jumped off the porch. "Come on." She gestured with her head. Everyone moved to follow her. There was a heavy silence as the procession went into the woods.

Dean stayed beside the Annoras. He noticed his daughter whispering to Ethan. The boy was back to clinging to her. Dean looked at Silas. Most teenage boys would be mad at someone clinging to their girlfriend, no matter the circumstances. This boy wasn't jealous or angry. He looked worried. His black eyes kept looking at Ethan's back. Dean wished he'd had that level of emotional maturity as a kid. "Hey," he said to get the boy's attention. "He's gonna be fine."

"Have you seen this before?" Matthias asked the other man. He had an arm around Ariyah.

Dean shook his head. "Nope, never seen any of them shift." He smiled, "But if I know Ender, she won't let Ethan get hurt."

The group came to an edge of a clearing. The full moon above it was like a beacon. Lee gestured to Lavender and Ethan. The pair entered the open space. Sara passed off the blanket to Lavender. She spread it out on the snow.

Dean pushed his way through the people and stood beside Jerry. The other man was shaking, tears in the corners of his eyes. His chest was rising and falling rapidly. Dean reached out and took Jerry's hand, giving it a reassuring squeeze. The other man sighed in relief, squeezing Dean's hand back.

A scream made everyone start.

Ethan fell to the ground. His screeches were sharp and guttural. Lavender fell onto the blanket next to him. She looked at him frantically, trying to find where he was hurting. Unfortunately, the pain was everywhere. Ethan began clawing at his skin. His nails dug into his flesh, causing chaotic trails of blood to stream down his body. "Mama, mama!" he wept. Ethan wanted to reach out and grab her, but couldn't pull his fingers out of his wounds.

Lavender grabbed his wrists away. Instinct took over. "Breathe, breathe," she instructed.

Ethan began to retch. His stomach emptied. The gurgling noise that came from him was horrifying. "It hurts!" the boy cried. "It hurts!" Ethan choked, like his throat was seized by an unseen force. The words he wanted to spew became garbled and distorted.

The sounds of cracking bones filled the air.

Lavender watched in terror as his jaw dislocated. More cracking followed. Ethan went on all fours. He continued to retch and break. His spine popped upward and tore through his skin. He was finally able to scream. His voice waved and shifted into something animalistic. Drool and blood poured from his mouth.

His jaw hung loose, limp and swayed in the winter air. His body shuddered and rippled against the blanket. Ethan pushed his face into the fabric. It smelt like home. For a split second it made him relax. Another scream tore through his destroyed throat when his elbows snapped forward. "M..a..m..a," he managed to garble out.

110

Lavender swallowed her panic. There was something in her that knew what to do. Without hesitation, she trusted that feeling. She pressed her forehead on top of Ethan's head. "I'm here, I'm here," she reassured. "You have to let it happen." Lavender pressed her nose into his hair. "Relax, Little, relax." Lavender felt something hot in her chest. Her heart was in her ears. It drowned out the grotesque noises Ethan's body was making. Lavender let her mind slip away. The primal came to the forefront. Everything became automatic. She slipped into cruise control. Lavender started making noises. It started as a hum before it turned into a rumble. Deep and soothing. Hypnotic and lyrical. It was old. It was slow. It had been buried within her blood. The vocalizations soothed Ethan.

The boy untensed. The pain eased. His body stopped its rapid spasming. The sharp cracking of bones became gentle snaps. Ethan's distressed calls quieted. They turned into mewls.

Lavender gathered the boy closer, uncaring about the vomit and blood. She pressed his disfigured head against her chest. Pressing his ear against her heartbeat. Lavender closed her eyes. Then the humming stopped. She hadn't consciously done it. She could feel Ethan twisting in her arms, until finally, she heard him.

Mama?

Lavender opened her eyes. A wolf stared back at her. "Little?" The juvenile nuzzled her face. Lavender gasped in wonder. She pressed her forehead to the pup's. "Oh, Little!" Lavender kissed the boy's face over and over again. Even as a wolf, he smelled like Ethan. His eyes were Ethan's. Lavender smiled, tears finally streaming down her face. "I'm so proud of you!"

The crowd at the edge of the clearing cheered. They ran into the space and circled the pair. The collective joy was infectious. Jerry fell to his knees and hugged his son. "My boy!" he cried, kissing his son's furred face. "My strong boy!"

Lavender giggled and stood from the snow. Her legs were shaking. She did it. She actually did it! Dean wrapped an arm around her. "Good job, flower," he praised with a kiss on her temple. He turned to Matthias, "Told you!"

Ariyah was with the others who were reaching out to pet Ethan. The boy was soaking up all the attention. The other bitten kids were whooping and hollering. They danced around Ethan in a frenzy.

Ethan began to run around. His new form gave him a burst of energy. The moon was shimmering. The night air felt amazing. He howled, calling to his pack.

Aunt Lee screamed in joy and shifted. Her body did it in a blink. It was a smooth and practiced transition. She shook out her fur and raced after the boy. Lee was double the size of Ethan. The two raced through the trees.

Jerry turned to Dean, handing the other man his water. "Hold that for me," he said with a wink before shifting. Jerry raced after his son and sister.

Dean watched the trio as they traveled through the woods. He stepped away from Lavender to keep an eye on the group. Their howls echoed through the quiet forest. The rest of the shifters shed their human forms to run with the new packmate.

13.

13 wolves now in the pack.

The other bitten children came up to Lavender. They showed their bites to her. Their ages ranged from Lavender's own to as young as 10. All of them begged at once. She could only make out what a few of them were saying.

"Will you help me too, mama?"

"Me too!"

"Please, mama!"

Lavender nodded to all of them. "Of course, of course!" They all smiled at her. In an instance she seemed to be the center of their universe. They crowded around her, clutching and hugging at her. Lavender let them rub against her. Whether scenting her or taking in her scent, she couldn't tell.

Silas waited on the edge of the congregation. He tried to swallow his horror at what he'd just witnessed. People could say what they wanted about vampire turnings but werewolves were physically worse. Silas never wanted to see a new shift again. He watched as the pack raced around the clearing. At least the body breaking stuff was a one and done thing. Like adjusting to new shoes.

Lavender finally got out of the kids' hold. They ran off, following the pack on foot. She went to Silas. "Welp, that was…so much." Lavender looked at her clothes. "I should probably burn these."

Silas giggled, "Probably." He kissed Lavender's forehead. *That was fucking terrifying*

Lavender snorted, *You're telling me!* Lavender's lip quivered, she rested her head on Silas's shoulder. *I thought he was going to die. I was so scared he was going to die.* She choked and began to cry.

Silas, heedless of the mess on her, pulled Lavender into a tight hug. *You did amazing, motek.* He placed kiss after kiss on the top of her head.

Lavender sniffled and clung to him. *I love you.*

Silas chuckled, *I love you too.*

Nana emerged from the clearing. Some of the older members of the tribe followed her. They'd been cooking and preparing for the celebration afterwards. Lavender was here, a born female was here. They knew this shift would go smoothly, unlike River. That poor boy's death had caused an untold amount of nightmares. Even more than Combstock stalking their land.

Nana beamed as the pack ran by her. Ethan trotted up to her, joy visible on his face. "Oh, my boy!" she cooed, kissing his face. The other elders pet him as well. Nana scanned the clearing and saw Lavender in Silas's arms. Her breath hitched. She'd never seen the boy before. Only rumors and whispers. He was tall and reminded Nana of a boy she hadn't seen in decades. She made her way over to them.

Dean, Matthias, and Ariyah were at the edge of the wood. The 3 were allowing Lavender and Silas their moment. Dean tensed when he noticed Nana heading toward them. "Oh shit," he whispered. Dean turned to the doctor. "Hold this!" He handed Matt Jerry's drink.

112

Nana noticed the mess on Lavender's clothes. "I should have warned you about that." Her granddaughter unburied her face from the boy's neck. Nana opened her arms to her. "I'm so proud of you," she whispered.

Lavender hesitated but eventually hugged her. She hoped they could bury the hatchet. Knowing Rosemary though, it was highly unlikely. "I'm just happy I knew what to do." She pulled away and turned to Silas. "Nana, this is Silas." She gestured from Silas to Nana. "Si, this is my grandmother."

The two stared at each other. The silence weighed heavily in the winter air. Nana was staring into the boy's black eyes. They were too familiar for comfort. She put on a cheery face. "Hello, dear."

Silas gave her a tense smile, "Hi." He nervously stuck his hand out. Thankfully, Nana shook it. Silas stepped back and lingered behind Lavender. "It's nice to meet you."

Nana looked the boy up and down. She then turned to Lavender, "Is he always like this?"

"He gets nervous, leave him alone," Lavender chastised.

Nana rolled her eyes, "I'm just teasing."

"Flower!" Dean ran up to his daughter. He asked, "Are you ready to go?"

Nana turned to the man. She huffed, "Nice to see you too, Dean."

The man bit the inside of his cheek to keep from grimacing. "Hi, Magnolia." Dean rubbed his face. "Listen-"

"4 years!" Nana hissed. She got in the man's face. "You have some nerve to try and brush me off. You didn't even tell me she was here!"

Dean tried to explain, "Listen, Rose-"

"Rosemary took her and you did nothing!" Nana jabbed his chest. "4 years, barely a whisper! You just let her run off!"

"What was I supposed to do? Track her down and drag her back here kicking and screaming?!" Dean threw his hands up in hysteria. "How'd that go for you last time?! Does she ever call you back, mommy dearest?"

Nana slapped the man across the face. Her claws caught some of his skin.

Dean staggered back in shock. The entire clearing went silent. The wolves stopped their running. Everyone held their breath.

"You know nothing, Dean Amos," Nana hissed. The amount of venom in her voice could have poisoned a hundred men. Nana went for another swing.

Lavender jumped in, she grabbed the older woman's wrist. She couldn't contain her fury. "If you ever lay a hand on him again, I will kill you." The disgust she'd tried to stamp down was now in full force. She pushed Nana's arm away.

"How dare you!" The older woman screamed. She got into Lavender's face. "I should-"

The pack entered the clearing. They were advancing toward them. Ethan had his fangs bared. Nana looked at them in shock. She stepped back from Lavender. Tears flooded her eyes, but she didn't let them fall. It was no longer her time. Nana held her head high. Without looking back, she made her way into the woods and back home.

Lavender turned to Dean. "Dad." She touched his uninjured cheek. "Are you okay?"

Dean forced a smile, "Not the first time, Ender." He sniffled and wiped the corner of his watering eye. "Welp," he looked to Silas, "you all aren't her number 1 enemy now." The joke fell flat.

Matthias came over. Gently, he turned the man's face. Two of the gashes would need stitching. Matthias grimaced, "She scratched you quite deeply." His friend had mentioned how tumultuous his relationship with his ex wife and in-law was. Matthias never thought it was one that included physical violence.

"That explains the stinging," Dean chuckled. He hissed when Matthias's cool fingers touched his cut. "No drinking that," he teased with a wink.

Matthias chuckled, "Of course. I have a first aid kit in the car." He took the other man's hand, "Come."

Silas tensed. The pair were too close for comfort. "We'll go with you!" he announced, taking Lavender's hand. Thankfully his girlfriend agreed.

"Come on, dad. Let's get you cleaned up," Lavender helped guide her dad out of the woods.

Wait for me! Ethan called.

Lavender turned and smiled at him. The boy brushed against her leg. She reached down and gave him a scratch on the head.

As they walked, Silas noticed how tired the boy seemed to be now. The wolf pup was trotting behind them slowly. He must have used up all his energy running around like a maniac. "Want me to pick you up?" he offered.

Ethan's ears perked up and he came closer to Silas.

The older teen chuckled. He picked up the other boy easily. Ethan placed his head on Silas's shoulder.

Lavender looked back, "What are you doing?"

"He's tired." Silas looked to Ethan, "Aren't you?"

The wolf barked.

Chapter 18

Lavender sat on the trunk of the car. Silas and Ethan were running around the cul-de-sac. The younger boy seemed to have gotten a second wind. Other pack kids were playing with sparklers. Dean was sitting on Jerry's front porch while Matthias cleaned his cuts. Ariyah was talking to Aunt Lee. Other members of the pack and the tribe were on their porches. The elders brought out the food. Stew and bread and pies lined a table in the center of the cul-de-sac.

Ethan tackled Silas to the ground. The pair kicked up dust, thankfully they were far from the table. Lavender giggled. She took a sip of her hot chocolate. Everyone was there, except for Nana. Lavender frowned and looked to her grandmother's house. It was located away from the other pack homes, closer to the shore. The half circle was filled with a warm bright light. Nana's home was a lighthouse in the sea of darkness.

"Ah!" Silas yelped. He grimaced as the wolf pup continued to lick at his face. "Stop!" he whined and pushed the boy away. Silas chuckled and wiped his face clean. "Gross, dude."

Ethan barked. He nudged at Silas. The other boy didn't react to his words though. Strange. Ethan tilted his head and nudged Silas again.

"What is it, bud?" the vampire asked.

Ethan huffed and ran over to Lavender. *Hey, I don't think he can hear me!* He noticed that Lavender's golden eyes were trained on Nana's house. *Mama?*

Lavender shook out of her thoughts. She put on a smile, " Sorry, Little. No, he probably can't. He's a different species."

"Is he talking?" Silas asked. He'd gotten beside them in a blink.

Both Ethan and Lavender jumped.

"Don't pop up like that!" Lavender scolded, "You're gonna give me a heart attack." She sighed and turned to Ethan, "Yea, he definitely can't."

Ethan turned and nipped at Silas's ankle. The vampire jumped up in shock, landing on top of the car.

"Dude!" Silas scolded. Ethan barked at him.

Lavender giggled. The pair were such rowdy boys. Silas jumped off the car and Ethan raced after him. They started playing again. Her thoughts wandered back to Nana. She stared at the gravel. Her grandmother and mother were two sides of the same coin. Lavender wouldn't be like them. She wasn't going to continue the cycle of resentment and silence.

Lavender looked into the dark again. The beacon of Nana's house glowed in the abyss. Lavender hopped off the trunk. Time to gently parent another adult. She carefully made a bowl of soup and grabbed some bread. Lavender then started for Nana's house.

Ethan trotted after her. *What are you doing, mama?"*

"I need to talk to her." Lavender explained, "The longer she stews, the deeper the resentment." She chuckled sadly, "If she's anything like my mom, I only have a few minutes." Lavender picked up her pace.

Ethan got in her way, making the girl stop short. *I don't think this is a good idea.*

Lavender rolled her eyes. "I know my family, Ethan."

I know, Ethan poked his paw into the ground, *but she might hurt you.* His ears pressed against his head, *I don't want you to get hurt.*

Lavender smiled and crouched down. She looked into Ethan's eyes. "I'll be fine, little. If I need you, I'll scream." Lavender kissed his forehead. When she stood, Silas was there. "Ah!" Lavender nearly dropped the food, but Silas thankfully caught it. "Silas!" she scolded. By some miracle all of the soup had stayed in the bowl.

The vampire winced, "Sorry, sorry." He handed the food back. "I don't mean to." Silas tugged at his shirt sleeve. "I just wanted to make sure you were okay," Silas sheepishly admitted.

Lavender couldn't stay mad at him. He was too sweet. She kissed his cheek. "You're lucky you're cute." With a pat on his chest she ordered, "Make sure Ethan doesn't get in my way." Lavender walked off toward Nana's house.

Silas and Ethan stared after her then each other. "I feel bad I can't hear you," Silas toed at the ground. An idea popped into his mind. "Oh, maybe we can learn morse code!"

Ethan tilted his head. *God, you're endearing.* The wolf rubbed against Silas's legs.

"I'm glad you like the idea, bud." Silas gave the pup a pet.

Lavender stepped into Nana's house. The door had been unlocked. Which was a good sign. She could hear the older woman in the kitchen. The soft clink of mugs and the beginning whistle of the kettle were drowned out by sobs. Lavender frowned. She announced her presence. "Nana?" she called into the warm home. The sobs stopped and turned to sniffles.

Nana kept her back toward the entrance of the kitchen. "What is it, Lavender?" She mechanically placed a mug on the drying rack. .

Lavender set down the food on the table. She noticed that her grandmother's shaky shoulders were settling. "Brought you some soup. It's really good." Lavender nervously dragged her finger along the table. "Did you help make it?"

"Of course I did," Nana snapped. She huffed, "Did you think all of us old timers were doing nothing?"

116

Lavender sighed and collapsed into a chair. "Just like mom," she mumbled in utter exasperation.

Nana whipped around, "Excuse me?!"

"I said you're just like my mom!" Lavender snapped back. "You two love to not talk. To just bottle everything up and take it out on me instead of telling me what the hell's wrong so I can-" Lavender covered her face with her hands. She needed to calm down. This wasn't going to help the situation.

Nana's face twisted in rage. "Guess what, princess, you're just like your mother too!"

Lavender slammed her fist on the table. "Fuck you!" She stood and made her way to the door but stopped herself. No, no, she wasn't going to be like them. Lavender turned around. "We're talking about this!" she demanded. "You're not going to make me leave by pissing me off. What did you do to my mom? Why did dad say you dragged her back?"

"What did I do? What did I do?!" Nana wailed in hysterics. She threw a mug against the wall. "You want to know what I did?!"

"Yes!" Lavender begged. "Will you please just tell me!" She wept, "Why won't you two ever talk to me. All you do is scream. I don't understand why you can't just talk." She hiccuped and tried to clear her blurry vision. The tears streaming down her face kept coming. "Just talk to me." Lavender coughed and shook. "Why can't we just talk?"

Nana sighed and rubbed her forehead. "We are blessed. Blessed, Lavender! Your mother never accepted it! She never gave a shit about our people, about our tribe, or our pack!"

"Did you ever stop to think she didn't want any of this?" Lavender asked. She hated she had to defend her mother, but that wasn't fair. "Maybe your expectations of her were too much?"

"Our pack is dying, Lavender!" Nana screamed. "We're dying out because of her selfishness." Nana threw the kettle of hot water across the room. "She's a selfish brat! I gave her everything in me. All I wanted was for her to stay. She couldn't even do that! She could have had your father. She could have lived off the reservation. I just wanted her to help the bitten. One tradition, just keep on tradition. I told her she didn't have to do anything else. That you would be old enough to lead by the time I was this old."

Nana staggered to the table, clutching her chest. She collapsed into the chair at her table. "She just screamed and said you'd never want to be a Den Mother. That you would hate me. That she'd make sure you knew what the pack was really about." Nana wept into her hands. "She tried to kill Jerry, Lavender. She let him get stuck. She ran and I had to drag her back to fix him." Nana bared her teeth, "I made her help him. She never forgave me for that. The fact that you, younger than she was, can understand the importance of shifting shows how immature and selfish she was and still is."

Lavender frowned. "Did she almost kill Jerry because of dad?"

Nana scoffed, "Of course. Because she wanted to act like a petty child."

Lavender looked at the floor.

Nana looked at her. "Well, how do we fix it?" she spat.

Lavender sighed. "I can't fix it for you. You and mom would have to talk." She sucked in a breath. "I'm here to fix this." She gestured between the two of them. "My mom already hates me. I'd rather not you hate me too."

Nana sighed, "Your mother doesn't hate you, Lavender."

"She has a very funny way of showing it," Lavender growled out. "She thinks you hate her."

Nana huffed. "I don't hate her, she just makes everything so complicated." Nana looked at the now cold soup. "I just wanted her to have the life she deserved."

"You mean you wanted her to be your clone?"

Nana slammed her fist on the table. "This is what we all want!"

Lavender shook her head. "No, it's not. You resented her for wanting to be herself. You resented her for not wanting a shit ton of kids and taking the title of Den Mother with grace."

"It's a gift, Lavender. One she squandered and threw away, and for what?! To marry a townie and burn up in who the fuck cares Arizona!" Nana couldn't believe she had to explain this to a child. "And you, you think you're above us?" She glared at the teen. "News flash, our blood is in your veins."

Lavender looked the older woman up and down. "I got the best of my father, which cancels out the worst of you." She walked over to her grandmother, who was staring at her in shock. "I'm not above you, just a better you. You made my mom hate herself. She made me hate myself." Lavender placed her hands on the table. "My child will never stay up all night wondering if their mother hates them. And if they get older, and don't want to deal with the pack, I won't make them."

Nana growled, "You have no right-"

"I have every right!" Lavender screamed. "I'm the one that had to live through what *you* did! I'm the one that had to grow up never knowing if my mother loved me. I'm the one that had to grow up on the run! My mom tried so hard to be everything you aren't that she turned out exactly like you. I refuse to do that!" Lavender leaned forward. She got in Nana's face. "I'm not letting either one of you hurt me anymore. I'm not letting either of you make me bitter and cruel."

Nana stood. "I never wanted her to be like that!" The older woman wept. She touched the pendant on her chest. It held a lock of Rosemary's hair. "When your mother was born, I was so happy. She gave me a reason to live. To keep going. After-" Nana looked at her husband's photo. "I wanted to kill myself. Then I was given this little life. I was then given an entire pack. Being a Den Mother made me whole. Your mother was so broken, I just wanted her whole."

Lavender wiped her face. "She needs to hear this. Not me."

Nana sniffled. Her throat was clogged. "I want my baby back."

Lavender wondered if her mother cried like this over her. If she only had the ability to feel guilt and regret when Lavender wasn't present. "You need to apologize to my mom."

That made Nana snap her head up in shock. "Apologize?" she spat. "She should be apologizing!"

"You both need to fucking apologize!" Lavender snapped. "I'm so fucking-" She felt like she was going to explode. Lavender needed to expel this demon. Why was she having to tell grown adults to act like adults? Why did she have to be the one to try and mend this broken family?! Lavender doubled over and screamed. A scream that had been building inside of her for over a decade. It seemed to shake the entire house. It shook the world around her. It ratted her very bones. The dam broke and the flood was unyielding.

Nana had backed up against the wall in terror. Tears streamed down her face. The pain of the cry made her heart shatter.

The front door slammed open. The force shattered the small glass window inside the wood. Silas noticed the absolute distress Lavender was in. He gathered her into his arms. "Lavender," he tried to calm her down, "Lavender." He wiped her tears. "Motek," he whispered. Silas kissed her forehead. *What do you need? I'll take you home. You can go home. You're safe. I'm here. What do you need, motek?*

The flurry of assurance cut through Lavender's wailing. They probably weren't even sent to her intentionally. Silas was just that worried about her. Lavender stopped her screams with a violent cough. Her throat hurt. It felt like she'd swallowed shards of glass. Lavender nuzzled into his shoulder. Cool hands were a balm on her burning skin.

Silas kissed her temple. "I love you," he whispered aloud. Silas could hear Dean coming. His fast footfalls were followed by Ethan's. Apparently the boy had shifted back into his human form.

Lavender sniffled and turned her head so she could see Nana. The older woman looked horrified and was unnaturally still. Lavender turned away and pulled Silas with her. The pair left the house.

Dean was running up the porch. The man sighed in relief. "Oh, Ender." He reached out and hugged his daughter. "Oh, my baby, my baby." Dean kissed her face. "Are you hurt? Did she hurt you?!" Dean had never hit an old woman, but he would tonight! The only reason he didn't storm into the home was because of Lavender. His girl was hugging him tightly.

"I want to go home," Lavender whimpered. "I want to go home, daddy."

Dean felt his heart break. "Okay, baby, come here." She may have grown, but she was still his little girl. Dean always made sure he could lift well beyond his own weight, so he could always carry his daughter.

Lavender let her father pick her up. She was too tired to fight or to talk. Lavender wanted her bed, wanted her room, and wanted to sleep.

Chapter 19

Lavender laid on her side. She stared at the sea glass wind chime. It glittered in the moonlight. Her body felt like it'd run a marathon. Lavender gripped her necklace. *Can you come over?*

Silas slowly peaked his head over the windowsill.

Lavender sat up on her arm. "Were you waiting outside?" A smile slowly spread across her face.

Silas came to her bedside and sat on the floor in front of her. "I was worried." he picked at her sheet. "Hearing that scream," Silas shuddered. He pressed his forehead against the edge of her bed. "I thought the worst."

Lavender reached down and played with Silas's hair. "Hey," she said to get his attention. Those beautiful black eyes warmed her soul. "Come here," Lavender urged. With a fistful of his shirt, she pulled him onto the bed. "Cuddle me?"

Silas immediately nuzzled into her neck. He reached down and pulled the blanket over them. "This is my favorite," he muttered into her curls. Silas wrapped his arms around her. "You're so warm."

Lavender giggled and snuggled closer to him. "Wait, I wanna look at the window." She tried to shift around.

Silas held her tight and turned them around together.

Lavender screamed out a laugh. "Si!" she scolded and playfully hit his arm. The blankets were all tangled up. Both of them had to kick out their legs to free themselves. "Release me!" commanded Lavender to the fabric.

Silas snorted and giggled into her shoulder. After a lot of wiggling, the pair were finally comfortable again. "You need a bigger bed," Silas mumbled. His ass was currently hanging off the edge.

Lavender rolled her eyes, "Well sorry, didn't think I'd be dating a giant."

"I'm not a giant, you're just tiny," Silas teased, planting a kiss on Lavender's cheek.

The girl growled, "You are so lucky you're cute." She turned in his arms and gave him a kiss.

Dean sat at the kitchen table. His head was pounding. Memories replayed in his mind. The room was warmer. Laughter and the smell of spices. He could still see the chilis his mother hung by the window in front of the sink.

Why had he taken those down? Had they rotted beyond repair, or was it to keep Lavender's little hands from getting ahold of them? When did he take down the pictures of him and Rose? Was it the last time she left or the one before?

Dean rubbed his temples. Why did he always open the door for her? Why didn't he take Lavender away? Moving so much couldn't have been good for her. Did he really think a mother knew best or was he terrified of being the parent that messed her up?

Dean stood up. He needed a smoke. He hadn't smoked in years, but he needed one. An old kitchen drawer was violently ripped open. Dean dug around the junk drawer for the long unused cigarettes. It was crumpled and over 3 years old. There was a lighter among the sticks. Dean pulled it out. The design on the plastic casing had nearly faded away.

Dean took them and his flip phone outside to the porch. The night air was freezing. It felt wonderful on his feverish skin. Dean collapsed into the beat up chair by the door. He dialed Rosemary's number and hoped she picked up. His leg bounced with the ring. Dean lit one of the cigarettes. At least smoking would pass the time.

"Hello?" the voice on the other end sounded hoarse. Like she'd been screaming.

Dean huffed, "Didn't save my number?"

Rosemary sighed, "What do you want, Dean?"

He decided to cut to the chase. "Our daughter thinks you hate her for being born." Dean was surprised by the silence on the other end. If it wasn't for the shifting on the other end he would have thought she had hung up. Dean frowned, "I can't blame her either," he added.

Rosemary was still quiet.

Dean felt hot tears flood his eyes. "Ethan Shifted. He shifted tonight, Lavender helped him."

"She what?"

Dean cringed. He thought Rose would have been at least a little proud, instead she sounded horrified. "He did his werewolf thing-"

"You let her go!" Rosemary roared. "One thing! I asked you to do one thing, Dean!"

The man growled, "All bets are off when you throw our kid away!"

The other end went silent again.

Dean wanted to scream. He now fully understood Lavender's scream. It was such a maddening cycle. All he wanted was for his daughter to have some healing or some closure. Dean wept, "Rose, I didn't call to fight. You know I hate fighting. Why does it always have to be a fight?" The line was still silent. He took another drag of his cigarette and tried to quell his sniffles.

"Are you smoking again?"

Dean barked out a laugh. "Really, that's what you're focusing on?" He rubbed his eyes with the back of his hand. "Yea, I'm fucking stressed out. There's vampires and werewolves running around my hometown. Also it turns out the woman I loved and trusted with our daughter fucking traumatized her! Also, there's a serial killer running around. I'm a little fucking stressed!" Dean tried to catch his breath.

The other side of the line kept silent.

Dean growled. "Our daughter thinks you hate her, Rose. Our daughter thinks you wish she'd never been born. Your mother also didn't fucking help."

"My m-mom?"

Her voice sounded so small. So broken. Dean nodded then remembered she couldn't see him. "Yea, your mom. She also smacked the fuck out of me, needed a couple stitches."

"That's why I didn't want Lavender near her!" Rosemary growled.

"Did you tell her that? Or did you just tell her 'no' and when she asked why you blew up at her?" Dean continued, "Cause I sure as fuck didn't know anything, because you never told me. You'd just fly off the handle!" He finished his cigarette and stomped the butt out on the porch. "I want my daughter to have a mom." Dean warned, "If you want her to have one too, you'll come here and actually talk to her." He drove it home. "She's hurt, Rose. You hurt her."

"She left," Rosemary growled.

"Lavender was right, you're just like your mom." Before she could scream in his ear, Dean hung up. He sighed and sat back down. A thump above him made him pause.

Silas jumped down and landed in the grass. Thankfully on his feet. The moment of pride ended quickly when he looked up and saw Dean.

"You ever gonna use the front door, Dracula?" Dean teased.

Silas tugged at his shirt sleeve. "Sorry, she ask-" the boy hung his head, "I just wanted to help her sleep."

Dean raised an eyebrow. "Do I need to buy a pregnancy test?"

Silas gave him a confused look. The question was strange. "I mean…if you think you're pregnant?"

Dean was gobsmacked by the response. "If I-" he snorted and doubled over. God it felt good to laugh. "I meant for Lavender!"

"Oh." Silas thought for a moment till the realization hit him, "Oh!" His face went red, "N-no sir, no!"

Dean tried to reign in his chuckles. "Boy, I'm worried about you," he said through happy tears.

"My mom says that a lot too," Silas admitted. He kicked at the grass. "She is asleep though," he pointed toward Lavender's window, "and she's okay, Still sad obviously but…not as sad."

Dean nodded. He sighed. "I called her mom."

Silas winced, "Yea, I…heard."

Dean frowned, "And you still decided to jump down?"

The boy shrugged, "I..." He looked away.

Dean snorted. The poor kid was obviously anxious. "Well?" he urged gently.

122

Silas tugged at his sleeve. "Well," he stepped up on the porch, "I wanted to tell you something." He frowned, "I can't remember though." He gestured to the phone. "Can I help?" The boy took a seat on the porch's railing across from Dean.

It looked uncomfortable and Dean couldn't comprehend how the teen was doing it. An awkward silence followed. Finally Dean said, "I don't think there's much to do, bud."

"Maybe my mom could help?" Silas offered. "She was a therapist at our last home."

Dean smiled. "You really see them as parents?"

Silas tilted his head, "Why wouldn't I?"

"Well," Dean tried to ask as delicately as he could, "What about your parents before?" The boy was giving him another confused look. "Your human ones?" Dean clarified.

"Oh!" Silas laughed, "I ugh...I didn't know them." he shrugged, "Was raised by my grandparents."

Dean nodded, "I see, sorry."

"Why?" Silas tugged at his sleeve. "You know, people do that a lot and I don't get it. They ask a question and then I answer and then they say sorry." He rested his head against the beam that went to the roof of the porch.

Dean shrugged. "I can't speak for everyone. I just know I feel bad for you. Because 1 you never got to know your parents and 2 you lost them." He noticed how still the boy was. Such a subtle thing that gave away his supernaturalness. It also didn't help that the boy's face was free of the usual acne found in his age group. Leaning on the porch like that, he looked like a strange art piece. Or like he'd been paused in real life.

Silas finally snapped back to life. "I guess that makes sense." He remembered why he'd wanted to talk to Dean in the first place. "Oh, um Lavender said something in her sleep. I think she wants it."

"Yeah, what was it?"

"Soapa..." Silas furrowed his brow, "pee-ya?"

Dean chuckled, "Sopapillas, they're a pastry." He remembered the first time he'd fed one to Lavender. How the little girl's eyes widened at the taste. She'd grabbed it out of his hand. Her chubby cheeks and little fingers were covered in crumbs by the time she'd finished. Dean remembered her tiny voice. She'd begged for another and another. "You can put cinnamon or powdered sugar on them. Ender always liked cinnamon and honey."

Silas smiled fondly, "Makes sense. She has a sweet tooth." He thought of how happy Lavender would be to wake up to them. "You should make some for her in the morning." Silas began to rock side to side. "Or I could make them, if you can't." He wondered if his house had any cooking supplies. Probably not. Matthias did give him that credit card. Silas wondered what stores would be open. He'd probably have to wait till the morning.

Dean smiled at the boy's passion. "I can make them. You might burn yourself." Silas looked up at him hopefully.

"Cool, she'll be so happy!" Silas couldn't help the smile spreading across his face. The way Lavender's eyes brightened at the sight of sweets always warmed his heart. It was such a simple thing to get excited over. A part of him wished he could still experience those small joys. "One time, when we got candy at school, every time she'd pull out a piece she'd get really excited and wiggle around." Silas moved his body the same way she did. "It was really cute."

Dean chuckled, "Yeah, she gets that from me." Young love was so precious. The way Silas talked about Lavender warmed Dean's heart. A part of him felt bad for threatening to seduce the boy's parents. "I'll make them for her in the morning."

"Yay," Silas whispered. He hopped off the banister. "I know it won't fix the-" he gestured to the phone, "but it'll make her feel a little better."

"Definitely," Dean agreed. He stood. "Get home safe, kid."

Silas beamed, "I will."

Dean blinked and the boy was gone. "Holy shit," he muttered. Now alone, winter air seeped into his bones once more. A shiver ran down his spine. Dean went inside. He looked through the cabinets for ingredients. Since Lavender had moved back in, he started keeping food around. Eating out was becoming rarer with his daughter here. Dean laid everything out on the counter for the morning.

His phone rang. The shrill jingle made him hiss. He quickly answered it before the tune woke up Lavender. The girl's ears were as sharp as a tack. "Hello?" Dean tried his hardest to not sound angry. He probably failed though.

Rosemary's voice came from the other end. "I'll be there after new years."

Lavender woke up to the smell of cinnamon. Sleep tried to weigh down her eyes, but she fought it. Her arms searched the bed. Lavender frowned when she noticed Silas was gone. While it made sense, it still disappointed her.

The scream of the fire alarm made her jump up. Lavender growled when her feet tangled in her sheets. She kicked the fabric off and rushed down the steps. "Dad!" she called in distress.

Dean was waving a dish towel at the fire alarm. "Shut up!" he screamed at it. He shook his head. A whiff of controlled smoke and the thing screams. Finally it stopped its shouting. Dean jumped up and ripped it out of the ceiling. He threw it into the closet. "Begone!" Dean huffed and turned to his daughter. Who looked both worried and incredibly amused. "Hey, flower!" Dean took his hair down then re-tied it into another messy bun. "Hungry?"

Lavender snorted out a laugh. "What are you doing?" The kitchen was a mess. Ingredients lined the counters and there was something popping on the stove.

Dean went back to the pan. He strained the fresh pastries out of the oil. "I made sopapillas!" With a dusting of cinnamon, he set the edible pillows on a plate. "I also made some eggs, bacon. There's honey on the table and-"

"Did you read my mind?" Lavender asked. She grabbed the full plate. "I had a dream about these last night!" The teen sat at the table and drizzled honey on the sopapillas.

"Don't eat all of them," Dean warned. "Remember last time?"

124

Lavender rolled her eyes, "Last time I was like 9."

"And you threw up so hard chunks shot out your nose." Dean sat across from her.

Lavender made a disgusted face. "Ew, dad!" She lightly kicked him under the table.

Dean giggled, "You did!" He took a sip of his coffee and watched as she devoured her food. Lavender swayed back and forth in joy. Her little dance caused more crumbs to get on her face. Dean sneakily took out his phone and snapped a picture of her. The shutter made her look at him.

"Dad!"

Dean rolled his eyes, "Calm down, it's all blurry." He looked at the picture. It was from a bad angle and his phone's quality was low, but he saved it. "Your boyfriend told me you were mumbling about them last night."

Lavender's face turned red. "Um...well-"

Dean rolled his eyes. "I don't care if your boyfriend comes over, Ender." He added, "If you need condoms though-"

"Dad!" Lavender wanted to crawl into a hole. The embarrassment couldn't be repelled by her tasty treats. "Please stop!"

The talk wasn't anymore comfortable for Dean. However, the discussion needed to be had, before it was too late. "Lavender, I want you to be safe."

"I know!" Lavender covered her eyes in shame. "We're not doing that, okay. I'll tell you if that changes." Her face felt hot. She stuffed another pastry into her mouth.

Dean reached across the table and extended his pinky. "Promise?"

Lavender quickly wrapped her little finger around his. "Promise! Please don't ask again."

Dean chuckled. "How are you both so much like us and yet nothing like us?" He shook his head in amusement. "Smarter than we were."

Lavender's embarrassment ceased. "You and mom?"

Dean nodded. "Her and I ran wild."

"Is that why your nickname was the town bicycle?"

Dean balked. It was now his turn to go red with shame. "Who told you that?!"

Lavender giggled. "Miriam." The old woman had said the nickname with an eye roll years ago. Took Lavender till now to fully understand what she'd meant.

"Well," Dean set his coffee down, "I think I need a new receptionist."

Lavender snickered, "You can't fire Miriam, she'll kick your ass."

Dean snorted, "I hate that you're right." Rosemary's words replayed in his head. Across the table Lavender was happily eating. Cinnamon crystals were scattered over her cheeks and fingers. Dean frowned.

He'd tell her later.

"Dad?"

Dean snapped his head up. "Sorry, what is it, flower?"

Lavender repeated, "Silas invited us to a New Years party." She licked her hands clean.

Dean huffed, "Really?" He gently kicked her under the table and tilted his head to the sink. The way Lavender rolled her eyes made him chuckle. "I think Matt mentioned that the other day."

The teen washed and dried her hands. "So…are we going?" Lavender shut off the stove top. Something her dad had forgotten to do. "I mean, I know you've met some of them…"

"But meeting the whole family is a big deal?" Dean nodded. "I get it. Speaking of which, anyone I should worry about."

Lavender thought for a moment, "Maybe, Eden?" She forced a smile, "She's intense." Lavender began wiping down some of the counters.

Dean nodded, "Alright, guess we'll go. I'm wearing my light up sweater." He made his way to his bedroom. Unfortunately duty was going to call soon and yell at him for being late.

"Dad!" Lavender groaned. The light up sweater was tacky. Which she'd normally be fine with but the Annora's were a classy bunch. Granted Matthias did work with Dean.

"You can't talk me out of it!" the man declared from his room.

Lavender shook her head in disbelief. She looked at the messy kitchen and began to clean up. Was only fair since her dad cooked.

Chapter 20

The amount of lights on the Annora house would be concerning to most. Especially since they were strung far higher than a human could reach. Thankfully the pair coming for the party were well aware of the family's true nature.

Lavender clutched her present like a vice. The box was small and messily wrapped with snowflake covered glossy paper. Anxiety was building in her chest. She hoped Silas liked it. They hadn't been able to see each other for a while. The Annora family had gone on a trip for Chrismukkah. Silas had said it was a family tradition. She hoped her present was good enough. What do you get a boy who could literally have anything?"

"Stop your freakin', the boy adores you," Dean assured. He ruffled his daughter's hair. "Come on!" he urged.

Lavender huffed. "Easy for you to say!" She fixed her hair. The insane sweater her dad wore was flickering. Little LEDs illuminated dancing snowflakes and reindeer prancing. At least it'd take any awkward attention off her.

"Listen, I've never been here! If anyone should be nervous, it's me. Look at what I'm wearing!" Dean gestured to his crazy sweater.

Lavender burst out laughing. She nuzzled into her dad's side. The man wrapped an arm around her. Warm lips pressed against her temple. The pair made their way up the steps and to the front door. "You're right, I shouldn't be worried," Lavender looked her dad up and down, "but you should be."

"Cheek," Dean pinched his daughter's face. He knocked on the grand door.

It opened slowly. A blast of heat hit Lavender and her father. Warm light flooded the dark winter air. Jonathan and Matthias stood in the doorway. Their sweaters blinked with LEDs.

The 3 men rejoiced. "Hey!" they cheered in unison.

"Sweater bros! Sweater bros!" Jonathan chanted. He picked up Dean with ease and began hooting and hollering.

"One of us! One of us!" Matthias clapped.

Lavender snorted and buried her face in her hand. "Give me strength," she begged to whatever was listening.

"Guys," Everett sighed. He was also wearing a LED sweater. It was light blue with gold dancing snowflakes. Everett had tried to say no but Jonathan used those signature puppy dog eyes. Said man went from dancing with Lavender's dad and their own vampiric father to throwing snowballs. Everett groaned in embarrassment.

Lavender went to the blond. "Hey, at least your sweater brings out your eyes." She gestured to Dean. "His looks like Christmas threw up on him."

Everett giggled, "At least his is on theme." He gestured to Jonathan. The black man's sweater was an obnoxious orange. It also had light up snowflakes.

Lavender scrunched her nose, "I didn't even notice. Why orange?"

"That's what I said!" Everett whined.

"Don't diss my sweater!" Jonathan defended. A snowball got him in the face.

"Ha ha!" Matthias cheered. "You have been owned!" A snowball got him in the face. The ice entered his mouth. The man hacked out a cough.

Dean snorted, "Sorry, Matt!" He looked at the house. "Oh hey, Ariyah!"

The vampire mother smiled. She called out, "Please stop abusing my family with ice, handsome man!"

Dean blushed and dropped the second snowball he had in his other hand.

Lavender and Everett jumped and turned around to look at Ariyah.

"Hello, Lavender," the woman greeted. She then turned to her eldest. "Oh, that sweater looks lovely on you, dear." Ariyah took his pale face in her hands. "It really does bring out your eyes."

Everett snorted when she kissed his cheek. "Thanks, mom."

Lavender felt a twinge of jealousy at the display. She stamped it down though. It wasn't the time to drown in her mommy issues. She forced a smile. "Is Silas-" Before she could finish asking, warm arms wrapped around her.

Silas nuzzled her neck. "You smell like happy."

Lavender burst into laughter. She reached down and covered the arms around her middle with her own. Silas's arms were warm. Something she wasn't used to. The boy normally ran cool. Room temperature. It was probably from just eating and whatever roaring inferno they had going inside the manor. She turned and gave him a kiss on the cheek. The boy let out a quiet whine and buried his face into her shoulder.

"Hey!" Dean threw a snowball and hit Silas on the top of the head. The boy immediately let go of his daughter and hissed.

"Dad!" Lavender growled. Some of the snow had gotten on her.

"I'm too young to be a grandfather!" Dean cried.

Lavender screamed. She ran across the lawn and tackled her father into the snow.

"Help!" Dean cried as he went down.

Everyone was gathered in the sitting room. The fire was lighting up the lounge. The TV was screaming as the ball dropped in Time Square. Dean was chugging 200 year old wine like a frat boy. Jonathan and Hana cheered the man on while he drained the bottle. The pair had already guzzled down their own. "Go, go, go!" the vampiric siblings cheered.

"Mr. Amos, you're a fucking legend!" Hana laughed. She'd never seen a human keep up with them. Granted, they'd never had a human over for New Years.

"He's a fucking machine!" Jonathan added. He loved working for this wild man. "The guy won the badge through a fist fight. Roosevelt can suck it, this is a real bull moose!"

128

Dean finished his wine. "Whoo!" He set the bottle on the side table. His legs gave out. Thankfully the couch caught him. "I think I need some water!" Wine drunk was another beast to beer drunk. Especially aged wine that apparently was strong enough to affect vampires.

"I got you," Hana patted the man's shoulder and stumbled to the kitchen.

Lavender sat next to Silas on the couch. Eden and Ariyah were chugging their own bottles by the window. Matthias was cheering his wife and daughter on. "So," Lavender nudged Silas, "You guys can get drunk?"

The boy nodded. "High too, can't have synthetic stuff though." Silas nuzzled Lavender's face and kissed her cheek. "They always get turnt on New Years."

Lavender snorted, "Turnt?!"

"Crunk?" Silas offered instead.

Lavender wrapped her arms around the puzzled boy and kissed him. "You're such a dork." She gave him a few more kisses for good measure.

"Yea," Silas agreed. His smile was dopey and blissed.

Everett came into the room. A bottle in his hand. "Want to join us this year, Si?" He knocked the bottle gently against the boy's cheek.

Silas shook his head. "No thanks."

Everett shrugged. "Lavender," he offered.

"I'm not old enough," Lavender reminded him.

"What?" Everett uncorked the bottle.

"Kids can't drink, Ev. Got to be 21," Jonathan explained.

"What?" Everett's southern accent came out full force. This day and age stayed vastly a mystery to him. One good thing he did notice was that Jonathan and him could walk side by side down the street. People didn't bat their eyes like they used to. "When did they do that?" he asked.

Jonathan giggled and came over to the blond. "When kids like us kept getting into trouble."

Everett rolled his eyes. "We only stole a few horses."

Jonathan added, "And a wagon, and a car, and a few bottles, and-"

Everett covered the man's mouth with his. "Shouldn't be talkin' about your crimes, Mr. lawman."

Jonathan rolled his eyes. "When are you gonna let that go?" He wrapped his arms around the other man's neck. "Listen, think of it like this. As a cop, I can bend the law when it suits me."

Everett rolled his eyes, "So you're every cop ever?"

Jonathan frowned, "Alright you got me there." He smiled, "But think about it, darlin'. I'm a cop!" The black man giggled, "Couldn't have been one of 'em a few decades ago." Jonathan hugged Everett close. "Could you imagine me as a lawman when we first turned?"

The blond rolled his eyes again. "You did try in Alabama," Everett tugged the man's shirt, "and almost got lynched." The memory made his fangs itch. A bunch of hooded men had come to their cabin. Those men didn't get the chance to leave.

Jonathan snickered. "We ate good that night." He kissed Everett's cheek. Jonathan laughed and looked at the red head. "We ate good at Buchenwald too, didn't we E?!"

Eden cheered, "Hell yea, drainin' nazis!" She smashed her wine bottle into the fire, "The family business!"

"Here, here!" Everett began to chug his bottle. Jonathan snorted and buried his face in the pale man's shoulder. Everett offered the bottle to Jonathan.

Hana laughed and collapsed next to Dean. She handed him a glass of water. "Happy, whatever year this is!" Hana opened another bottle of wine. It was chugged down in seconds.

"2007," Dean told her. "It's on the screen." He pointed to the massive TV above the fireplace.

Hana squinted at the flashing numbers on the screen. "I'm not reading all that." She uncorked another bottle and began to chug it down.

Dean laughed and knocked shoulders with the girl. "You're my favorite." Hana was the type of girl Dean would've befriended in his youth. They would have raised hell. The lime green streaks in the asian girl's hair were shining in the fire light. Dean wished he'd dyed his hair more when he was younger. "Especially 'cause you've got cool hair." Hana tossed her chopped locks, which made Dean laugh.

"Hey!" Matthias whined. He was sitting in his wife's lap. "I thought we were friends."

"We are, but your daughter's cooler." Dean looked at Lavender, "Just like mine."

Lavender giggled and leaned against Silas. At least now that her dad was drunk he wouldn't tease her about cuddling with her boyfriend. "Drink your water, dad."

Dean waved his hand dismissively but gulped down his glass.

Matthias turned to Ariyah with a pout. "Am I not cool?"

"You're adorable," Ariyah answered, kissing her husband's forehead. She polished off her bottle and tossed it in the fire.

"Mazel Tov!" Matthias giggled. He kissed his wife.

Silas jumped at the shattering of glass. It was getting too much. Someday he hoped to join in their revelry, but not this year. He stood up and told Lavender, *I need quiet*

Want to be alone? Lavender was still holding his hand.

I wouldn't mind being quiet with you, Silas smiled.

The pair slipped out of the party and into the foyer. It was cooler and quieter here. Lavender hadn't realized her own overstimulation till she was no longer bombarded with it. The chandelier was dim. The ceiling had a honey glow to it. This was the perfect opportunity. Lavender laid down on the floor and looked up at the paintings on the ceiling.

Silas watched her go down. He smiled and laid down next to her. Slowly, he snuck his hand across the tiled floor. His pinky finger tapped Lavender's. Those big golden eyes stared into his own. Without hesitation, she took his hand.

"You're cute," she whispered.

Silas blushed and scooted closer to her.

130

Dean noticed Lavender and Silas wandering off. It didn't concern him. Lavender sometimes needed a breather. Silas didn't seem to be one for parties. He had teased the pair enough for one night. They seemed happy. They were happy. Dean hoped that happiness never soured. He wished his own relationships didn't always fall apart. His mother used to say "Oh hijo, eres demasiado amable." Dean didn't think he was kind though. Just a bleeding heart push over. He opened his home to his ex every time, but he was pissed while doing it. Dean was the best man at Jerry's wedding, but he cried his eyes out afterward. The other failings weren't worth mentioning. Dean hoped Lavender and Silas made it work. He hoped even if they did break up they could stay friends.

"Your brain's loud, dude," Hana poked at the man's forehead.

Dean flinched, "Can you guys read minds?"

"Not clearly. It's all muffled cause I'm fucked up," Hana rested her head against the back of the couch. She pointed to Ariyah. "Má, use your mind powers."

Ariyah giggled, "Do you mean my master degrees?"

"Yeah those," Hana waved her hand.

Dean turned to the oldest woman. "You a shrink?"

"On and off," Ariyah answered. She gently moved Matthias off her lap. The man sat on the ground and placed his head on her lap. Ariyah patted her husband's head. "What is ailing you, love?" She leaned forward, placing two fingers under the man's chin.

Dean cleared his throat. The woman's beauty and voice were not helping his drunken state. "Well ugh...I'm bad at relationships."

Ariyah narrowed her eyes at him.

Dean's breath hitched. He could feel her in his mind. She was poking and prodding. It was like a plumber tapping pipes with a wrench. Eventually she retreated and relaxed into her chair. "I see you try to fix others so you don't have to work on your own needs. You fix others in the hope that they will turn around and fix you. Instead you get taken advantage of." Her face morphed into one of pity.

Dean sniffled then burst into tears.

"Oh, Dean," Matthias crawled over to the other man. "It's okay," he opened his arms.

Dean slipped onto the floor and let himself be hugged. Matt was cool. The same temperature of the room around them. The fire was dying. A slight chill settled in. Dean knew he should've felt revolted by the unnaturalness of it, but he wasn't. Matt was a good guy. A kind man. He'd admitted to Dean he became a doctor because he couldn't stand to see suffering. Those cool fingers were soothing his curls. Dean wept into his shoulder.

"There, there, motek," Matthias cooed. He was still drunk as hell. Dean's sadness was palpable. Matthias was too inebriated to make out the man's muddled thoughts.

Dean wailed, "I just wish she'd stay. I don't even want us to get back together! I just want Lavender to have a mom and dad!" Dean choked on his sobs. "Lavender thinks her mom hates her. She might have abused her and I just left her with her!" Dean cried harder.

"Oh Dean," Matthias looked at his wife and mouthed 'Help'. He continued rubbing the crying man's shoulders.

Ariyah sighed and gestured to Hana. Her youngest daughter rolled her eyes and moved off the couch. Ariyah sat on the other side of Dean and wrapped her arms around him. "Motherhood is complicated. My children didn't trust me at first."

"Hell no we didn't!" Jonathan agreed. He and Everett were now laying on the floor. "Came in and we thought you was gonna be a Combstock clone."

"Thought you was gonna kill us," Everett drawled out. He hugged Jonathan closer. "Was so mad I didn't try to turn you. Thought I was going to lose ya."

The black man kissed the blond's forehead, "Hush." Jonathan then looked at Ariyah, "Eden tried to take a bite out of you."

"I sure did!" The red head was laying across the chaise lounge. Hana had decided to just sit on Eden's prone form. "I didn't know what to expect. America was always painted as a hellscape." She looked back at Hana. "You actually bit us."

Hana rolled her eyes, "I didn't know what you guys were saying!" She laid against the couch.

"Learnin' Vietnamese was hard as hell," Everett bemoaned.

"We did it though!" Matthias cheered. He looked to Hana, "For our little flower."

Dean stopped his crying for a moment. "Your name means flower?"

Hana beamed, "Sure does."

"She's our little sunflower," Ariyah began to cry. "You're so big now."

Dean turned the tables and hugged the woman. "I know how that feels." He recounted, "When Lavender was 3 she wouldn't answer to anything but Flower. Rosemary and I used to call her 'Lavender!', 'Ender!', and she would put her hands on her hips and turn away from us till we called her 'Flower!'."

"So she's always been stubborn?" Matthias giggled.

"She's my daughter," Dean nudged the other man with his elbow. He then looked at Ariyah, "You blink and they're fully grown." Dean wept, "What if she never comes home?!"

"You have 2 more years," the woman comforted. Ariyah kissed the man's forehead. "There's time to mend bonds and heal wounds. Besides, Lavender adores you. I've seen it in her. She loves her mother as well, but…"

Dean sniffled. "I know, I know." He wiped his eyes, "I haven't cried this hard in years!" Dean pulled himself together, "She's coming. Rosemary will be here soon and we can talk. I'll make sure she actually talks!"

Ariyah sighed, "You can't force her, my dear. I may be able to help you get her to talk though."

Dean nodded, "Please. If Lavender can't have a mom, I at least want her to have closure."

Lavender gasped, "Your room's fucking huge!"

Silas giggled. He stayed back in the doorway while the girl explored.

Lavender noticed the walls were a deep maroon. A giant bed sat against the wall. It looked rarely used. Band posters and fairy lights were along the walls. "Wow!" Lavender went to the bookcase. The shelf was twice as big as her own. "You have so much cool stuff!" Books, CDs, DVDs, and knicknacks. All sorts of shinies that Lavender wanted to touch. "What's this?" she picked up the strange spinning top. It was smoothly carved with symbols she'd never seen before.

"It's a dreidel. I made it with mom during my first Hanukkah." Silas touched the carvings on the wood. He then showed Lavender the fragile ornament. "Made this with Jon. He can blow glass. It was terrifying."

Lavender looked at the multicolored ball. It was a red and white swirl. The topper was a glittering gold. "Were you scared you were going to inhale and drink the glass?" Silas placed his forehead on her shoulder.

"You know me so well."

Lavender snorted and quickly placed the glass ball back on the shelf. She noticed some of the music. "So, did you get Hana in the scene or did she get you?"

Silas snorted, "She infected me." He picked up some other albums. "We listen to a lot of different stuff though. Jimmy Eats World, AFI, Fall Out Boy." Silas put those ones back and pulled out more. "Also Brittaney Spears, Salt-N-Pepa, Evanescence."

Lavender giggled. She sang, "One of those things is not like the other~" She looked through more of the music. "Do you like Queen?"

Silas rolled his eyes. "I'm Bi, of course I like Queen!"

"Just had to make sure. Otherwise we would have had to get divorced." Lavender helped Silas reorganize his albums. "My dad got to see them when he was like 12." She remembered the pictures her dad had shown her with glee. "Turns out it was their last concert in the states. His dad had gotten a good job. They saved for a whole year, made the trip, and dad said that was the night he turned gay."

Silas laughed and had to lean against his bookcase for support. "That's hilarious!"

Lavender was laughing as well, "The first time he said that to me I screamed." Lavender felt the box in her pocket. "Oh, yea," she revealed the present. "I got you something."

Silas looked at the gift. He took it gently. Silas went to the bed and sat on the edge.

Lavender watched as he untied the ribbons and undid the paper. He seemed mesmerized by it. The slow process made Lavender want to scream.

Silas swallowed when he saw the note on top of the cardboard jewelry box. He opened it. It read:

I heard if you loved someone enough, you'd be willing to carve out the earth for them. So I did.

       -Love, Lavender

Silas looked up at the blushing girl. He opened the jewelry box. It was the stone Lavender had picked up from the waterfall. The black stone that reflected red in the light. The one she said looked like his eyes. It was carved into the same shape Lavender's stone was. Etched into the rock were leaves and branches. Silas let out a shuddering breath. "Lavender," he whispered in awe.

The girl walked over to him. "I hope you don't mind. I know it's your family tradition, but I wanted to-" Lavender gasped when arms wrapped around her in a flash. She melted into the hug. "You like it?"

Silas laughed, eyes wet with tears. "I love it!" He immediately put on the necklace. Silas wiped his face and asked, "How does it look?"

Lavender placed a hand on his chest. She took the necklace in hand and shifted the stone back and forth. Black and red. Black and red. Lavender leaned in and kissed Silas. "You're beautiful."

Silas bit his lip and looked down at Lavender's necklace. He touched the purple stone. "You're my everything."

Lavender stared into those black eyes. Pools of ink that held so many stories yet to be told. They were like the night sky. Every reflection in them was a star. Lavender kissed him again. After she pulled away, she rested her head on his shoulder. That was when she caught sight of the bed. She turned to Silas. "Hey," she said to get the boy's attention, "Can…can we jump on that?"

Silas looked to the bed then his girlfriend. "Absolutely."

Lavender pumped her fist in triumph. She kicked off her shoes and threw off her sweater. The bed had a load of spring in it. "Whoo hoo!" Each bounce made her smile bigger. Her own bed was too worn down to be jumped on anymore.

Silas joined her. The two tried to reach the ceiling.

"I can do it!" Lavender declared, her fingers were inches away.

Silas used more force and managed to reach the ceiling. "Ha!"

"No fair!" Lavender tried to jump higher. The bed under them groaned in protest.

Silas smiled deviously. He wrapped his arms around Lavender's waist. Besides a surprised squeak, she didn't protest. "I got you, motek!"

Lavender snickered, "Go! Go!"

Silas used more force then he should have. He even extended his hand. Both teens touched the ceiling and when they landed on the bed, it broke. The crash was loud and made them both wince. "Oh shit!" they screamed in unison.

Multiple pairs of running feet stormed down the halls.

"Silas Clearwater-Annora!" roared Ariyah as she crashed through the door.

Dean slid in after her, "Lavender Maria Amos!"

Both teens stood in the center of the demolished bed. They looked at the woody carnage around them. Silas winced, "Sorry, mom."

Everyone took in the damage, then burst into laughter.

The teens were confused, but were happy they weren't in trouble. Silas kept Lavender close. They're necklaces touched and it made him feel warm.

Being back on the reservation was strange. She was alone this time. It was daylight, so no one was worried about the possibility of Combstock intruding. Well, if the vampire decided to, he'd most likely be killed. Lavender was again in the clearing.

3 of the children all began to shift at once. Lavender was told shifting during the day was harder, but not impossible. Elora was 12. Dan was 15. Willow was 14. All 3 were currently clutching at Lavender as their bodies cracked and twisted. They weren't screaming as much as Ethan did. Lavender didn't know if it was because she had practice now, or if they hid their distress better.

The new Den Mother simply let the call carry her. After a few minutes, Lavender was staring at 3 happy wolf pups. Dan was bigger than the two girls. Lavender hugged them all. "I'm so proud of you!" she cheered. The pups all tried to nuzzle her face at once. Lavender giggled, "One at a time!" She gave them each a kiss before standing. She'd made sure to wear some disposable clothes. The trio began sprinting through the softening snow. Ethan shifted and joined them. His transition was now just as smooth as Aunt Lee's.

Uncle Jerry came over to Lavender. He hugged the girl tightly. "Just 3 more to go," he said with a smile. Said 3 children were running after the pups. The parents of the newly shifted joined them.

Lavender nodded. Just Jack, Levi, and Winona to go. "This time felt a lot easier," she admitted. Lavender looked at uncle Jerry. "How are you doing?"

Jerry shrugged. "Been nice having a break. Those Annoras put that bastard out of commission long enough for me to get some sleep."

Lavender chuckled. The pups were rough housing on the edge of the forest. Some of the Elders were leaving to go back and bring out the food. The hole Nana left was palpable. "How has she been?"

Jerry frowned, "She's alive. People have been giving her food." He never realized how similar Rose and Magnolia were. "How are you? I know that situation had to be…a lot."

Lavender shrugged. "I'm okay. I'll be okay."

Jerry nodded. He called to Ethan, "Bubba! Come on back, time to eat!"

Everyone ran back to the cul-de-sac. At 5 Lavender naively thought the circle was all there was. At 10 she learned there were other little neighborhoods. Wasn't until recently she learned that there was so much more. A few stores. The school building. A large building to hold indoor celebrations and meetings. There was even an RV park and restaurant. Lavender never knew about the tourism. For the first time, Lavender had gotten the full tour. The rest of the reservation made the pack's section feel small.

The large table was brought out again. Food was once again laid out on it. Someone even brought fried chicken. Lavender snorted at the sight of it. "Who brought that?" she asked Jerry. Her uncle snorted.

"I think it was Travis," Jerry answered. He did take a piece.

"Mama!" Ethan called. The pups were sitting on someone's porch.

Lavender looked at Jerry.

The man just smiled and gestured to the 7 kids. "Go to your pups."

Lavender took her food and went over to the other kids. "Hi!"

"Hi, mama," they all said in near unison. Some of the kids said it more sarcastically than others. Levi was only a year younger than Lavender. Lavender realized she'd be 18 this year. Next year she'll graduate. Wild.

Lavender stepped onto the porch. The kids made space for her. She sat and Ethan nuzzled the side of her face. Lavender giggled and returned the gesture. Chatter began. School. Possible work. Love.

"So," Willow's voice was teasing, "are you 2?" She pointed between Ethan and Lavender.

The pair gagged at the notion. "No!" Lavender looked at Ethan, "He's like- no!"

Ethan violently shook his head. "She's like my mom, Willow!"

Said girl put up her hands in surrender. "I didn't know! She hasn't been here in 4 years! Even when she was, she never played with us." Willow ate some of her bread. "You always talked about her so…much so I thought." She waved her spoon in the air. "Besides, you're very pretty, Ender."

Lavender snorted, "Thanks Willow." She noticed Jack from the corner of her eye. He'd gone from smiling to solemn in seconds. His dark eyes were staring into his stew. A knowing smile spread across Lavender's face. "I'm about to be an adult. I'm taken. Ethan is a little brother at least and a son at most." She watched as Jack's shoulders untensed. A little grin was on his lips. Lavender dug into her food.

Winona asked Ethan, "Does the shift hurt?" She was nervous to let out her wolf. She was the youngest of the group, only 10. "The bones snapping is." The girl shuddered.

Ethan smiled, "Mine hurt at first, then everything felt fine. Hasn't hurt to shift since then."

That made Winona perk up. She looked at the stew and then everyone else. "I miss River," she whispered. A tear rolled down her face. Death was such a strange thing. Such a final thing.

All the kids paused. The porch went quiet. Lavender took a deep breath. The scent of sadness came off them in waves. She set her food aside. "Come here, Winona." Lavender opened her arms to the girl. Once in her arms, Lavender hugged her. "I won't let that happen again. I won't let anyone ever get stuck again."

Levi began to hum. Dan, the second eldest at 15, joined in. The other kids joined in and began to sing. Some made a beat by tapping the wood of the porch. Others clapped their hands.

Some of the older pack members joined in. They sang from their own seats and porches. Lavender's eyes watered at the sound of the song. It was like something she'd been missing was finally back. The song itself wasn't mournful. It was in fact cheerful. A thumping beat that synced with your heart. Still, it made Lavender want to weep.

Winona looked up at her Den Mother. The girl's brown eyes were full of mirth. Her mourning was forgotten as she was reminded that she wasn't alone. "Sing with us, Mama," she encouraged the teen.

Lavender sniffled and nodded. She joined in the song and harmonized with her people.

Chapter 21

Ethan and Silas sat on the rocky bank while Lavender gathered rocks from the warmed water. The waterfall hadn't frozen like some of the small lakes and ponds around the area. Silas convinced Lavender to wear her thick rubber boots. "She was going to go in bare foot," Silas huffed.

Ethan snorted. Lavender's hands were bare as they reached into the water. "Don't doubt it." She would wrap him in layers, but go out into the snow in a simple jacket. She'd cover Ethan in sunscreen, but never put it on herself. Thankfully Dean would normally catch her and slather her in the white paste too. Those memories made Ethan smile. "She's better at taking care of others than herself."

Silas nodded. "Yea, I noticed." Lavender was holding a stone up to the gray sky. "Thankfully we're here," he bumped shoulders with the boy. The pair chuckled.

"I can hear you!" Lavender called with a smile. The boys straightened up with a start. She giggled. The rocks in her pocket clicked and clacked as she moved. The air around her was crisp. Her fingers were getting stiff. The haul she had was enough. Lavender walked back to the shore.

"Got your rocks off?" Ethan teased.

Lavender pursed her lips to stop a forming smile. "You're too young to be joking about that." The responsible tone of her voice was dampened by the mirth in it. She sat on the rocks and tried to warm her hands.

Ethan took them and flinched. "Geez, Mama!" He quickly rubbed his hands over hers. Lavender's hands were like ice. "You need to wear gloves!" he scolded. Thankfully he had been running hotter since his shift. Lavender was warmed up in minutes.

Silas frowned at the display. He couldn't do that. The cold stuck to his skin. Warmth escaped him. He'd never be able to warm up Lavender. Silas swallowed the bitter taste in his mouth. A rock was placed in his field of vision.

Lavender showed off the stone. "Isn't it cool?" The rock was amber in color. She hoped the rock would get her boyfriend out of his head.

Silas took the rock and shifted it around. "No mosquitoes, no dinosaurs."

Ethan laughed and Lavender joined in.

Silas smiled. He couldn't warm up Lavender's body, but he could light up her face.

A loud grumble made everyone stop.

"Was that your stomach?!" Ethan asked in disbelief. Lavender's cheeks turned red. He got up. "Come on, let's go to Chee Z's." He took the girl's hand and got her on her feet.

"Chee Z's?" Silas asked. He walked with the pair. They all began walking back to the car. Lavender's warmed hand intertwined with his. She pulled his hand up and kissed it.

Ethan gagged at the display. Lavender lightly swatted his arm. He answered, "It's the pizza place in town. Really good." He asked, "Are you hungry?"

Silas smiled, "No, I ate last night."

Ethan frowned. "So, you guys only eat once a day?" His knowledge of vampires was sparse.

Silas mused. "It depends. Mom and dad like to have one big meal. Jonathan and Everett have three throughout the day. Hana and Eden go back and forth."

Ethan was confused. If he had the ability to just eat once a day he would. Eating could be so cumbersome. Granted, he wasn't the best cook. "Why do Jon and Everett do it three times a day?"

Silas shrugged, "It's how they've always done. They lived together for years before Jonathan was born. Everett would drink from him after Jonathan ate a meal." The pair rarely discussed their time being held captive by Combstock; however they happily discussed their time after. "They lived in this little cabin together for 3 years before mom and dad found them."

Lavender furrowed her brow. "Wait, so Everett's had human blood?"

Silas nodded. "Hana and I are the only ones who've never drank human blood." He unlocked the car. Everyone piled in. Once sat inside he continued. "Dad says we're proof we don't actually need it."

"So you're veggie vampires?" Ethan teased.

Silas snorted at the comment. The joke made him think about it though. "I don't think we can be vegetarian in the human sense. Like people are omnivores and choose to take one out. We need blood, there's no alternative to that. The species doesn't matter." He started the car. "You only see us as merciful and vegetarian because you're spared."

A chill went up Ethan's spine. "Jesus Christ dude, what the fuck?"

Silas stared ahead. "I think I got possessed by my dad," he whispered in horror.

They all laughed and headed back into town.

Snow was melting off the trees. The sunlight cut through the gray. It illuminated the world. The temperature jumped to 60. Winter was on the way out. The streets of downtown were sparse, not that they normally were packed. Lavender was indulging in a 'girl's day'. Belle had called and begged her to come out. It had been a week since she'd last seen her friend.

The final 3 pups had shifted, so Lavender felt she was free enough to have some fun. Silas had been visiting nightly. Sometimes staying till she fell asleep. Sometimes leaving while she was still awake. Lavender couldn't explain why, but this felt like the calm before the storm.

There was a family run restaurant everyone in town frequented. It had been around in some way, shape, or form since the town's founding. The food was good. The atmosphere was light. A part of Lavender wished Silas could eat so he could experience places like this. Belle had dragged Carrie out of her house too for this little lunch date. Lavender had driven herself, just in case. The trio were currently sitting by the window. Lavender had finished her meal and was now people-watching.

Belle was going on and on about prom. Color coordination. Limo route. Timing. Pictures. A possible personal photographer. It was a lot and Lavender was zoning out during most of it.

"It's like 5 months away!" Carrie whined. She turned to Lavender. "Tell her!" she begged. The book she'd been trying to finish was long forgotten on the table.

Belle cut in, "I like being prepared!" She looked at the trees. "I'm so happy the snow is melting." Belle leaned forward. "I heard you and Si are getting serious."

Lavender smiled at the mention of Silas. "Yea. Got to meet his family." She noticed a man walking his little dog.

"Are they just as weird?" Carrie asked, drinking her coffee.

"In a cool way, just like Silas." Lavender giggled at some people on the street. It was that time of year where no one knew what to wear. Some people had on t-shirts while others were still in layers. One man had on a sleeveless puffer jacket and shorts.

"Does he have any cute brothers?" Belle giggled. "For Carrie, I'm happily taken!" The blonde showed the promise ring Blake had given her.

Lavender snorted, "Silas is the youngest, everyone else is an adult."

"I don't want to date anyone anyway," Carrie picked up her book. "Stop trying to play matchmaker."

Belle huffed, "You should get a boyfriend, or a girlfriend!" She smiled brightly, "Maybe one of the boys on the rez?"

Carrie groaned, "I told you, I don't want to date, Belle." She shook her head, "I don't see the point of it."

Belle pouted. "I don't want you to be alone forever."

"I'm not alone, I have friends." Carrie used her book to gesture to Belle and Lavender. "That's all I want."

Belle huffed, "Fine, but don't complain when you're dateless for prom."

Carrie smiled, "I won't." She continued reading. "Besides, Jeremy and I are going to go as friends."

Lavender wondered how the pair became friends. Belle probably just latched onto the bookworm and refused to let go. Golden eyes went back to the few people on the street.

One caught her eye.

Lavender's heart stopped. Across the street, going into an alley, was Combstock. His face was clean shaven and his hair was chopped short, but it was Combstock. The man looked healed, though he had a noticeable limp. Lavender dug into her pocket and clutched the knife her father gave her. Slowly, she rose. "I need to do something." Before the other girls could ask, Lavender ran out of the shop. She kept her eyes trained on the man. There wasn't a plan in mind, only an urge to rip the bastard apart.

The alley was one way and Lavender made sure her back was to the opening. She wasn't foolish enough to go all the way inside yet. Lavender flicked the switchblade out.

"Ain't those illegal, little gold?" Combstock lit a cigarette. Although his dead lungs no longer needed air, he did enjoy the burn of nicotine.

"Isn't being a murderer illegal?" Lavender snipped back.

Combstock chuckled. His face still had a few faint scars, but nothing that would turn anyone's head. "You going to kill me with that?"

"I could," Lavender smiled, "You're weak in the sun." She gripped the handle of her blade. "Nearly human, if I recall."

Combstock planted his feet. "I'm still a man."

Lavender glared at him. "And I'm still a girl," she added, "just like Anna."

Combstock's eyes widened. "I see you learned your history."

"Those who don't learn, repeat," Lavender quoted. "You seem to like getting your ass whipped then crying like a bitch and running."

Combstock stomped out his cigarette. "You got a mouth on you." He gave her a sickening smile, "Wonder what else it can do."

Lavender growled, "Bite." She ran up to him, knife in hand. With a slash, she caught his cheek.

"Bitch!" he smashed his fist into her face.

Lavender coughed. The punch knocked the wind out of her, but not the fight. She stabbed him in the stomach. "Yep," Lavender pulled out the knife and stabbed him again.

Combstock slapped her.

Lavender stumbled back. She spat out some blood and lunged again. With all the force in her, she tried to stab him in the heart. Unfortunately, her strength wasn't enough.

"That's the sternum," Combstock laughed. His cold hand grabbed her wrist. While she gasped in surprise, he slammed her into the wall. "Her blood always made me stronger," Combstock smiled, "bet yours is even sweeter." He tilted his head back and bore his fangs.

Lavender struck first. She bit into his neck. Her teeth were blunt but did a decent job. The man howled in shock. Lavender shook her head. Instincts took over. Something changed in her. Something snapped. She felt her teeth sharpen into his skin. Cold unyielding flesh suddenly popped open. A rush of fire went through her. Gushing blood choked her. Lavender kept up her biting and shaking.

Combstock grabbed the girl's curly hair and pulled.

Lavender took a chunk with her when she went. Her back hit the brick with a startling thunk. Her head hit the brick with enough force that her vision blurred. She spat the flesh into Combstock's shocked face. "Told you," she snickered.

Combstock punched her in the face. It knocked the girl to the ground. "You little bitch. You savage little c-"

"Lavender!" Belle called from the entrance of the alleyway.

"I'm calling 911, asshole!" Carrie warned. She blew the whistle her mother gave her.

"Get out of here!" Lavender warned them. She tried to stand but her vision swam.

Combstock raced out of the alleyway. He barreled past the two girls and down the street.

"Fuck!" Lavender tried to get up but fell back down.

"Lavender!" Belle ran to the girl, "Holy shit!" She helped the other girl up. "Call an ambulance!" she ordered Carrie.

Lavender shook her head, "No, no. I need to go home." She pushed past her friends and raced to her car. She could hear the other girls calling after her but didn't stop.

She needed to get her dad.

Rosemary sat across from Dean. She hadn't seen him in years. Being in the same room as him was so surreal. She'd run and come back to this house so many times. It hadn't changed. It always looked the same.

The house.

The town.

…Dean.

Her handsome and kind Dean. A part of Rosemary was so sad she never took his last name. They never got married, not legally. A ceremony on the reservation but nothing on paper. They didn't have the money at the time. Dean had been perfectly fine with it. He was just happy to be with her. His warm brown eyes and curly hair. Rosemary would fall asleep petting that mane.

"Thanks for getting me," Rosemary finally said. She took a sip of her water. "I know that drive from Seattle is a bitch."

Dean shrugged, "No problem." He drank his tea. Getting drunk or even tipsy around Rosemary wasn't ever a smart idea. Lavender didn't need to come home to a fight…or new sibling. "Thanks for coming."

"Yea," Rosemary looked at the bay window. "Can't believe you kept those." She pointed to the sea glass wind chimes. "I threw mine away ages ago."

Dean frowned, "Lavender helped make them." His voice sounded small, even to his own ears.

A twinge of pain went through Rose. "She did?"

Dean nodded, "She got the sea glass, remember?" The memories were still so fresh. "She was so proud she found all those pieces." He saw flashes of memories. Lavender's little smile and sand covered hands. "She helped you wire them together too. I still have her fishing pole."

Rosemary grimaced, "Why would you keep that?"

"Cause I missed my child and never knew when I'd see her again," Dean bit back. He looked at the table. Starting a fight wasn't smart.

Rosemary took a deep breath. She swallowed. "Dean."

Dean raised a hand, "I don't want to hear it." Any excuse she gave wouldn't soothe the ache in his chest. He wished he'd made a report. Wish he'd fought harder to find them. "Lavender's home, that's what matters now."

Rosemary frowned. "This isn't her home."

142

Dean chuckled. "From what I heard, this is her first home in a long time."

Rosemary slammed her fist on the table. "Not everyone can get a house, Dean."

"And not everyone has a house they can always come back to," Dean spat back. Guess it was going to be a fight. "I told you there's a spare bedroom and-"

"I don't need your fucking charity!"

"But our daughter did!"

Rosemary sat back. She felt hot. Her face was probably scarlett. "I did my best."

Dean hissed, "Like you did with Jerry?"

Rosemary's eyes went wide. "Who-"

"He told me eventually," Dean's lip quivered, "Saw shifting for the first time. How could you do that?"

Rose began to cry. "Fuck you, Dean."

"Have you ever apologized for that?" Dean asked, "Or in general?"

Rose stood, "This was a mistake."

"You're going to run away again?" Dean snapped. "I'm glad I didn't tell Ender you were coming. Lord knows you've done enough damage to her!"

"Excuse me?!" Rose rounded the table. "You think you're so fucking great? Got this house and cushy job and you think you're the big man don't you? Not around for 4 years and you think you know everything?"

"How could I be there when you took off?" Dean wouldn't cry. He was going to cry his eyes out later, but not now. "I talked to a psychiatrist yesterday. A really smart and kind woman who's a mother of 5. 5 kids who she adores. 5 kids who all have traumas we can only pray to never get. She loves her kids. She makes sure she says it and acts like it."

Rosemary rolled her eyes, "I'm glad the rich lady you met has the ability to love her children enough."

Dean stood. "You think you need to be rich to love your children?! My mom and dad were dirt fucking poor but they always made sure I knew I was loved. It's the little things, Rose! It's keeping the things she made!" Dean pointed to the windchimes. "It's telling her, saying it out loud. It's watching a show with her on the couch, even after a long day of work. It's listening when she needs you. It's hugging her when she's crying." Dean began to hyperventilate. "Rose, if you'd heard her scream. If you'd seen her face. If you heard how she begged to know why you don't love her-"

"I never heard my mother say she loved me! I never got any apology! She never kept what I made, never showed any pride in what I did!" Rosemary snapped.

"So you're okay with being your mother?!"

Rose stepped back. The words smacked her in the face. "I'm not my mother."

"You sure?" Dean moved toward her. "Cause all I'm hearing is you want to do to Lavender what your mother did to you. All I'm hearing is you want her to hurt like you have. All I'm hearing is you don't love her."

Rosemary smacked Dean. "You know nothing, Dean Amos."

With a burning cheek, Dean smiled. "That's the exact same thing your mother said," he pointed out the faded scratches on his cheek, "And did."

Rosemary gave him a horrified look. Tears streamed down her face. "I know I'm a fuck up. I know I'm a terrible mother!" Rage filled her again. "You don't have to rub it in!" She began swiping at the man.

Dean grabbed her wrists. For the first time, he stopped her. "I never turned you away! I never made you leave! I never made you sign papers! I only wanted us to be happy. I wanted Lavender to be happy. We were so happy, Rose. Do you remember?" Dean was sobbing now. "We were so happy. Do you remember those first 3 years? After Lavender was born. We were so happy. What happened to us, Rosie? Why did you leave?"

"I don't know!" Rosemary screamed. "I don't know!" She wept. "I didn't want Lavender to feel…" She coughed and stopped struggling. The weight of regret slammed into her. Rose freed her arms and wrapped them around Dean. "I didn't want to be my mom," she cried. "I didn't want to, I don't want to." Rose clutched at the man's back. "She was here, you wouldn't leave."

"I can't leave, you know that." Dean growled, "You remember what the cops were like before me. You remember what they did to us as kids. You want others to live through that?" Dean would never forget how patrol cars would wait outside the reservation. How one step outside of it could lead to being slammed against the hood of a cop car.

Even Dean, someone who wasn't indigenous, wasn't safe from their abuse. He remembered being called every slur under the sun by cowardly men hiding behind a badge. To those bastards, anything brown was the enemy. "Fontaine was a monster. I'm not going to let another one of him get power."

Fontaine. That was a name Rosemary hadn't heard in forever. She laughed through her tears, "You knocked that bastard on his ass." She sniffled and buried her face in his shoulder.

Fontaine, the old sheriff, was truly a two headed snake. The man had won the election in the 80's. He'd platformed himself as a kind man. Someone who saw and would treat everyone as equals. That all changed when he got the title of sheriff. For a decade, he had the town in his grip. Folks were too afraid to run against him. Fear did things to people. Especially when they adopted the saying 'better him than me'.

Rose remembered Dean winning the title of sheriff. It was on a dare. A man's audacity knew no bounds and Fontaine was a full blooded man. They'd been having a celebration. A powwow. Dancing, eating, singing. Fontaine and his gang had come in like a bat out of hell. Batons raised and guns posed.

"Son of a bitch thought he had a chance against me," Dean chuckled. The deal they made was if Dean could knock Fontaine out, Fontaine would make him sheriff. The 18 year old sent the racist prick to the hospital. Fontaine was a known liar, but in this case, a deal was a deal. Dean had legitimately won the position every election after. Fontaine disappeared. Probably too ashamed to stick around.

"You always wore those baggy shirts. Made you look small." Rose fell in love with Dean that day. The boy she'd met while running in the woods had knocked out the man that'd been making her people miserable for years. "You were so brave."

"I was stupid," Dean rested his cheek on the top of her head. "He underestimated me though."

Rose looked up at him. "You've barely aged." She touched the couple of lines that'd formed on his face. "Black really doesn't crack, huh?"

Dean snorted. He wanted to kiss her. He wanted to ask her to move back. Then he remembered the last time…and the time before that…and that…and that…

Dean shook his head and stepped away. They weren't good for each other. They made the worst come out of each other. He had to remind himself she'd just slapped the shit out of him not 5 minutes ago. "Rose…"

The front door slammed open and Lavender staggered in, "Dad!" She noticed her mom and her blood ran cold. "What are you doing here?"

"Ender!" Dean raced to his daughter. He took her face in his hands. "Flower what happened?!" She was covered in blood. Her mouth. Her clothes. Her knuckles. Her eye was black and her lip was busted.

"Most of it isn't mine," Lavender explained, "Listen, Combstock, I saw him in town and-"

"Combstock?!" Rosemary went to her daughter. "Why do you know that name?!" She glared at Dean, "Why does she know that name?!"

"Would you let me talk?!" Lavender roared. She pushed past her fretting parents. They made the air too thick. Lavender told her mom, "Listen, Nana told me about Combstock. He's here for me. He's killing people. Caught up, good?" She turned to her dad, "Anyway, I saw him while I was out, got in a fight, ripped a chunk out of his neck, stabbed him a bunch. Lost the blade by the way, sorry. Anyway, he's weak and bleeding. If we can get the pack to sniff him out, I can call Silas and-"

Dean took his daughter's face in his hands. "Flower, stop!" The girl was a mess. He tugged her over to the sink.

Lavender frowned. She was panting and looked at him in disbelief. "Dad, we could get him now!"

"Yes, we, not you!" Dean sat her down at the table. He grabbed a towel. Her eyes were dilated unnaturally. He checked her teeth. Her canines were longer. What the hell? There was also something sweet beneath the scent of blood and sweat. All these things made Dean worry more. He checked the back of her head and found blood. "Jesus, Ender. What the hell were you thinking?!"

"They're weak in sunlight!" Lavender defended. She hissed as the towel was pressed to her wound.

"Weaker," Dean hissed, "Weaker, Ender. They can still fight. We need to go to the hospital."

"Just call Mr. Annora or Silas. I can drink their blood."

Dean was bewildered, "What?!"

"Vampire blood can heal!" Lavender blinked, her head was still swimming. How did she get home? Lavender couldn't remember driving. Why was her mom here?

"You've been taking their blood!" Rosemary screeched in horror. She grabbed her daughter's face. "Have you lost your mind! Their blood is poisonous!" Rose glared at Dean. "You've been letting her run around with leeches?!"

Dean growled, "Matt's a good man. Silas has been a good boyfriend to her-"

"You're dating one?!" Rosemary buried her hands in her own hair and tugged. "I can't fucking believe this!" Rose began to pace, "I leave you alone for half a year and your head first in this!"

"Maybe I wouldn't be head first if I had a mom who'd actually explained shit!" Lavender roared. "If she didn't throw me out when all I wanted was some fucking answers!" She threw the salt shaker at her mother. "If I had a mom who wasn't a selfish bitch!"

Dean scolded her, "Lavender stop!" At this point Lavender was going to pass out. They needed to do something, but not this!

"You always defend her!" Lavender cried. "Why do you always defend her?!" She pulled away from her dad. "Why is she here?" Lavender sobbed. "She didn't want me anymore. She doesn't love me."

"That's not true!" Rosemary defended. "That's not true at all. I do love you! I tried to keep you away from this damn place. I didn't want you involved."

"Then maybe you shouldn't have thrown me out!" Lavender screamed. "You threw a duffel bag at me and told me to find out for myself. Congratulations, mom, I did!" The girl coughed. Blood sprayed from her mouth. Her back hurt. That collision with the brick wall was settling in. Adrenaline was rising and falling within her. Blocking and revealing her pain. "I hate you!" she seethed. "You're just like Nana. You didn't want to protect me! You just wanted me to be your clone!"

Rosemary's lip quiver. "Lavender," she began. Her throat closed as despair choked her. "I-" Rose looked at Dean. The man's head hung in shame. He was gripping the towel. It was drenched with their daughter's blood. "Let me help you," she begged. Rose reached out to her little girl.

Lavender slapped her mother's hands away. "You've done enough," she hissed. Lavender ran out the house.

"Ender!" Dean screamed. He grabbed his shoes and started to run after her. "Flower, stop!"

Rosemary followed. She was faster than Dean. The wolf in her was roaring. Rose stamped it down. She wanted that part of her to be silent. Being away from the pack had put it to sleep. Being here though, its eyes were opening. The scent of her child's blood was making it howl.

Dean pushed through the burn in his chest. He pushed through the trees and scratching branches. Lavender was bleeding enough to leave a trail. A stark red path on the melting snow. Good for him since he'd lost sight of her. He was starting to lose sight of Rose. They were so fast.

Lavender screamed. A blood curdling scream. Her legs fell out from under her. The ground was hard and made her wounds scream. Her body was throbbing in pain. Something was broken. Many things, most likely. The forest began to scream with her. Cracking branches and running feet. The vibrations were rumbling against her temple. Something was coming and fast. It wasn't her mother or father. The slush on the ground was helping the ache in her. In fact, most of the pain was numbing. The edges of Lavender's vision were going black. Was she going to die?

"Lavender!"

Said girl blinked her bleary eyes. A cool hand touched her cheek. Lavender smiled up at Silas. "Hi," she croaked out.

"What happened?!" Silas lifted her into his arms. He cradled her in his lap. There was so much blood on her. It wasn't all hers, but the fact some of it was, made him distressed. Silas bore his fangs and punctured his wrist. "Here, here!" he urged, pressing his wrist to her lips.

Lavender giggled in delirium. "I already had blood today." She grunted when Silas forced his wrist against her mouth.

"Drink!" he demanded.

Lavender groaned but did. Only a couple sips.

"Get the fuck away from her!" Rosemary barreled into the boy. Her jaw was already cracking into a maw.

Silas kicked the woman. "Fuck off!" He tried to get to Lavender. The woman tackled him again. Silas was furious. He turned and buried his fangs into her arm. He was weaker in the sun, but he did have one thing.

Venom.

Rosemary howled in pain.

Dean broke through the trees. He saw his daughter on the ground. Silas was there though. Rosemary was thrashing against the snow. "What did you do?!" Dean went to Rose. The veins in her arm were turning black. Her eyes rolled back so far they were white.

"She wasn't…Lavender's," Silas clutched at his girlfriend. "I-"

"Make it stop!" Dean demanded.

Silas didn't know why Dean cared about this stranger. "Who is she?"

"She's Lavender's mom!" Dean cried.

Silas's eyes widened in horror. "Oh shit."

Chapter 22

"Silas, what did you do?!" Eden shook the boy.

Silas wept. His face was stained with bloody tears. "She wasn't letting me help Lavender. I panicked. She was strong. I didn't-"

"Leave him be, Eden!" Ariyah pulled her oldest daughter away. She wrapped her youngest in her arms. "I know you had good intentions, my boy. Hush now."

Silas clung to his mother. "I'm sorry. I'm sorry."

Ariyah kissed the top of his head. "Go to your love, stay in your room. We'll get you when her mother awakens."

Silas choked on his sobs. He nodded. The boy raced to his room.

Ariyah sighed and turned to Eden. "What is wrong with you?"

The red head hissed. "What's wrong with me?!" she threw her hand up in rage. "We're going to have to move again! They'll bring their pitchforks and torches. Those hounds will be on us and-"

"E, stop," Hana hugged her sister. "Stop, please stop." She soothed the panicking girl. "Dean understands. Lavender has more sway with the pack then that woman. We're fine. We're going to be fine."

Eden turned and hugged Hana tight. "I can't…I can't see the fire again," she wept.

Ariyah left her girls to their consoling. She went to Matthias's lab. It was quiet, which was good. The door was unlocked, another good sign. She could hear the men talking on the other side of the door.

"When will she wake up?" Dean asked.

Matthias answered, "A few minutes to an hour. It really depends on her. We can move her out of the lab, if you want. I think waking up in a bed would be better than in here."

Dean remembered how Rose could wake up swinging. Better to spare his friend a black eye or, more likely, Rose a broken hand. He shook his head, "No, leave her be. As long as someone's here, it should be fine."

Ariyah opened the door fully. She took stock of everything. The woman, Lavender's mother, was laying on the steel table. She was hooked up to the blood transfusion machine. The woman and Lavender shared a face, but not much else. "She's more of you," Ariyah mused while looking at Dean.

The man shrugged, "If you say so." His shoulders relaxed a fraction. "Just glad your little cobra's bite wasn't that deadly." Dean had no idea how he would've dealt with Magnolia if Rosemary died.

Matthias frowned. "True, it is a good thing Silas is young and unpracticed." He checked Rosemary's vitals again. "The older we get, the worse it is."

"Ages like a fine wine?" Dean joked, hoping to cut through his own anxiety.

Matthias nodded, "Exactly." He went to his work table. Papers and diagrams littered the surface. "You said Lavender fought Combstock."

Dean nodded. "Her plan wasn't bad but," he gestured to Rosemary, "Also she was all beat up."

"We should be grateful she was not bit by him."

Dean shuddered, "Why's that?"

Matthias tried to find a way to explain the danger without causing hysterics. "Combstock is over two centuries old. Silas's venom would have taken at least an hour to be fatal, Combstock's could take minutes."

Dean's eyes widened in horror. "How…" he looked at Rosemary. Just hooking her up to the machine took 5 minutes.

"The venom would have to be sucked out," Ariyah explained. She sat on top of Matthias's desk. "If none of us were there…"

Dean looked between the pair in disbelief. "Holy shit," he whispered. Dean's leg bounced with anxiety. "You two smoke?"

Matthias frowned. "As a doctor, I do not condone smoking."

Dean snorted, "As a friend?"

Matthias smiled, "Are you okay with menthols?"

Silas stared down at Lavender's prone form. He couldn't tear his eyes away from her chest. The sight of it rising and falling was so minute. Silas slipped a finger under her nose. Faint air touched his skin.

Silas sighed in relief and laid down next to her. His ears hyper focused on her heartbeat. The steady rhythm calmed his own. Silas rubbed the necklace she'd made for him. "I love you," he whispered to her. "I'm sorry I bit your mom." Silas tugged lightly at the black gem. He stared up at the ceiling. "I'll say this again when you're awake."

Silas nibbled on the stone. He turned to Lavender. Her face was so placid. Peaceful. Silas looked at his ceiling fan again. He let the necklace fall from his mouth. "I really love you. I know I say it, but words don't feel enough. Like it feels fake. I don't want to say it feels fake though cause then you might think I don't mean it, but I do." His lip quivered. "I'm bad at this. I was never good at it but being like this…" Silas blinked the blood tears out of his eyes. "I feel like you're always in danger when you're with me. I know that's dumb though. I just hate how powerless I feel. There's no right answer. I can't keep you 100% safe, whether I'm away from you or near you."

Silas covered his eyes with his hands. "If you die I'd…" A warm hand was laid on his chest. Silas jumped in shock. He whipped his head toward Lavender. The girl's eyes were cracked. "How long have you been awake?" Silas asked. His voice was barely a whisper.

149

Lavender's voice was rough. It was like she'd swallowed sand. "A while," she croaked out.

Silas frowned. "I'll get you some water." He moved to sit up, but her hand gripped his shirt. Lavender was shaking. Silas could hear her breath becoming more labored.

"Stay," Lavender begged.

Silas immediately fell back. He gently pulled Lavender to him. Her head rested on his shoulder. Black curls tickled at his nose. Silas smoothed them down. Those clutching fingers relaxed. They stayed over his heartbeat, but no longer shook. Silas inhaled deeply. Lavender smelled calm. No longer the bittersweetness of illness. No longer the spicy scent of pain.

Lavender nuzzled into his neck. Silas was sniffing her, which she was used to at this point. Lavender draped her arm over his chest. While she knew he'd stay, because she asked, it didn't hurt to have some reassurance. Cool arms wrapped around her in turn. "You're a dork," she whispered.

"Cause I talk to myself?" he asked.

Lavender frowned. She moved to look at him. "Because you're worried about protecting me, as if it's not a two way street." Lavender laid back down. She shifted so she was half laying on him. His coolness was a comfort, like her warmth was to him. "You don't think I'm scared to lose you? I've thought about letting Combstock take me. That if I did, you all would be safe." Silas squeezed her tighter. Lavender chuckled, "I know you'd all come after me though. I think about how you all were fine till I came along." Lavender furrowed her brow. "But that's bullshit too. Because none of this is our fault, Silas. We didn't ask for this. Didn't seek it out. It just happened. Like a hurricane or the economy crashing."

Silas snorted. "All I can think about is Combstock spinning like a ninja star around wrecking things."

Lavender burst out laughing. It hurt to do with her sore throat but it didn't stop her. "See!" She leaned up and kissed him. "That's why I love you!" Lavender scooted up so she could press her forehead to his. "You make me happy. You make me stronger. You make me feel safe."

Silas leaned up and kissed her. "You make me feel safe too."

Rosemary felt like a train had hit her. She felt cold. It was cold. Where was she? Rosemary turned her head. Which was an effort in itself. A flash of silver made her realize she was on an examination table. Rosemary groaned and tried to sit up.

"Relax."

Rosemary started and turned toward the voice. She hissed in pain. Her eyes squeezed shut in agony. There were footsteps coming toward her. Rosemary desperately tried to open her eyes, but the ache was too sharp. Cool hands soothed her fiery nerves. Those talented fingers massaged her back into relaxation. Rosemary sighed and was finally able to open her eyes. The woman above her was gorgeous.

Luscious brown curls and emerald green eyes. The woman's smile was kind. Rosemary nearly fell for it. Then she noticed the woman barely had a scent. Her skin was like marble. Not a pore in sight. Her fingers though, were room temperature. Rosemary felt her body lock up in terror. "What do you want from me?" she growled.

Ariyah rolled her eyes. "Retract your fangs. I want nothing from you." She walked to Matthias's desk.

Rosemary watched as the woman began to make something. "What is that?" she asked. The woman was humming to herself. Her voice was beautiful. Deep and lulling. Rosemary shook her head. She couldn't fall under this thing's spell.

Ariyah could hear her movements. "Try and lie still. The venom is out of you, but you're still healing from the effects."

Rosemary paused, "Venom?"

Ariyah finished making the tea. She went back to the woman. "Yes, our poison. Thankfully, Silas is young. It has not had time to…how do you say? Ah yes! 'Age, like fine wine'." Ariyah snorted thinking of Dean. She lengthened her fang and punctured her finger. She squeezed a drop of her blood into the mixture. "Here," she offered the concoction to the woman.

Rosemary sneered, "I'm not drinking that."

Ariyah shrugged. "If you would like to heal the old way, then fine. Though it will take weeks, even months. During that time, you will probably have to stay here and-"

"Alright, alright!" Rosemary rolled her eyes. "I'll take it."

Ariyah smiled, "Wonderful." She helped the injured woman drink. "You're lucky. Silas is still young, his blood would take a couple gulps to heal. Ours only takes a drop."

Rosemary finished the drink. "Why the rest of the stuff then?" She gestured her head to the cup.

"Oh," Ariyah giggled, "That's to help your throat."

Rosemary felt a wave of relief hit her. She sighed in joy. The woman helped her sit up fully. "I guess…thanks." Rosemary jumped off the table. She stretched and her spine popped. "Where's Dean and Ender?"

"Dean is currently smoking his stress away and your daughter is with my son in his room."

Rosemary hissed, "Seriously?!" She made to leave but Ariyah stood in her way. "Move! My daughter-"

"Is fine. Lavender didn't inherit her parents' promiscuity," Ariyah teased.

Rose scoffed, her cheeks tinted pink. "Fuck you, lady."

Ariyah made a show of looking Rosemary up and down. She then smiled. Her eyebrow raised flirtatiously. "Ask again when you're fully recovered."

Rosemary balked. Her face turned even redder, this time not from anger. "Shut up!" she rebuffed and pushed past the woman. The woman let her go but followed close behind. "This place is dark as night!" Rose touched the wall.

Ariyah giggled. "Well, our nature…"

Rosemary rolled her eyes, "Oh hush!" She made it to what looked like a living room. There were others in it. Two men and two women. "Hi," Rose greeted awkwardly.

"Holy shit, Lavender's a clone!" the black man cackled.

"The resemblance is uncanny," the red head mused.

"She's got straight hair though," the asian girl pointed out. "Also lighter."

"And cold eyes," the blond added.

"Fuck you!" Rosemary snapped. The 4 jumped in surprise.

"So that's where the temper comes from," the red head quipped.

Rose growled.

"Children, please," Ariyah placed a hand on Rose's shoulder, "Calm yourself."

Rose pointed at them, "They-"

"Are young," Ariyah finished.

"I'm over a hundred years old," Jonathan huffed.

Ariyah raised her brow. "Yet you still act like the young man I met all those years ago." In a flash she was by her son's side and ruffled his curls.

"Ma!" the man whined. Jonathan pressed himself into Everett's side to try and escape. The blond laughed at his attempt.

"You never ruffle my hair anymore!" Hana whined. She immediately regretted her outburst when her mother's hands began shaking through her hair. "Wait! Wait! I didn't mean it!" Hana giggled and pushed at her mother's arms.

Ariyah laughed but quit her attack. She turned to Eden.

The redhead sneered, "Don't even think about it!"

Ariyah rolled her eyes. She teased, "What is the saying? Oh yes. No fun!"

Eden snorted and stuck her tongue out at her mother. Ariyah returned the childish gesture, which only made Eden giggle.

Ariyah came back to Rosemary, "Come, Dean is outside." She guided the stunned woman out of the sitting room.

"The fuck was that?" Rose asked when she thought the 'kids' were out of ear shot.

"What?" Ariyah paused at the stairs. The room around her was silent so she pushed her ears past it. Up the halls and through a door. Silas and Lavender were laughing. Ariyah relaxed. "Lavender is awake. I think you and Dean should speak first." She took the woman's hand, so she wouldn't be tempted to run up the steps. "Come," Ariyah urged.

Rosemary stared at the woman's hand in hers. It was unnaturally smooth and cool. She frowned but let herself be led.

Chapter 23

Dean laid in the grass. The stars were beautiful. His cigarettes were snuffed out. They were in a little pile on top of the handkerchief Matt apparently carried. Speaking of said vampire. Matt was laying beside him and was currently going on about Copernicus.

"It is incredible he was able to hypothesize correctly. Imagine what he would think of the moon landing!" Matthias giggled, "Him and Galileo would have been good friends."

"You know, I always forget you're old as fuck," Dean teased.

Matthias rolled his eyes, "Oh, please, Dean. Fucking is far older than I am."

Dean laughed. "You can't say stuff like that with your accent!"

"Why not?!"

"Cause it's too funny!" Dean snorted and wiped happy tears from his eyes. He turned and saw Matt was giving him the snootiest face known to man. Dean screamed, laughed and turned away from the other man. He could hear Matt laughing as well. "Dude!" Dean snorted, "What is wrong with you?!"

Matthias giggled, "I'm almost 700 years old."

Dean shook his head. "I can't think about that too much or my brain will explode."

Matthias frowned. "I am a good doctor, but I can not fix exploding brains."

Dean lightly smacked the other man's shoulder. "Cut it out." He sighed and covered his eyes with his arms.

Matthias felt Ariyah coming closer. "Ah, she's awake." The vampire smiled at Dean. "Ready?"

Dean was utterly confused. "What?"

"Dean!"

Said man flailed into uprightness. "Rose?!" Dean scrambled to his feet. Unfortunately he was knocked back down again by Rosemary. The pair hit the cold ground with a harsh thump. Dean groaned in pain.

"Sorry, sorry!" Rosemary sat up. She could hear the two vampires snickering at them. Rosemary pursed her lips.

Dean yelped when he was pulled to sit up again.

"Come on, let's get Lavender and go," Rosemary urged. She glared at the vampiric couple. "These guys are fucking weird," she whispered.

"You are not the only one with big ears, little pitcher," Ariyah teased.

Rose huffed and stood, dragging Dean up with her. "Just take us to our daughter."

Dean shrugged Rosemary off. "Don't be shitty." He rubbed his face. The spark of joy at her awakening now felt like a brand of despair. "Come on, let's get Lavender and head home."

"You can stay the night," Matthias offered.

Dean smiled, "I appreciate it, Matt, but..." He quickly glanced at Rose. Matt gave him a tight lipped smile and didn't push.

The drive home was weird.

Lavender sat in the backseat. Seeing her mom and dad next to each other was jarring. Rose was quiet as they pulled up. Lavender wondered if she'd notice the new window. If she'd already commented on it. The teen got out of the car and followed her parents inside.

Dean grimaced. The blood Lavender tracked in had dried onto the hardwood and tile. He noticed Rose was heading to his room…their old room. It was like she was on autopilot. Lavender noticed the blood too and started for the broom closet. "Flower," Dean redirected her to the stairs. "I've got it. Why don't you shower first?" Her gold eyes stared at him in disbelief. "It's okay," he reassured.

Lavender stepped back and took a deep breath. She headed upstairs. The faint sounds of water and rummaging in the closet eased her. The blood on her shirt had dried and encrusted itself onto her skin. A wave of disgust washed over her. How could Silas stand to hold her? She threw her stuff in the hamper and went to the bathroom.

Dean waited till he heard the shower kick on before leaving the kitchen. He stalked into his bedroom and found Rose standing in the center of it. She was eyeing the fishing pole.

"You weren't kidding," Rose chuckled. She noticed that all the pictures of them were gone throughout the house. She'd hoped maybe Dean had kept one in his room. There wasn't one. Only Lavender. It was a photo strip that hung over his bed like a cross. Jealousy was an ugly feeling. Especially jealousy over your own child. Rose tried to shake it off. "The bed's the same," she noticed the messy sheets.

Dean opened and closed his hands. "Your room's still made up." Rose finally turned to him. Her face was forlorn. "I have spare sheets if-"

"Really, Dean?" Rosemary felt her lip quivering. She bit it. Getting back together wasn't an option, but they could at least have something. Couldn't they?

Dean felt his chest tighten. "Rose…" he steeled his nerves. Ariyah's words played over and over in his mind. "You can't sleep in here." To his surprise, she went without a fight. He waited for her to ascend the stairs before releasing a breath he hadn't known he'd been holding. Dean covered his face with his shaky hands. He shook his head and went back to the kitchen. He hoped he'd be able to get at least some of the blood out of the wood.

Lavender felt lighter after her shower. She leisurely got dressed and brushed her teeth. After drawing a face in the mirror, she wrapped a towel around her hair. It'd take awhile to dry, but she could at least read before bed. When she opened the door, a puff of steam escaped into the hallway. Lavender headed down the hall. Something smelled off. She stopped at the door.

With another deep inhale, it clicked. Someone was in there. In her room. Heart pounding, Lavender slowly opened the door. She expected a threat.

Instead, Rosemary was on her bed.

Lavender sighed. A part of her ached. She didn't know the smell of her own mother. She didn't recognize the woman's presence.

Rosemary looked up. "Who did you think it was?" She noticed how Lavender's eyes were welling.

Lavender shrugged and wiped at her face. She scrunched her hair in the towel.

Awkwardly, Rose asked, "You're using your father's soap?"

Lavender shrugged again. "I like it. Plus, I didn't have time to grab my own."

The dig made Rose wince. "Lavender…" she mulled over her words. None of them felt like enough. Words felt meaningless. Empty. "I shouldn't have-" Rosemary wanted to scream. She didn't know how to express her regret. Didn't know how she could make Lavender understand. "I'm sorry, Lavender." It was the only thing she could manage. It didn't feel enough.

Lavender frowned. The towel landed heavy on her floor. "Why are you sorry?"

Rosemary frowned. "What?"

"Why are you sorry?" Lavender asked again. "I need to hear why, mom," she hissed the title. Like the word burned her. In a way, it did. "Why are you sorry?"

Rose dreaded the burn that came with tears. She hated the way her throat would tighten and her nose would clog. "Because I hurt you," she sobbed.

"Then why'd you do it?" Lavender pushed, "Why did you do it?"

Rose cried, "Because I'm a bad mom!"

"No!" Lavender stamped her foot. "No, you don't get to do that! Tell me why!"

"Because you chose this place over me! Everyone, everyone has always chosen this place over me! My mom! Dean! You! I only had you-" Rosemary sobbed. "All I had was you." She hiccuped, "And you didn't want me either." Rosemary felt her body shaking. She wrapped her arms around her stomach. "I was so scared you'd hate me like everyone did here. That they'd make you hate me." Rose bent forward and buried her nose in Lavender's blanket. "I wasn't what my mother wanted. I was always her disappointment. Always the pack disappointment. I-I…"

Lavender frowned. Tears were streaming down her face. She looked at the windchimes in her window. "I don't hate you." She sat on the edge of her bed. "I thought you hated me. Since I was 13, I was convinced you hated me."

Rose looked up at her. "Why?"

Lavender laughed in disbelief. "You stopped saying I love you. You stopped taking interest. You stopped helping me with my hair. You stopped listening. You just…One day I had a mom, the next I had a roommate." Lavender looked at her hands. "I would stay up at night and wonder why. What did I do? Why didn't you love me anymore? I have your face. I have your voice. I was good, you ignored me. I was bad, you ignored me. You were all I had and you acted like you didn't want me."

Rosemary sat back up and scooted closer to her daughter. "My mother- Nana, wanted to take you. Wanted me to leave you here."

Lavender looked at her in shock. "Why?"

Rose sniffled. "Ethan got hurt that summer, remember?"

Lavender nodded. "Yea, he fell off the dirt bike."

Rose continued, "When you were comforting him, you were using a Den Mother's call."

Lavender's eyes widened. She didn't remember that part. The memory of Rose and Dean going to the reservation without her was clear. The memory of Rose coming back without Dean was clear. Being thrown into the car. Driving until the sun came up. All of those memories were clear. "I did?"

Rose nodded. "Nana, Jerry…everyone- They got so excited. Mother was about to go into menopause. Her call was growing weaker. I…they didn't want me and I didn't want them. So there you were, the youngest born female. Not even into puberty and already able to soothe and call." Rosemary wiped her eyes. "The elders, my mother, everyone begged me to leave you there. That I could go be free. That even leaving you with Dean would be fine. They just wanted-"

"Me, but not you," Lavender finished.

Rosemary looked off in shame. "I…I didn't realize I was-"

"Showing your resentment?" Lavender finished again.

Rose buried her face in her hands. "I- I'm sorry, Lavender. I never…I never wanted to be like her."

Lavender didn't know how to feel. She didn't know what to do next. Her universe was flipped on its head. Insecurity. Anxiety. Pain. Lavender looked at her mother. This broken woman. The weight of the world had cracked Rose. Lavender wouldn't crack. They could fix this. It wouldn't be easy. It would take time, but there was a chance. Lavender took that chance. "I want a hug," she admitted.

Rose opened her arms. It hit her that she hadn't done that in years. The guilt of that realization was soul crushing. To her shock, Lavender actually crawled into them. She wrapped her arms around her child. Had it really been 4 years since she'd done this? It felt like it. When was the last time they'd talk? This entire time, she hadn't even tried to talk to her daughter. She'd left her girl to the wolves of the world. Rosemary buried her nose into Lavender's curls. Underneath the soap and shampoo, was Lavender. Lavender's floral scent. Her namesake. Rosemary remembered spending hours holding her baby, smelling that sweet scent. She used to smell Lavender's head when she was stressed. "I love you, Lavender. I love you so much." Rose kissed the top of her daughter's head. "I love you. I love you. I love you."

Lavender wept into her mother's shoulder. She clutched at Rose. Years of isolation. Years of being neglected. She'd built up walls to keep out the anguish of it. The dam fell away. Lavender cried harder. Time robbed. Time wasted.

"I'm so sorry, Lavender." Rosemary held her daughter tighter. "I'll be better. I'll do better. Please let me make it up to you. Please let me fix this."

Lavender hiccuped and nodded. She placed her ear against her mother's chest. The rapid beating of her heart was paradoxically soothing. Her mother was here. Her mother wanted her. Her mother was holding her.

Her mother loved her.

Her mother loved her.

Her mother loved her.

A knock at the door made the women pause. Dean slowly opened the door. He looked at the pair with worry. "You alright?"

Rosemary manically laughed. Tears were still flowing down her face. She nodded and reburied her face in Lavender's hair.

Dean frowned and looked at Lavender. His daughter gave him a small smile. He stepped into the room and sat on the bed.

They somehow ended up laying down. The 3 were squeezed onto Lavender's small bed. It wasn't entirely comfortable, but no one wanted to move. Rose and Dean were on either side of their daughter. They used to sleep like this when Lavender was little. When nightmares would scare her, she'd run to their room and climb in between them. They'd wrap their arms around her.

Lavender used to think nothing could hurt her while she was in their arms. The outside world didn't stand a chance against her parents. No boogeyman could snatch her. No worries could find her. "I think I need a bigger bed." Dean and Rose chuckled and held her tighter. Lavender smiled. She was warm.

She was safe.

She was home.

Chapter 24

The next morning, Lavender woke up alone. She stretched and looked around her room. The house felt warmer, lighter. There was chatter from downstairs. Lavender rubbed her eyes and made her way to the first floor. Her mom and dad were chit chatting. There were sounds of pans and popping oil.

Lavender walked into the kitchen. Dean was at the stove. Rose was at the table, coffee in hand. They were close, but had a silent understanding. "What are you making?" she asked. Her mom and dad both looked at her and smiled. Lavender felt warmth explode in her chest.

"Your favorite," Dean answered. He held up a sopapilla with a pair of tongs.

Rose gestured to the table. There were other breakfast foods laid out. "Come eat, flower."

Lavender smiled and sat at the table. Dean set down the plate of pastries and took his seat. Lavender began loading her plate and so did her parents.

"How's school?" Rosemary asked.

Lavender was taken aback by the question. She thought for a moment. "I have friends," she then added, "also my friend got Mr. Johnson fired."

Rosemary beamed, "Hell yea!" She remembered when the man would harass her as a teen. "You remember Homecoming?" she asked Dean.

The man snorted, "You mean us hiding cracked eggs in his car?"

Rose giggled, "I meant us TP-ing his house."

Dean corrected, "No, that was Halloween."

Lavender smiled, "So he was awful before too?"

Rosemary sighed, "He was a nightmare. If I sneezed wrong he'd try to have me expelled.

Dean nodded, "I had to transfer out of his class. He was a racist and homophobic curmudgeon back then. Had to hide it better over the years."

Lavender huffed. "Not too well." She looked at her mom. "Would you make my prom dress?"

Rosemary stared at her in awe. "Of course, flower."

Lavender beamed. "Good, cause Carrie said Belle was a nightmare to dress shop with." She began to scarf down her food.

Rosemary looked at Dean. The man gave her a smile and went back to eating. Rose picked up a still hot pastry and took a bite.

Rosemary stared at Jerry's house. It was the same. Lavender's warm hand was in hers. Rose looked down the road at her mother's house. One step at a time. Rose went up the steps and knocked on the door.

Jerry opened it. His eyes widened in shock. "Rose?" He saw Dean on the hood of the car. The man gave him a tight lipped smile and a short wave.

Lavender could feel her mother shaking. She squeezed Rose's hand.

Rosemary nodded. "Hi, Jerry."

"Dean said you might be coming." Jerry rested against the frame of the door. "You look well." He could see Ethan out of the corner of his eye.

"Hi, Rose," the boy greeted. Ethan saw Lavender. He pushed past his dad in the doorway and wrapped his arms around her. "Hi, Mama!" he greeted.

Lavender giggled, "Hi, Little."

Rosemary was shocked. Ethan had changed so much. He was almost her own height. She watched the pair stagger off the porch. Ethan shifted and ran around Lavender. Her daughter laughed and chased the pup. Ethan howled. Rosemary watched as the cul-de-sac came to life. Other children raced from their homes. Soon a gaggle of pups were surrounding Lavender.

"She took to it well, takes to it," Jerry informed. He was surprised to see the joy on Rosemary's face. He'd thought for sure the woman would scream and cry at the sight. "The pack is now 19 strong."

Rose nodded. She watched as the kids ran around. Jerry was smiling brightly. He'd aged. They all had. Rose looked to Dean. The man was watching the kids.

"I got 'em," Dean told the pair.

Rose nodded. She looked at Jerry. "Can we talk?"

"About what?" Jerry asked.

Rosemary frowned. "I'm sorry." The look of shock on his face was priceless. It would have been funny if it also wasn't so sad. "I want to talk."

Jerry looked at the woman up and down. She didn't seem hostile. He nodded, "Come in."

Rose smiled and followed the man inside.

Dean smiled as the pair went inside. Spring healing seemed to be the theme. He sighed and laid back against the windshield of the car. Lavender was playing with the pups. The sun was setting and Dean watched as it went down. It looked beautiful over the trees. The sky was a fiery orange.

Dean looked at Magnolia's house. The lights were on. He looked at Jerry's house. He could see his old flames talking. Dean hopped off the car. He spared one last look back at Lavender and the kids before heading to the lone house by the shore. Dean stepped up on the old porch. He knocked on the door. The little glass window in the door was covered with a piece of cardboard.

Nana opened the door. She was shocked to see the man. His face had healed. "What do you want, Dean?"

"Rose is here," Dean informed her. The woman gasped. "She's talking to Jerry, right now." He gestured into the house. "Can I come in?"

Nana listened to the laughter of the children. The sun was setting. She sighed. "Fine. Make it quick."

Dean followed the woman inside. It was strange being in the house. He watched as Magnolia sat down at the little table by the bay window. She gestured to the seat across from her. Dean took it. He took a deep breath. "Rosemary wants to talk to you soon. Not today, obviously, but soon."

Nana grimaced. "Why would she want to talk to me?" She took a drink from her mug. Her daughter being back in town was both wonderful and terrifying.

"She wants to be a better mom. She's thinking about coming back to Branches." Dean looked out at the water. "I want to know if it's worth her trying to talk to you."

Nana frowned, "I…" She looked at her drink. "I should speak to her." The world was dark outside. The moon was a crescent. "I want to talk to her."

Dean nodded. "That's all I needed to hear."

A knock at the door made both of them look at it.

"I'll get it," Nana stood. There was a chance Lavender was on the other side. She hoped Lavender was on the other side. Unfortunately, it was some white man. He was clean shaven and his hair was short. Dressed in a collared shirt and slacks. A gold cross hung around his neck. Sometimes missionaries came to the reservation. During any other time of day, he wouldn't be completely out of place. "Can I help you?" she asked.

"Hello, ma'am. I'm here to talk to you about our lord and savior Jesus Christ."

Nana frowned. The man's voice made the hairs on the back of her next stand up. "It's 7 o'clock," Nana hissed. She went to shut the door but the man stuck his foot out. "Move," Nana growled.

The man smiled widely. "Oh, but ma'am, I'm here to save you little savages."

Nana looked up at him in fury. She took a step forward. "Excuse you?" The man's hand wrapped around her throat.

A blood curdling scream made Lavender freeze. It was coming from Nana's house. She looked to the pups, "Get your parents, now!" Lavender ran fast. The wind was flying past her. Blood. There was blood. Rot. Combstock. Lavender raced to the property. *Silas, Silas, he's here! Come to the reservation!* she screamed into the night. Lavender noticed her dad wasn't on top of the car anymore. Her blood ran cold. "No, no, no," she whispered in terror. Just then Silas answered.

We're coming

"Nana!" Lavender called, "Dad!" She barreled into Nana's front yard and froze. Combstock was holding Dean. The vampire's claws were at her father's neck. Nana was on the ground, unconscious.

"Oh, wolf blood just hits the spot!" Combstock laughed maniacally. "I wonder what you'd taste like, little gold." He licked his lips clean of blood.

Lavender was going to kill this bastard. She moved toward the man.

"Don't!" Dean cried. One of the claws punctured his skin. Hot blood trailed down his neck. He tried to kick at the man.

Combstock cooed, "Aw, you're feisty." He looked at Lavender, "I see where she got it from." He removed his coat and wrapped Dean in it. The man tried to bite at him. "Oh, how cute."

"Let him go!" Lavender demanded.

The vampire smiled. "Aw, you want your daddy?" Combstock could hear the wolves and the Annoras. "Come and get him." He pulled Dean with him into the night.

Lavender pushed past her shock and raced after them. She tried to keep up, but it was useless. Lavender inhaled. Combstock's scent was everywhere. Leading in all different directions. There was no scent of her dad. Lavender wept. "DADDY!" she cried.

Silas's arms wrapped around the screaming girl. "Lavender, Lavender!"

"He has dad," the girl was hysterical. "He has dad!"

The rest of the Annora family joined them. "He has Dean?!" Matthias looked into the night. "Shit!"

Silas frowned. His father rarely cursed. He held Lavender tight.

"Lavender!" Rose called from out of the woods.

Said girl raced back toward Nana's house. "Mom!" Her mother was kneeling next to Nana.

Matthias went beside the passed out woman. He nicked his thumb and used his blood to close the puncture wounds. The old woman's heart was still beating. That was a good sign. "She's still alive. Open her mouth."

Rosemary was on autopilot. She listened to the demand and pried Nana's mouth open.

Matthias bit into his wrist and let a few drops fall onto the woman's tongue. "Get her inside and monitor her." He stood and turned to Lavender, "We need a plan."

Lavender looked around her. 19 wolves, the old and new generations came and stood at attention, waiting for Lavender's word. The Annora's looked to her too. If they all wanted orders, she'd give them. Lavender stood on Nana's porch.

"Alright listen up! We need to split up and follow the trails!" Lavender looked at the Annora family. "6 of you, 6 teams. You guys have telepathy and can call each other." She turned to the wolves. "Split up, groups of 3's. Stay in your team, howl if you find him. Ethan," Lavender pointed at the pup, "you're with me!" Lavender turned to her mother, "Stay here, mom, protect Nana."

"I need to help!" Rosemary begged.

"You will be by keeping Nana safe!" Lavender snapped. The authority in her voice was undeniable. She turned to Silas. "You're with me." Silas nodded without hesitation. "Get going!"

Lavender pointed to the forest. To her shock, everyone split up and was gone in seconds. Lavender hopped down. "Inside," she ordered Nana and Rose.

"Where are you going?" Rose asked. She had her mother in her arms.

"Home," Lavender informed, "to get the shotgun. Inside you two!" She pointed to the boys and the car. Lavender went to her mother. She gave her mom a hug before going to the car.

Silas opened the back door for Ethan. He then got in the front seat.

Lavender peeled out of the reservation. She sped. Most of the police force was home sleeping or currently running through the wood as wolves, so she didn't worry.

"What's the plan?" Ethan asked.

"He wants me," Lavender growled.

Probably 'cause you blew if head off, Ethan offered.

Lavender shook her head, "Apparently he's taking me somewhere."

Silas looked at his girlfriend then the pup. "I hate that I can't understand you."

Lavender giggled and took a sharp turn. She peeled through town and toward her house. She'd just gotten her family back. She'd just gotten her home back. She wasn't going to let this bastard take it all away.

The tires kicked up the gravel of her driveway. The car jolted as it came to a stop. Lavender raced out of the car and up to the front porch. She stopped. Silas and Ethan both froze as well. Lavender turned to the boys. *He's here*, she said to both of them.

Silas silently moved to stand beside Lavender. *How did he get in?*

Must have forced dad, Lavender clenched her fist. She turned to Ethan, *Stay back*

Ethan walked up to sit by the porch.

Lavender turned back to the door. Silas moved out of the way of the doorway. There were no sounds coming from inside. There were no lights on inside. Lavender opened the door. It creaked. The moonlight from the entrance illuminated Dean. He was bound and gagged to a chair. Dean was beaten and a tad bloody, but alive.

Lavender slowly moved into the house. Dean looked up at her and shook his head. The door slammed closed behind her. *Stay*, Lavender ordered the boys. She could feel Combstock. The weight of his presence was like an anvil on her chest. He inhaled deeply. It made Lavender's gut twist in disgust.

"They named you well," the man came around and gave her a sleazy grin. "A lovely little flower." Combstock traced her jawline with his finger. "I knew you'd come to me."

Lavender's eyes widened in shock. She quickly returned her face to a neutral expression. "Please," she scoffed, "I came for my gun."

Combstock chuckled, "You're cute. I almost want to keep you for myself. I don't think the old ones would mind if I had a taste though." He sneered at the tied up man, "Would you mind, dear old dad?"

Dean began to struggle. He screamed against the gag.

"Has your little boyfriend drank from you yet?" Combstock teased. He bared his fangs, "Too bad he won't get a chance."

Lavender realized Combstock thought she was alone. "You only want a taste?" she teased. Luckily it worked to throw him off balance.

Combstock retracted his fangs and laughed. "You love cracking jokes, don't you girl?"

Lavender smiled. She moved, not too fast. With a cheeky tone, she said, "I mean…if you got it, flaunt it." They made a little circle. Combstock followed her lead till she had him right where she wanted him. Right in front of the door. *On my mark,* she told Silas.

Combstock sneered. "You're lucky Mother and Father want you alive." He twirled the girl's hair with his clawed finger. "They want a shiny new toy to chew on. So why don't you just come quietly? I'll even leave your daddy and pack alive." He moved to be eye level with her. "Have you ever been to Europe? We can have a little vacation before I hand you over. They ain't expecting me back for a couple years. That'll give me just enough time to break you."

Lavender gave him a sweet smile. She leaned in close, shocking the man. "That sounds like fun."

Combstock smiled and leaned in as well. "Aren't you full of surprises?"

Lavender grinned, "You don't know the half of it." She called to Silas, *NOW!*

The front door exploded into bits. Lavender jumped back.

Combstock flew through the air when Silas slammed into him. The colonel hit the couch and flipped over it. Landing on the ground with a deafening crash. The house wasn't like the forest. Nowhere to run. No cave tunnels to duck into. His only choice was to fight. "You little bastard!" the pale man roared.

Silas laughed, "I'm not just taking your arm this time." He charged forward and slammed the colonel through the wall.

Lavender raced to Dean as chaos erupted around them. The ropes were tight, too tight for her to get loose. Lavender called for Ethan, "Little!"

Ethan came bounding in. He saw Dean and immediately ripped through the bonds.

Silas was thrown across the room. He went through the front door and landed on the porch. Before he could get up, Combstock was on him.

"I've fed well, boy. That wolf blood is something special. Too bad you've never gotten a taste." The colonel pinned the boy down. "I heard you used your venom," he bared his fangs, "want to see mine?"

Silas's eyes widened in horror.

Lavender jumped onto Combstocks back and bit his neck. The man screamed and grabbed Lavender by the hair and ripped her off him. Throwing the girl off the porch, in front of him. Before he could fully stand, Silas kicked the man in the nuts. Combstock fell to his knees and clutched his junk.

Silas scrambled down the steps to Lavender. "Are you okay?" he asked.

The adrenaline was drowning out most of the pain. Lavender nodded and spat out a chunk of Combstock's neck. The pair looked up to see said man collecting himself.

Combstock hissed, "That's it! I'm going to kill you, boy." He pointed to Lavender, "And you, I tried to be nice, but now, I'm just gonna drain you and take that old bitch back with me!"

He stomped over to the pair. "You're more trouble than you're worth!" A hunk of his shoulder exploded. Comstock screeched and whipped around.

Dean kept his shotgun raised. He fired again, but the vampire was faster. The gun was grabbed and wrenched from his hands. Dean threw a haymaker. The punch seemed to only pissed the colonel off.

"You call that a hit, boy?" Combstock punched the man in the stomach. Dean retched. The force sent the father into the wall by the door. Combstock snapped the gun in half. A wolf came from the dark and bit into his ankle. Combstock punched the pup, successfully knocking him off. He was going to stomp the dog's head in when the other vampire tackled him back into the house.

Lavender went to Ethan. The boy was hurt but nothing seemed broken. "Get the others!" she commanded, "Run and get them!"

Ethan nodded and raced off, beginning to howl.

Lavender looked at the remains of the gun and then to her dad. She crawled over to him. "Dad?" Lavender sighed in relief when he looked at her. Hurt, but still alive.

"Run," Dean begged. "Run, Ender."

Lavender wept. "No, no way." Lavender racked her brain. Weaknesses, weaknesses. Lavender began to list them. All the ones Silas told her. Sunlight, dead blood, silver, oak- Lavender's eyes widened in realization. Oak. Oak! She got to her feet and scrambled into the house.

Silas and Combstock were grappling at each other in the living room. Combstock was thrown into the fireplace.

Lavender grabbed the chair her father had been tied to. She slammed it into the wall until it shattered. One of the legs snapped into a sharpened end. She grabbed it and went to the still fighting pair. *Hold him!* She told Silas. Lavender clutched the leg tight enough to bruise her hand.

Silas pinned Combstock to the ground. The colonel spat in his eyes. Silas cried out and unfortunately let his hold loosen.

Combstock kicked the boy away and turned to Lavender. "Guess I got to fight dirty with your kind." He charged her and knocked her to the floor.

Lavender positioned her makeshift stake. She pressed it over the man's heart. Sadly she didn't have the leverage. Lavender wrapped her legs around his back and tried to pull him down onto it.

"Oh, how forward," Combstock teased. He grabbed the wrist that was holding the stake. "Poor little-"

A choir of howls from outside made the man pause.

That was all Silas needed.

The boy came up behind Combstock and slammed his foot down on the center of the colonel's back.

Lavender got a front row seat to what happened next.

The man's face twisted in shock then horror. His body shook, as if it was filling up with air. He was a balloon that was about to pop, and pop he did. Blood exploded throughout the room.

Lavender somehow managed to close her mouth and eyes in time. She heard Silas yelp in disgust. Lavender kept the stake in her death grip.

Silas fell to his knees. He wiped his face and tried to get the blood out of his eyes. He spat out the chunks and clots.

Lavender finally opened her eyes. She gasped. The realization she'd been holding her breath hit her full force. "Holy fucking shit!" she wheezed out. Lavender stared up at Silas, who was now the one kneeling over her. She sat up and pulled him into a hug. Her boyfriend sputtered in shock but eventually wrapped his arms around her. Their necklaces clinked together.

"Holy shit. Holy shit," Silas chanted. His mind was going a hundred miles a second. He'd never killed another vampire before. In fact, he'd never killed anyone. Silas rested his head against Lavender's shoulder. They were both covered in gore. It was disgusting and sticky, but they were alive.

They were alive.

"Silas!"

"Lavender!"

The pair looked at the hole where the front door used to be. Their family was there. Their friends were there.

It was okay. They were alive.

Chapter 25

Eden bounced her leg and finished her cigarette in one drag. She sighed and looked at the mess around her. Also on her. Thankfully she had on work clothes, so they could stand to be drenched in blood. Eden finished her smoke and crushed it under her heel. Break time was over.

"I don't know why you do that." Everett was currently scrubbing the colonel's blood off the floor. It felt good to know his tormentor was dead. Though he was mad he didn't get to kill him. All's well that ends well, he supposed.

"Memories I guess." Eden took the dirty bucket water and went to throw it out the door. She turned to Hana, who was scrubbing up the porch. "You okay?"

Hana looked up, utter boredom plastered on her face. "This shit sucks." She went back to scrubbing up the blood.

Eden snorted and went back inside. She refilled the bucket, got more soap and went to work by Everett again. The pair got most of the mess up. The blood stained rags would most certainly need to be burned later. Hana was now hosing down the porch. Hopefully they'd be able to get the Amos family back in their home soon.

Jonathan emerged from the dark. "I found something!" He'd been trying to get some debris up in the back bedroom.

Everyone dropped what they were doing and were beside Jonathan in a flash.

"What is it?" Everett asked.

Jonathan produced a notebook. Compact enough to fit into a coat pocket. "Ev?" He looked at his partner. The man's icy eyes had gone wide with shock.

"That's his," Everett confirmed. He took it from Jonathan and looked at the first page. "This was started a few years ago." That was good. Everett flipped through the pages till something caught his eye.

December 12, 2005

The mother and father want to know more. They demand more. I can't leave. Her voice is inside me. Her blood's in my veins. If I manage to find my way out, she'll make me come back. She makes them all come back. They'll eat me. Like that foolish Mariana. They'll eat me alive. They wanna pet. Something new. Something to entertain them. We aren't entertaining enough. They made us, they know us, they're inside us. Mother wants new. Something fresh.

Mother needs a dog. A dog. I'll get her a dog. I told her, I'll get her a pretty little wolf. With pretty golden eyes. She was so happy. Now I can leave. Now the cave will show me the way out. Once I bring a pup back, she'll get out of my head. She'll take her blood back. The wolves have caught their interest. I'll bring mother a wolf, and she'll let me go.

Everett slammed the book shut. A chill went up his spine. "We need to give this to Matthias," he whispered in horror.

Hana frowned, "How bad?"

Everett didn't answer. He turned and headed home. The others followed him.

Dean chugged the concoction Matt gave him. He sighed as his body mended. The pain slowly faded and left him feeling refreshed. Dean jumped when a chilled stethoscope pressed against his back.

"Sorry," Matthias whispered. He listened to his friend's breathing become normal. The man's heartbeat slowed to a usual pace. Matthias pressed his nose against Dean's neck and inhaled deeply.

"Whoa! Let a guy heal first," Dean joked. He rolled his shoulders and was glad to find it didn't cause a lightning strike of agony to shoot through him.

Matthias chuckled, "I was making sure your internal bleeding had stopped." He stepped back and gently checked the man's sides. "Ribs have healed too." Matthias smiled, "You heal well, Dean." The vampire placed his stethoscope around his neck. He walked back to his workbench. "Of course, if you feel any discomfort, let me know."

Dean nodded, "Got it, doc." He stretched up. The night had been horrifying. Traumatizing. He wanted to erase it, but couldn't. It replayed and replayed. Dean then thought about one of the things that crazed killer had said. "Hey, Matt."

The vampire smelled the anxiety flowing off of the other man in waves. "What is wrong, Dean?"

"That guy, Combstock." Dean rubbed his arm nervously. "He…he mentioned old ones…that wanted Lavender."

Matthias dropped the glass he was holding. He was in front of Dean in a flash. Gripping the man's shoulders, he asked "What else did he say?!"

Dean felt a pit open in his stomach. "He…he just said he had to take her to 'the old ones' and some mother and father?"

"Anything else?" Matthias gripped the man's arms harder than he probably should have. This was important. More than important.

Dean shook his head. "No. I mean he said they weren't expecting him for a couple years." The terror in Matt's face was concerning. "Matt, what's going on?"

Matthias sighed and tried to reign in his panic. "It's…it's probably nothing."

"Bullshit!" Dean hissed and hopped off the table. "You don't freak the fuck out like that over 'nothing'."

Matthias frowned. "The old ones…Mother and Father…" He looked away and went to one of the bookshelves. The notebook he selected was worn and tattered. "I met them centuries ago." Matthias looked through his old journal. He handed it over to Dean.

Dean looked at the opened book. The sketches inside were strange. Dean flipped through a few pages. There were portraits of people. No, these weren't people. They had a basic humanoid shape. Everything else was wrong. The eyes were big, black voids. Thin elongated arms that ended in bat-like claws. Pointed ears and near androgynous. Only some carrying traits of smoothed over breasts. Some were nude other wore what seemed to be silk. Jewels and chains adorning them. "What is this?"

Matthias tapped one of the monsters. "Those are the old ones."

Dean gulped. "These…they…"

Matthias explained. "They've lost their humanity and live underground. " He turned to the next page, showing the intricate cave systems. On the next page were pillars of carved stones and detailed rooms. "They keep some human comforts. Rooms, trinkets, music, books." Matthias turned the page again, revealing the feast.

Dean jumped. "Holy shit!" He looked at the sketch then Matt. "What the fuck is this?!"

Matthias's frown deepened. "They feed by dragging stray humans underground. They rip them apart afterward and consume their flesh. They've also been known to cannibalize other vampires." Matthias turned the page to reveal Mother and Father. "These two," Matthias explained, "proclaim themselves to be the progenitors. It was the reason I went to them. I wanted to know our history. They offered their blood to me." Matthias was glad his younger self had some semblance of sense.

"What does their blood do?" Dean asked. The Mother and Father sat on what seemed to be thrones. They appeared much larger than the other old ones.

Matthias took the notebook back. "Mother's blood will give you immense power, but also will make you one of her thralls. She'll have complete access to your mind and be able to take over your body. Father's blood could either kill you or give you a gift. I never was able to figure out why some die and why others don't."

"What kinds of gifts?" Dean asked.

Matthias rattled off, "Flight. Telekinesis. Pyrokinesis. The ability to see the future. It varies wildly." He placed the book back on the shelf. "The old ones are dangerous. Most have shed their morals and see humans as livestock. Like how you see cows. Sure, some keep them as cute pets, but at the end of the day…they'll still eat them."

Dean shuddered. "Why would they want Lavender?"

Matthias grimaced. "I hope Combstock did not tell them the specific gift he was bringing for his freedom. Otherwise, it will not end well for any of us."

Dean frowned. "Jesus Christ."

"They're older than him."

The door to the room swung open. Everett held up a journal. "You need to read this." He handed it over to his father.

Dean didn't know how, but Matthias got paler. "What is that?" Matt took the journal and flipped through the pages. Dean realized he was holding his breath and inhaled. His heart was pounding.

Matthias read fast. Going through the words like a bullet through the air. When he finished, he shut the book. His grip on it caused the worn leather to creak. The weight of what he knew now was overbearing. He looked at Dean. A single tear rolled down his face. The pounding of his friend's heart would only get worse. Matthias whispered, "I am so sorry."

What the Mother was promised, the Mother would get.

Lavender licked her lips clean from Silas's blood. She relaxed back against her boyfriend's chest. The pair were clean and lounging on Silas's stupidly big bed. A slow heartbeat was drumming against her back. Cool lips pressed against her cheek. Lavender traced her finger along Silas's arms. They were a bit bigger than hers. There were fine hairs on his forearms, just like her's.

Silas broke the quiet, "I'm sorry about your house."

Lavender chuckled. "I'd rather have you all safe than the house. "Besides," her voice took on a light and teasing tone, "I'm not against chilling in a mansion for the foreseeable future."

Silas giggled. His feet unconsciously wiggled in glee. "Sleepover."

Lavender laughed. She turned around to see Silas's face. He had the goofiest smile on his lips. "You're too cute!" Lavender couldn't help but kiss him.

Silas giggled into the kiss. "I love you." he whispered as they pulled apart.

"I love you too," Lavender looked down at the carved necklace Silas had given her then at his matching one. She noticed the shine in his eyes. That flash of red. The way his flawless skin seemed to glow in the low lamp light. "I was so scared we were going to die, or even worse, you'd die and I lived. I saw my whole life flash before my eyes when he was over me." Lavender hugged the boy close to her. "I kept replaying meeting you. Us in that cafeteria. I kept replaying it over and over again." Lavender kissed his cheek. "And all I could think was, 'I'm so glad I met you.'" She laid her head on his shoulder. "I still think that. I love you, Silas."

Silas wept. He couldn't help it. The tears spilled out of him. Waves of relief and the sweetest devotion. He didn't like crying. It was messy. It was a lot. In this situation though, with these emotions, there was nothing else he could do. "I'm so happy I met you too." He gripped her tight. "I love you, Lavender."

The pair shared little whispers of sweet nothings. They slipped down onto the bed, still wrapped in each other's arms. Lavender kicked the blanket up so she could pull it over them. Silas reached over to the lamp and shut it off.

The room went dark.

The pair fell asleep.

Epilogue

Lavender let her mom lace up the back of her prom dress. The fabric was soft, thank goodness. She knew everyone was waiting for her downstairs. Getting her hair into the style she'd wanted had taken longer than she'd expected. Thankfully Belle was a sweetheart. Carrie was patient, Jeremy grumbled but kept his mouth shut, and Blake knew better than any of them how textured hair could be.

"Alright, flower," Rosemary said, smoothing out the fabric. She stepped back and gasped in wonder. "Oh, flower." Tears filled her eyes. Rose hadn't been able to go to prom. Her and Dean had a party in the woods. Which was fun. This though. Seeing her daughter, not only being able to go but having the ability to attend everything Rose was shunned from, made her heart swell with joy. "You're beautiful."

"Please don't cry, mom," Lavender sniffled and tilted her head back. She had to sit for 30 minutes to finish her makeup. It was not going to be ruined now.

"Sorry, sorry," Rose turned Lavender toward the mirror. "Look at you, Ender."

And look Lavender did. The dress was everything she'd hoped for. Nana and Rosemary had worked together to sew it for her. The pale blue and white were stunning against her dark skin. It was an a-line shape. The top layer of the skirt was shaped like an opening curtain. The bottom layer was white. The sleeves were puffy and off the shoulder. Dangling from their hems were sea glass beads. Around her waist was a thick tan leather belt. Embedded in the center of it was a full moon made out of pieces of sea glass. It reminded Lavender of stained glass windows. 2 trailers of glass pebbles extended from either side of the moon and around Lavender's waist to the back where the belt tied.

Lavender felt like a princess. Especially with her moccasin boots. She turned and hugged her mother. "Thank you." She batted the tears forming in her eyes away.

"You're welcome, flower." Rose kissed the top of her daughter's head. "Come on, let's get you downstairs." She ushered her daughter out the door.

Lavender realized she was going to have a 'coming down the stairs moment'. The thought of this being like a scene from a cheesy movie made her giggle. Lavender hopped the last two steps. "Ready!" she announced.

Belle hopped up and clapped. "Oh, Lavender! You look gorgeous!"

Silas was staring at her in awe. She was a queen. She was his queen. She was the moon and the stars and-

"Silas?" Lavender waved a hand in front of her boyfriend's face.

Silas blinked out of his daze. Her golden eyes were shimmering in the dying sunlight. "I love you," he whispered in wonder.

Jeremy giggled, "He's so whipped!" Carrie smacked him with her clutch. "What, he is! He's gonna be like Blake!"

Silas chuckled. He still hadn't looked away from Lavender. "Already there."

"Alright kids! Line up, let's get a picture!" Dean ordered.

"Is that a polaroid?" Carrie asked as she stood next to Belle.

"Sure is!"

"Don't worry," Rose showed her camera, "I have something this decade." Dean stuck his tongue out at her and she returned the gesture.

Dean instructed, "Alright, say cheese."

"Cheese!" the teens all said in unison. The group then headed to the limo that Belle's father actually rented. None of the teens, aside from Belle, had been inside one before.

"Your dad is crazy loaded," Jeremy started clicking buttons.

Belle rolled her eyes. "Oh stop it you!" She smacked Jeremy's hand away from the air controls.

The limo pulled up to the school just as the sun set. They got the attention Belle was hoping for. Gawking teens watched as they exited the stretched car. Lavender hooked her arm with Silas's. She could hear both whispers of condemnation and appreciation. Lavender ignored both.

The rest of the night was a blur of dancing, singing, and drinking crappy punch. An hour later, Lavender went outside. The stone steps of her school had never looked so inviting. Lavender collapsed down and sighed in relief. Thankfully, she hadn't worn heels like some of the poor girls resting their feet. The night air had grown humid with the summer approaching. Cool hands rubbed her shoulders. Lavender inhaled Silas's scent.

"You okay?" he asked.

Lavender nodded, "Just needed some air." She looked up at him. He was beautiful in all light, but especially moonlight. *Sit with me*, she urged.

Silas sat without hesitation.

Lavender rested her head on his shoulder. She took his hand in hers. The sounds of laughter and tapping heels were drowned out by Silas's slow heartbeat. The smell of sweat and teenage hormones were replaced by Silas's earthy notes. Lavender melted against him. A strong arm wrapped around her and pulled her closer. Lavender inhaled deeper. Everything was alright. They were okay.

They were alive.

42874606R00096